An unknown visitor, with some unguessable purpose, who had come and gone before Valdemar had caught more than a glimpse of him—or her—had just made the young grape-grower a present of one of the Twelve Swords. The recipient felt overwhelmed by the discovery. And yet—even in this tremendous moment when Valdemar first glimpsed the ebon hilt, he found himself thinking that he ought to be more surprised at the gift than he really was.

He had a strange feeling that he had always known, had never doubted, that something like this—something truly great—was fated to happen to him sooner or later.

Well, here it was. And whatever unconscious anticipation might be keeping him from being properly astonished, he was certainly beginning to be afraid...

Tor books by Fred Saberhagen

THE BERSERKER SERIES

The Berserker Wars
Berserker Base (with Poul Anderson, Ed Bryant, Stephen Donaldson, Larry Niven, Connie Willis, and Roger Zelazny)
Berserker: Blue Death
The Berserker Throne
Berserker's Planet
Berserker Lies
Berserker Man

THE DRACULA SERIES

The Dracula Tapes
The Holmes-Dracula Files
An Old Friend of the Family
Thorn
Dominion
A Matter of Taste

THE SWORDS SERIES

The First Book of Swords
The Second Book of Swords
The Third Book of Swords
The First Book of Lost Swords: Woundhealer's Story
The Second Book of Lost Swords: Sightblinder's Story
The Third Book of Lost Swords: Stonecutter's Story
The Fourth Book of Lost Swords: Farslayer's Story
The Fifth Book of Lost Swords: Coinspinner's Story
The Sixth Book of Lost Swords: Mindsword's Story
The Seventh Book of Lost Swords: Wayfinder's Story

OTHER BOOKS

A Century of Progress
Coils (with Roger Zelazny)
Earth Descended
The Mask of the Sun
A Question of Time
Specimens
The Veils of Azlaroc
The Water of Thought

WAYFINDER'S STORY

THE SEVENTH BOOK OF LOST SWORDS

FRED SABERHAGEN

A TOM DOHERTY ASSOCIATES BOOK
NEW YORK

THE SEVENTH BOOK OF LOST SWORDS

A Tor Book
Published by Tom Doherty Associates, Inc.
175 Fifth Avenue
New York, N.Y. 10010

Tor® is a registered trademark of Tom Doherty Associates, Inc.

ISBN: 0-812-50575-1
Library of Congress Catalog Card Number: 92-858

First edition: June 1992
First mass market printing: December 1993

Printed in the United States of America

0 9 8 7 6 5 4 3 2 1

ONE

HIS huge, work-roughened hands shaking with excitement, young Valdemar turned up the sleeves of his farmer's shirt. Squatting on the earth floor of his solitary hut, peering intently by firelight and fading daylight, he reached for the long, heavy bundle that lay near the fire and began very gradually to undo its wrappings of gray cloth. The bundle was neatly made, tied with strong cord. As Valdemar worked to undo the knots, he did his best to keep himself from thinking of what he might expect to find within. He told himself he had no right to expect anything at all. But it was as if he wished to shield himself from an enormous disappointment . . .

The wrappings loosened and began to fall away. As soon as an area of unrelieved blackness came into view, unmistakably part of the hilt of an edged weapon, the young man's fingers ceased to move. Like many other people, he had a sensitivity to the presence of powerful magic, and he was already beginning to realize just what kind of weapon he had been given.

Valdemar thought that he could feel the blood drain from his face. Leaning his enormous weight back on his heels, he did his unpracticed best to formulate a prayer to beneficent Ardneh.

Whatever prayer he at last managed to say went up in

silence. Outside, spring wind howled fiercely, shoving against the rough stone walls of his lonely hut, rattling the crude, ill-fitting door, spattering rain through the hole in the roof that served as chimney, so that the small fire, fueled mostly by last year's dried vines, hissed as if in pain.

He had a serious mystery to contemplate.

An unknown visitor, working alone in pursuit of some unguessable purpose, who had come and gone before Valdemar had been able to catch more than a glimpse of him—or her—had just made the young grape-grower a present of one of the Twelve Swords. The recipient felt overwhelmed by the discovery. And yet—even in this tremendous moment when Valdemar first glimpsed the ebon hilt, he found himself thinking that he ought to be more surprised at the nature of this gift than he really was.

He had the strange feeling that he had always known, had never doubted, that something like this—something truly great—was fated to happen to him sooner or later.

Well, here it was. And whatever unconscious anticipation might be keeping him from being properly astonished, he was certainly beginning to be afraid.

Scant minutes ago, the unexpected shadow and the silent form of the mysterious caller had moved almost simultaneously, and with a swiftness almost magical, past the door of Valdemar's isolated dwelling, interrupting the young man in the midst of preparing his evening meal. The door had been left slightly ajar for more light, and to let the smoke-hole draw.

Until that moment, Valdemar had had no suspicion that any other human being was anywhere within a couple of kilometers. By the time he had jumped up and run outdoors, the figure of his anonymous visitor was already almost out of sight in mist and rain. Valdemar had caught only a single glimpse of a human shape, so muffled in gray garments that it might have been either man or woman.

The gigantic youth had started in pursuit, swiftly bounding up one, two, three of the narrow cultivated terraces that rose above his hut. But by the time he had reached the third terrace, his caller had already disappeared into the wet twilight shrouding the domesticated vines, the scant wild bushes, and the granite outcroppings of the lonely mountainside.

Shouting for his vanished visitor to stop, Valdemar had continued the chase a little farther, almost to the boundary of his cultivated land, but without success. Returning to his hut a couple of minutes later, the young man had picked up the bundle which had been so mysteriously deposited at his door. He had paused to reassure himself that at least it was not alive (he had heard stories of babies being left at the doors of lonely huts) and carried it in by the fire. After closing the ill-fitting door again, and shaking his garments dry as best he could, Valdemar had hesitantly begun to unwrap his present—a process which came, moments later, to a shocked halt.

Though he was scarcely past the age of twenty, and for most of the past year had dwelt in this lonely place, Valdemar could not claim complete innocence or ignorance regarding the affairs of the great world.

Like every other thinking person, he knew something of the history of the Twelve Swords, magical weapons created almost forty years ago by the gods themselves. Valdemar knew also that two of the Swords had been destroyed not long after they were made. This black hilt partially visible before him, if it were genuine, might belong to any of the remaining Ten. And though like most people he had never seen, much less handled, any of the Twelve, Valdemar could not doubt the authenticity of this one. A heavy elegance of magic flowed into his fingertips the instant they brushed against it; and to magic he was not a total stranger.

It was common knowledge in the world that four Swords—Shieldbreaker, Dragonslicer, Stonecutter, and Sightblinder—had for some years been gathered in the royal armory of Tasavalta, under control of that realm's powerful and unfortunate Prince Mark. Among the six others now lost to public knowledge were the two Valdemar considered the most abominable of the god-forged weapons, Soulcutter and the Mindsword.

No one, as he understood the case, could ever be sure of the whereabouts of Coinspinner, a tricky blade given to randomly moving itself about. Nor was there any way to guess the whereabouts of Farslayer, Wayfinder, or Woundhealer. That last was the only one of the surviving ten that Valdemar would have rejoiced to find in his own possession.

Crouching near the fire, alone with his mysterious gift, the youth hesitated for a long time before continuing the process of unwrapping. His irresolution was grounded in the fact that he feared certain of the gods' Swords more than others, and at this point it was still at least theoretically possible for him to refuse the knowledge of which one he had been given. At this point he would still be able, if he chose, to tie up the gray cloth again, carry the whole still-mysterious bundle back out into the rain, and drop it, lose it, deep in some rocky crevice among the nearby crags, hoping that no one else would ever discover the presence of the thing of power, or be able to come near it.

For what seemed to Valdemar a long time he sat there on his heels. The wind battering at his door seemed to mock his fearful hesitancy, while outside the clouded daylight slowly faded. Still, enough light remained inside the hut, around his dying fire, for him to see whatever white mark might be emblazoned on the Sword's hilt, when his next tug at the gray cloth should reveal it.

Of course, one Sword had no white symbol at all. If that was what he found, it would mean fate had put into his hands Soulcutter, the Tyrant's Blade.

The young giant's eyes closed briefly. His strong, almost-handsome face was troubled. Awkwardly he uttered words aloud: "Ardneh, let it not be that one. I do not want the responsibility of trying to hide that demon's Blade. Or of trying to destroy it." He understood full well that breaking any Sword, or otherwise rendering it ineffective, would be far beyond his powers.

"Therefore let it be any of them, except Soulcutter, or . . ."

Valdemar's prayer stumbled to a halt, as he realized that for him the second most fearful of the Blades would probably not, after all, be that called the Mindsword. Given that one, he could simply refrain from drawing it; for him, he thought, the power to bend others to his will would pose no great temptation. Farslayer would be far more likely to be his downfall. There were certain people in the world, oppressors of humanity, for whom—though he had never met them—the youth felt a dislike that threatened always to spill over into personal hatred; and if the life of one of those persons, wherever they might be, should be so helplessly delivered into his hands, Valdemar feared his own latent capacity for violence.

Yes, it would be better if he got rid of this unknown Sword at once, not tempting himself by looking for the symbol which it must bear upon the hilt . . .

Valdemar's hands quivered. Because he might, for all he knew, be holding Woundhealer, the Sword of Mercy. That glorious possibility was enough to eliminate any thought of plunging the mysterious gift into a crevasse before he had identified it.

After minutes of immobility, the youth with a sudden jerk stripped back the gray cloth completely from the black hilt.

A small white arrow-symbol, pointing upward to the pommel, leapt into view. Neither the best nor the worst of possibilities had been realized. The weapon in Valdemar's hands was Wayfinder. The Sword of Wisdom, it was also called—Ardneh grant it bring him that!

Valdemar breathed somewhat more easily. Toward Wayfinder he felt timidity and awe, but no overwhelming fear. Gently he peeled away the remaining wrappings, exposing a plain leather sheath. Without pausing for further thought, he clasped the hilt and drew forth a full meter of incomparable double-edged Blade. The faint light of fading day and dying fire gleamed softly on steel smoother and sharper than any human armorer had ever crafted, at least since the lost civilization of the Old World. Beneath the surface of the metal a lovely mottled pattern was perceptible.

Valdemar ran a tremulous finger along the flat side of the tremendous Blade. No, despite his youth, he was no stranger to the touch of magic. But he had never in his life felt anything the like of this.

A happy thought struck suddenly. Some of the new strain and worry vanished from his youthful face.

"Powers who rule this Sword," he said, self-consciously—then paused for a deep breath, and started over. "Powers of this Sword, whoever or whatever you may be—I understand that giving guidance is your function. Guide me, therefore—guide me to the person—to her—to the woman I have—I have almost despaired of ever finding. The one who is most fit, most suitable, to share my life."

Though he was utterly alone, the young man could feel his cheeks warming. Frowning suddenly, he quickly amended: "Let all be done in accordance with the will of Ardneh."

Having concluded this awkward speech, Valdemar arose, gripping the black hilt firmly in both of his great hands, fingers overlapping. Tentatively he moved the great Blade in a horizontal circle. One direction alone, almost straight east, set the Sword's tip quivering. At the surge of magic he cried out, wordlessly. For just a moment the movement had become so violent that the weapon had almost leaped free of his grip.

On a warm spring afternoon, seven days after the day when Valdemar had unwrapped the Sword, and more than a hundred kilometers distant from his hut, two pilgrims were making their way across a heavily wooded hillside that formed one flank of a deep ravine.

The first of these gray-clad travelers was a woman, apparently about sixty years of age, but still vigorous and hearty. There was nothing feeble in the way she moved across the steep slope, among the thickly-spaced, narrow trunks. Her silver hair was long, but bound up closely. The strains of a long life showed in the woman's face, but no burden that seemed too much for her present determination. Like many other female pilgrims or travelers, she wore boots, trousers and a loose jacket, and was armed for self-defense with a short sword.

The crowded treetrunks made it all but impossible for two to travel side by side. The woman's companion, who walked three or four paces behind her and carried a similarly serviceable but somewhat more impressive weapon at his belt, was a man in his early twenties, sturdily built, of average size. The young man's appearance, like the woman's suggested both the weariness of long travel and a remaining capacity to deal with formidable difficulties.

The woman halted suddenly. She frowned and

squinted at the sun, which shone brightly from beyond the canopy of the tall trees' small spring leaves. Then she inspected the terrain, as well as she could in the midst of a forest.

"This hill curves round," she announced to her fellow traveler at last. "And I see no end to the curve ahead. It carries us farther and farther to the east."

"And that, my lady, is not the direction in which we want to go," the young man responded. "Well, then. Shall we try climbing to the top of the ridge again? Or going down into the ravine?"

The lady sighed. "Zoltan, we are well and truly lost. No reason to think the bottom of this ravine will be more hospitable than any of the others we've struggled through during the past two days." In those dark gorges, the ubiquitous thin-trunked trees had grown more closely and ever more closely together, until it became impossible for adult humans to force a passage anywhere between them. An army of men with axes would have earned their pay clearing a road.

"And no reason either," replied Zoltan, "to suppose that the leather-wings are going to let us alone this time if we come out of the trees up on the hilltop." He rubbed at his left arm, which was still bandaged—though fortunately not disabled—from their last encounter with flying reptiles, two days ago.

"I suppose we might risk trying the hilltop just before sunset," the woman said thoughtfully. "If we were able to see far enough to get our bearings—" She broke off abruptly, holding herself motionless. Above the high canopy of leaves a silent, broad-winged form drifted; a half-intelligent enemy, cruel-clawed and implacably hostile.

When the wind-borne reptile had drifted out of sight and hearing, Zoltan spoke again, his voice cautiously low. "Anyway, we're soon going to need water." Each was carrying a single small canteen. "We'll have to go down into the ravines for that, of course. This one may be dry, but the next—" He fell silent at the woman's imperious gesture. Her face had abruptly turned away from him, and she was listening intently for the repetition of a small sound just detected from ahead.

In a moment Zoltan, looking over his companion's shoulder, could see a tall human shape, garbed in dull colors, moving among the dun-colored trunks, still fifty meters off, approaching along the hillside.

Both travelers watched in ready silence, hands on swordhilts. The single figure approaching seemed to be making no effort at stealth. The towering, broad-shouldered man was clad in what appeared to be a farmer's rough shirt and trousers and woolen vest. In both hands he gripped a long-bladed sword with which he steadily swept the air before him. Zoltan, watching, felt the hair stir on the back of his neck. This could be a Sword indeed!

The stranger continued moving along the slope directly toward the pilgrim pair, though as yet he had given no indication that he was aware of their presence.

Zoltan, staring at the approaching figure with intense, frowning concentration, whispered: "Is that—?"

"Shh. We'll see."

Amid the dun trunks the seeker so superbly armed had approached within ten meters of the two motionless travelers in dull gray before he saw them. When he did, he stopped in his tracks, startled, continuing to hold the Sword leveled in their direction. Then, looking somewhat flustered, he grounded the bright point.

For a long moment all three remained silent.

At last the young farmer—for so his clothing made him appear to be—said: "Greetings." His voice was soft, but the pair who heard him got the impression that only a conscious effort made it so. "Greetings, in Ardneh's name." He was peering closely at the lady, and appeared to be trying to conceal growing disappointment and confusion.

"And to you," replied the lady. "May you find peace and truth." Zoltan at her elbow murmured similar sentiments.

"My object is entirely peaceful," the other assured them, gesturing with an enormous hand. He seemed now to be recovering from his initial shock, whatever might have been its cause. He was a head taller than most men, and of massive build, his body carrying a minimum of fat. His clothing, particularly his boots, gave evidence of an extended journey. He carried pack and canteen, as any traveler most likely would. A long, plain, leather sheath belted at his waist, of a size to hold his Sword, looked vaguely as if it should belong to someone else.

He added: "I am called Valdemar."

"I am Yambu," the woman told him simply. "This is Zoltan, who has chosen to travel with me. We are both pilgrims, of a sort."

The young farmer nodded and smiled, acknowledging the information. His hair was dark and curly, his blue eyes mild, flanking an interestingly bent nose. The more one looked at him, the bigger and stronger he appeared.

"Yambu," he repeated. "Yes, ma'am." His eyes moved on. "And you are Zoltan." Then some memory visibly caught at Valdemar, so that his gaze went back to the silver-haired woman. "An unusual name, ma'am." he remarked.

"Mine? Oh yes. And an unusual weapon that you are carrying today, young sir."

Perhaps Valdemar flushed slightly; in his weathered face it was hard to be sure. "Lady, in my hands I hope this Sword is something other than a weapon. It has guided me here—to you. Your pardon, lady, if I aim the blade at you again; I promise you I mean no harm."

Taking care to remain at a distance well out of thrusting range, Valdemar lifted his Sword's point again. All three could see distinctly how the fine blade quivered when it was leveled straight toward Yambu.

The lady did not seem much surprised. "And what desire of yours," she asked, "does Wayfinder expect me to satisfy?"

This time there was no doubt that Valdemar was blushing. "I see you know this Sword's name. So I suppose you know what it is. That should—that ought to—make it easier for me to explain. As I said, my goal is peaceful. I . . . "

"Yes?"

"I am a farmer, lady. Actually I have a vineyard, which I have left untended. And I am looking for a wife."

There was a pause.

"Ah," said Yambu at last. A thin smile curved her lips. "And you confided this wish to the Sword of Wisdom?"

"Yes ma'am."

"And the Sword has brought you to me."

"Yes ma'am."

"And I am not quite the bride you have been imagining. Well, rest easy in your mind, young man. Were you to make me a proposal of marriage, I would not accept it."

"Yes ma'am," repeated Valdemar. He looked partly relieved and partly chagrined.

"We must discuss this," said the lady, "but just now my companion and I face problems of greater urgency. Have you experienced any particular difficulty along the way, in the last day or two of your journey?"

Valdemar blinked at her. "Difficulty? No. What sort of difficulty? Oh, do you mean bandits?" The young giant smiled faintly. "I never worry much about that sort of thing. And if there were any who saw me, no doubt they kept clear when they saw how I was armed."

Zoltan cleared his throat. "No trouble in finding your way through this forest, perhaps? Or in dealing with flying reptiles?"

Valdemar looked up, concerned; at the moment the sky was free of drifting shadows. "No trouble finding my way; I simply walked the way Wayfinder told me to go. And no reptiles of any kind; I've never seen one that could fly."

"*Any* kind of trouble?"

"None. Well, several times, for no good cause that I could see, the Sword counseled me to change direction. And once, when I saw no reason not to move on, it kept me walking in a tight circle for an hour, so in effect I was held in one location. But nothing that I would call trouble. Why?"

"Then would you now ask your Sword," put in Yambu gently, "to put aside for the moment the matter of your bride-to-be, and lead us all three safely out of this damned wildwood?"

Openmouthed, Valdemar gazed at her for a long moment. Then he nodded.

Less than an hour later all three travelers were resting comfortably at the bottom of another ravine, where a spring of clear water bubbled gently out of a crevice between rocks, and the trees grew just closely enough together to keep all sizable airborne creatures at a safe distance. Yambu and Zoltan had already satisfied their thirst at the spring, and were now refilling their canteens. Valdemar meanwhile had sheathed his elegant weapon and was bringing out generous portions of dried meat and hard bread from his pack.

Far upslope, too far to be of immediate concern, an ominous, silent shadow drifted overhead, above the canopy of leaves; drifted and came back and went away again, as if it were no longer certain of where its prey might be.

"Those creatures hunt us, young man," said Yambu, almost in a whisper. "Leather-wings—and sometimes worse than that. You say you have never seen them before?"

"I know them only by reputation." The youthful giant looked vaguely horrified, and at the same time fascinated. But not particularly afraid. "Why do they hunt you?"

"I believe they are in the service of some much more formidable enemy. Serving as his scouts. Then, too, it is my belief that any of the Twelve Swords tends to draw trouble to itself. And that one you are carrying in particular."

"And yet I have asked this Sword only to help me find a bride. And now to guide all three of us to safety." Valdemar seemed more disappointed, and gently puzzled, than alarmed by Yambu's reading of their situation.

"You've heard the Song of Swords? You remember how the verse about this one goes?" Zoltan asked him, and without waiting for an answer proceeded to recite in a low voice:

"Who holds Wayfinder finds good roads
Its master's step is brisk.
The Sword of Wisdom lightens loads—"

" '—but adds unto their risk,' " Valdemar concluded. "Yes, I've heard that song since I was a child. Never thinking . . . "

The gigantic youth let the matter drop. Then he looked at the silver-haired woman again. His gaze was timid, but resolute. "I can remember hearing, long ago," he remarked, "of a lady named Yambu, who was once known as the Silver Queen."

She who bore that name ignored the invitation to discuss her past. Having finished filling her canteen, she sat at ease on the mossy bank beside the spring.

"Zoltan and I thank you for your help, young man," she said graciously. "Where will you ask your Sword to point you next? And may I ask you just where and how Wayfinder came into your possession?"

Valdemar looked up at the treetops. "I still seek a wife," he declared stubbornly. "Why this Sword has led me to you, lady, I confess I do not understand."

"There may be an easy explanation. When the object sought is otherwise impossible, or very difficult, to obtain directly, Wayfinder leads its master first to the necessary means to bring the goal within reach. You may be sure the Sword of Wisdom is not suggesting that you propose marriage to me, who could be your grandmother. At least let us hope not. Sword or no, that would be far from wise. Besides, I have no wish to spend my last years growing grapes."

"Why, then, has Wayfinder brought me to you?"

Yambu shook her head. "It would seem that, somehow—I do not know how—I can help you to achieve your goal."

Valdemar sighed. More to himself than to the others he murmured: "I will now repeat my first request. I want this Sword to lead me to the woman, of all the women on earth, who will be the perfect, the ideal wife for me. Nothing more and nothing less."

And he drew Wayfinder from its sheath and held it out again in his great hands.

Once more the point reacted, quivering, only when it was aimed precisely at the lady.

Without comment the young giant re-sheathed the Sword of Wisdom at his waist. Giving up the puzzle for the moment, he recounted to his new companions the story of his enigmatic visitor, seven days past.

He concluded with a question. "Has either of you any idea who my strange caller might have been? It was someone who wore gray, even as you do. That's all I could really see."

Zoltan and Yambu looked at each other. Zoltan shrugged. The lady said: "A number of ideas; but no reason to take any of them seriously."

Her young companion nodded. "Certainly it was neither of us, if you are thinking that. A week ago we were nowhere near the region where you say you live. As for wearing gray, uncountable thousands of folk do that. Your own garments have acquired something of that tinge from travel."

The bigger young man nodded ruefully. "Then can either of you guess why this Sword should have led me to you?"

Zoltan only shook his head.

"I think," Yambu told Valdemar, "you will have to be patient if you want an answer to that question. It may be that the answer will never become clear, even if you do find your wife."

Valdemar took thought, running long fingers through his dark curly hair. A sparse beard was beginning to sprout on his youthful cheeks. Then almost shyly he inquired: "Might it have anything to do with the fact that . . . as I said before, a lady with your name was once the Silver Queen? But I had thought . . . "

Yambu nodded impatiently. "Very well, my history is no great secret. That was once my title. But I don't know why my past, good or bad, should have anything much to do with a young man who raises grapes and seeks a bride. You would have expected the Silver Queen to be a somewhat younger woman? Hold Soulcutter in your hands, my friend, throughout a day of battle, and you will be fortunate indeed if you do not look worse than I do."

Now young Valdemar indeed looked awed. "I apologize, my lady, for what must seem unwarranted curiosity."

"No apology is necessary."

The peasant-looking youth frowned for a while at the weapon hanging from his belt. Then he said: "Perhaps I must take the Sword's bringing me to you to mean that I should stay with you until it tells me otherwise. Perhaps it even means that I should turn over Wayfinder and its powers to you."

Yambu was frowning too.

Impulsively Valdemar said: "Let us try that!" In a moment he had unbelted his Sword, and was gallantly proffering the black hilt in her direction, the sheathed Blade balanced flat across his forearm.

Quietly she responded: "I do not know that you have hit on the right interpretation, young man. But . . . on the other hand, why should I fear this Sword?"

Her lips moved again, almost silently. Only Zoltan, who was close beside her, could hear her very low whisper: "Yet I do."

A moment later, she was reaching out to firmly grasp Wayfinder's hilt.

Having accepted the weapon, and drawn it from its sheath, Yambu stood up straight, her voice becoming a little louder. "It is a long time since I have felt the power of any Sword in my hands. Well, Sword of Wisdom, here you are, and here am I. If you can read my heart, show me the way which I must go to satisfy it."

The Silver Queen held out the blade in a strong two-handed grip, then swept it around the horizon, in unconscious imitation of Valdemar's first gesticulation with the weapon, seven days ago.

In her hands, Wayfinder's keen point quivered at one point of the compass only—almost straight east.

Yambu let the tip of the heavy blade sag to the earth.

She said to Valdemar: "I am favored with a definite reply. Now, do you want me to give you this weapon back?"

To the surprise of both the others, the giant youth put both his hands behind him, as if to make things difficult for anyone who meant to thrust the black hilt back into his possession. He said: "My lady, I wonder . . . "

"Yes?"

"Might the Sword's response to me mean that I am to stay with you, at least for a time? Travel with you?"

Yambu thought about it. "It brought you all this way to me. I suppose it might mean something of the sort," she conceded at length, as if reluctantly.

"And just now, in your hands, Wayfinder pointed east. Do you know what lies in that direction?"

Yambu smiled. "Half of the world," she said.

Zoltan, with his head tipped back, was leaning alternately to right and left, trying to peer upward through the canopy of leaves. He said: "Some days ago, we two were discussing the question of our destination, the true object of our pilgrimage, in philosophical terms. Then we began to be hunted. Being hunted limits one's time for philosophical discussion. In the process of trying to escape from the reptiles we became lost. Valdemar, you've helped us now to temporary safety. But as a practical matter, I must say that our next goal, whether east or west, ought to be some place of greater security. Somewhere completely out of the ken of those whose creatures stalk and harry us."

Valdemar looked from one to the other of his new companions, trying to assess the situation. There was no doubting the reality of those drifting shadows that kept reappearing no very great distance up the hill.

"And who might your enemies be?" he asked with concern.

"There are a number of possibilities," said Yambu drily. Again she took up the Sword in both hands. "But let us not become obsessed with safety. We are going east."

TWO

"HURLED to the ends of the earth, you say? Astride a demon?" The speaker, a startlingly handsome and apparently very youthful man, gave every indication that he found the prospect hugely amusing.

"Yes, to the ends of the earth, or farther for all I know. That was months ago, of course, and neither the Dark King nor his demonic steed have been heard from since." The youthful-looking man's informant, a short, blond woman or girl who appeared even younger than he, flashed a bright grin of her own. "Is it not entertaining, Master Wood?"

The two who spoke with such apparent carelessness of sorcerer's and demon's fate were standing casually just outside the massive outer wall of the world headquarters of the Blue Temple. The man was actually leaning against the building's stones. Squat granite columns, each thicker than the length of a man's body, and broad stone steps leading up to doors worthy of a fortress made the establishment an archetype of the substantial, or perhaps even a parody of such. The two appeared to be waiting for something; but what that might be, or why they had chosen this spot to hold their talk, was not immediately obvious.

The handsome young man nodded. His large, athletic-looking body was well dressed in tunic and cloak of rich fabric, though of no outstanding elegance. He might have been a prosperous merchant, or perhaps a physician. Surely not a warrior, for no trace of any material weapon was visible about his person.

He said: "Entertaining, yes. The demon was hurled away, I suppose, by the Emperor's name in the mouth of the Emperor's bastard, and that poor pretender of a magician, who likes to ride on demons, was whisked away helplessly with his mount—"

The young man laughed again, louder than before, and this time his companion laughed with him. She was garbed in a tight-fitting outfit of silver and blue that showed off her fine figure to advantage; the clothing suggested an expensive courtesan. The heads of passers-by turned in their direction; such merriment was uncommon here in the Blue Temple precincts.

Both parties to the conversation ignored the passers-by, even as they appeared to be ignoring the Blue Temple itself. But he who had been addressed as Master Wood soon sobered from his laughter. He stroked his chin in thought.

Almost wistfully he said: "And yet, Tigris—an alliance with Vilkata might well have been to our benefit."

Tigris had already assumed a more thoughtful expression too. She responded: "He may be able to return, Master, sooner or later. Or, if he cannot come back unaided, we might help him. That may still be possible. Yet, I fear that the Dark King was—or is—something of a bungler. Considerable skill in handling demons, one must admit that."

"Considerable. But finally insufficient," amended the other.

"Yes, Master, as I say—finally insufficient." The shapely young woman nodded soberly.

"And one of the Swords went with Vilkata."

"Yes, Master. The Mindsword, as you well know."

Wood allowed his displeasure at that accident to show. He had particularly coveted that weapon for his own. Then he brightened slightly. "Well, none of that can be helped now. Today we face other problems, quite sufficient to claim our full attention for a time."

"As you so accurately say, my lord."

In the bustle of the populous city, even a pair of such striking appearance did not draw a great deal of attention. Once or twice a beggar started to approach them, then, as if warned by some instinct, veered away.

Once a sedan chair, guarded on both sides by a file of mounted men, passed very close to them, entering the Blue Temple headquarters through a nearby gate.

The man called Wood appeared equally indifferent to potentate and mendicants. "So," he mused, "our erstwhile rival Vilkata, the Dark King, is probably not going to be available in the foreseeable future to discuss alliances. Nor is the demon who bore him away into—ought we to say into eternity? Nor, I suppose, can we hope to recruit any other demons from the Dark King's retinue." Wood's voice became abstracted. "That's all right, though—I can summon powers enough of my own whenever there's a need."

"Yes, Master, certainly you can." Impish little Tigris nodded violently.

Squinting at her, her master thought to himself that she was almost certain to prove something of a distraction in the staid Blue Temple offices, into which he planned to bring her very soon. Very likely, Wood considered, he would have to dismiss Tigris—or else effect a drastic though temporary change in her appearance—before the conference got very far. But that decision did not have to be made now.

The girl began to fidget, as if rendered uncomfortable by an overabundance of energy. She moved a step away, and with a dancing glide came back again. "If it is permitted to ask, Master, why are we waiting? Are those moneybags in the Blue Temple expecting us at a particular time?"

The young man grinned. He was not really a young man, for even now his eyes looked very old. "My dear Tigris, they are not expecting us at all. I expect that an unannounced arrival will produce a more co-operative attitude on their part, once they have recovered from their initial . . . yes?"

This last word was not addressed to Tigris, but to a sudden blurring of the atmosphere approximately a meter above her blond head. Out of this miniature aerial vortex proceeded a tiny inhuman voice, speaking to Wood in squeaky, deferential tones:

"The man Hyrcanus is now alone, Master, inside his private office. Do you wish me to accompany you inside the building?"

"Yes, but see that you remain invisible and impalpable in there. Unless, of course, you hear me suggest otherwise." Wood was standing erect now, the air of indolence having fallen from him like a shed cloak. "Tigris?"

The disturbance was already gone from the air above her head. "Ready, as always, Master."

Wood gestured, and their two human bodies instantaneously disappeared.

The locus of their reappearance a moment later was a tall, narrow, dimly lighted chamber deep in the bowels of Blue Temple headquarters. Though the room was obviously only an anteroom of some sort, the visitors found it elegantly furnished, with a thick carpet underfoot. The walls were paneled in exotic wood, subtly lighted by Old World lamps that burned inside their glassy shells with a cold and practically inexhaustible secret fire.

Wood and Tigris came into existence standing side by

side and almost hand in hand, before a cluttered desk behind which a male clerk or secretary looked up in petrifaction at their unanticipated presence.

The thin man in a tunic of blue and gold stared at them uncomprehendingly, his eyes watering as if from long perusal of crabbed handwriting and columned numbers. Even now, in what must have been a state of shock, the words that fell from his lips were trite; perhaps it had been a long, long time since he had spoken any words that were not.

Clearing his throat, the clerk said in a cracked voice: "Er—you have an appointment?"

Wood smiled impishly. "I have just made one, yes."

"Er—the name, sir? Er—madam?"

"I'm hardly that." And Tigris giggled.

The assured, undeniable presence of the pair seemed to place them beyond the scope of any fundamental challenge.

"I will see . . . I will . . . er . . . " Almost choking in confusion, the clerk bowed himself away through a door leading to an inner office.

The two visitors exchanged looks of amusement. A few moments later the thin man was back, ushering Wood and Tigris into the next room. There they confronted the Chairman of the Blue Temple himself, a man known to the world by the single name of Hyrcanus.

Here, in the inner sanctum of power, the furnishings were more sumptuous, though still restrained, their every detail tastefully thought out. Wood had expected nothing more or less, but Tigris was somewhat surprised.

"I thought to see more gold and jewels," she murmured. Wood shook his head slightly. He understood that splendor here would have been out of place; the finest appointments could have done no more than hint at the immensity of the temple's wealth.

The Chairman was small, rubicund, and bald, with a

round ageless face and a jovial expression belied by his ice-blue eyes. He was seated, flanked by ivory statues of Midas and Croesus, behind an enormous desk, engaged in counting up some kind of tiles or tokens. A large abacus, of colored wood in several shades, stood at the Chairman's elbow. The walls of the chamber were lined with account books and other records, some of them visibly dusty. Spiders had established themselves in at least two of the room's upper corners. The windows were barred, and were so high and dark that it was impossible for ordinary human eyes to see outside.

Raising his gaze from his desk, Hyrcanus stared at Wood in utter blankness for a long moment. His eyebrows rose when he looked at Tigris. Then he snapped irritably at his visitors: "Who are you? What are you doing here? I have made no appointment for this hour."

"But I," Wood retorted, "have made one to see you."

Such a response, from an utter stranger, evidently could not be made to fit into the Chairman's view of life's possibilities. Hyrcanus fixed a stern gaze upon his shaken underling, the thin clerk who still hovered near. "What possessed you to schedule an appointment at this time?"

The man's fingers fumbled with imaginary knots in the air before him. "Sir, I—I have scheduled no appointment. I thought perhaps that you had done so privately. I have no idea who these people are."

"My name is Wood," said the male visitor in a languid voice, speaking directly to Hyrcanus. "I should think it almost impossible that you have not heard of me."

The name took a moment to sink in. Then, with a slight movement of one foot beneath his desk, a gesture quite imperceptible to ordinary visitors (but noted at once by these two callers, and dismissed as harmless), the Chairman sent a signal.

Wood made a generous, open-handed gesture. "By all means," he encouraged, with a slight nod. "Summon whatever help will make you feel secure." Tigris, at her master's elbow, giggled. It was a small sound, almost shy.

In response to the Chairman's urgent signal, there ensued a subtle interplay of powers within the chamber's dusty air, much of it beyond the reach of the Chairman's senses, or those of his secretary. Powers charged with the magical defense of this room and edifice clashed briefly, trying immaterial lances, with the invisible escort of the two human visitors. The trial was brief but quite conclusive: the defenders of the Temple retreated, cowed.

Moments later came sounds of hurried human movement in an adjoining room. A door, not the one through which the callers had come in, opened quietly, and another bald man, this one obviously elderly, looked in with a wary expression.

"I assume," Tigris said to him, smiling brightly, "that you must be the Director of Security?" She almost curtsied.

The newcomer glanced at her, frowned, and kept silent, looking to his chief for orders.

"I would like to know," Hyrcanus grated at him, "how these two got in here."

The man in the doorway cleared his throat. "Sir, I recognize this man as the well-known wizard, Wood. The woman with him—"

"He has already told me his *name,*" Hyrcanus interrupted. "What I want to know is how—"

"And someday perhaps I will tell you how we got in," said Wood, interrupting the interrupter. "But there are other matters I wish to discuss first."

The Director of Security, seemingly unimpressed, stared at his fellow magician. "I know your name, and I warn you that you had better leave. At once."

"You? *Warn me?*"

The elder nodded impressively. His face had become

lugubrious. "I am indeed the Director of Security here. We here do not fear your powers."

Wood's eyes were twinkling dangerously. "Only because you do not comprehend them."

"I believe," the Director remarked drily, "that you are the same Wood who about two years ago visited Sha's Casino, a Red Temple establishment in the city of Bihari."

"And so?"

"On that occasion—correct me, sir, if I am wrong—you encountered certain enemies and were forced to make a swift retreat. It has further come to my attention that you entered Sha's Casino armed with the Sword Shieldbreaker, and that you left without that weapon—and lacking any compensation for it." The elderly man in the doorway smirked faintly.

Tigris, looking at her master, paled a trifle.

Wood put his fists on his hips. His voice was ice. "On that occasion, my man, I was opposed by forces well beyond your ability—let alone that of your money-grubbing masters here—to understand, much less to deal with."

A moment of silence followed. It was plain from their expressions that Wood's current hearers—except for Tigris, of course—remained unconvinced.

The wizard nodded briskly. "Very well, then. I see that a demonstration will be necessary."

The Director's expression became uncertain.

Hyrcanus behind his desk started to say something, then remained quiet.

Silence held for a long moment.

Wood's eyes closed. His left hand extended slightly in front of him, palm upward. The long fingers quivered. Then the hand moved, and the forearm, slowly, made a gentle lifting gesture. Near the high ceiling an almost imperceptible turmoil in the air grew briefly, lightly sharper.

In moments this gentle disturbance was answered by a much heavier vibration. An inhuman groaning and thudding seemed to start in the roots of the huge building and progress slowly upward. Soon distant frightened yells could be heard, rising from somewhere below the thickly carpeted office floor.

Tigris was smiling faintly now, watching the Blue Temple men for their reaction. Neither of them had moved, though the eyes of the Chairman seemed about to pop.

Wood's face, his eyes still closed, had hardened into an implacable mask.

The door to the secretary's anteroom burst open, to frame the large form of an armed guard officer. "Sir! The gold—" The man had trouble finishing his sentence.

Hyrcanus snapped: "What of the gold?"

The guard turned halfway round, gesturing over one beefy shoulder. "It's—coming—up the stairs—"

The Chairman leapt up from his chair, trying to see out past him.

The deepest rumbling, which had begun down around the massive, vaulted foundations of this Mother Temple, was now gradually shaping itself into a heavy, metallic rhythm. It sounded like a company, perhaps a regiment, of heavy infantry, clad in armor, marching upstairs in close formation.

There were continued cries of alarm, and more security people came pressing up behind the officer in the doorway.

Hyrcanus started to come around from behind his desk, and then went back.

The guards now crowding the doorway were pushed aside. But not by human force.

Bursting past them, into the Chairman's private office, came moving gold, coins and bars and works of art, all moving as if alive. The yellow treasure had somehow been conglomerated, magically held together, into the shape of a huge and heavy many-legged creature, a gigantic centipede. At intervals this animation broke apart into separate marching figures, all headless, some in the shape of men and some of beasts. Whether in the form of many bodies or only one, the gold tramped upward and forward, the several shapes enlivened by Wood's magic all glowing dull yellow in this chamber's parsimonious light.

The Director of Security, jabbering incantations, avoided the score of trampling golden legs. Gesturing, he intensified his magical efforts to undo what Wood was doing.

But it was obvious to all that the Director's attempted counterspells were failing miserably. Losing his temper, he rushed at his rival.

That was a serious mistake.

Halfway toward the object of his wrath, the Director slowed, then staggered to a halt. It was as if he had forgotten where he was going. Worse than that, it was as if he had almost forgotten how to walk.

Turning now to Hyrcanus, and then to all the others in the room, a smile of infantile imbecility, the Director of Security sank slowly into the nearest chair. Simpering vacuously at nothing, he appeared ready to be entertained by whatever might happen next.

His eyes lighted on the inexorably marching metal. "Gold," the old man whispered, obviously delighted. "Pretty, pretty."

Meanwhile Wood, his arms folded, had turned away from the Director and sat down on the edge of Hyrcanus's desk. He was watching the proceedings with an abstracted look, as if he were not personally very much involved. Tigris, taking her cue from her master, was now seated also, in a leather chair. From a purse that had appeared as if from nowhere she had actually brought out some knitting, with which she appeared to be fully occupied.

With the intrusion of the marching gold, and the ruthless disabling of his first assistant, Hyrcanus abandoned all pretense of calm control.

He jumped up onto his desk. With screams he rebuked his Security forces.

Then he turned to Wood, pleading: "Put the gold back! Send it back at once!"

"And you will listen to me if I do?"

"Of course, of course. And this fool here"—the Chairman indicated his chief aide, now smiling as he counted up his fingers—"can you restore him to what ordinarily serves him as his right mind?"

"If you will listen."

"I will. I swear it, by Croesus and Midas. What was it you wanted to discuss?"

Accepting this surrender graciously, Wood slid off the desk and with a few gestures quickly restored Blue Temple headquarters more or less to normality. The weird upward progress of long-hidden treasure ceased. The marching golden centipede and all its fragments, immediately obedient to Wood's most subtle command, reversed direction, and headed docilely downstairs. And at the same time the Director lost his carefree interest in his own fingers; his eyes closed and his head sank slumberously upon his chest.

Within moments after the tramping treasure had retreated, the building ceased to vibrate. Inside the Chairman's office only the shouts of guards, somewhere in the middle distance remained as evidence that something remarkable had occurred.

Slowly, shakily, Chairman Hyrcanus resumed his seat behind his desk. He wiped his brow. With a gesture and a few muttered words, he offered Wood and Tigris chairs. The three were now alone.

With the opposition satisfactorily crushed, Wood was calm and reassuring. He glanced at the Director, who was snoring faintly. "He will regain his wits—such as they were." Then Wood focused an intense look on the Chairman. "Hyrcanus, understand me. Your wealth is safe, for the time being—safe from me, at least. Every coin is now back where it was. I do not crave Blue Temple gold, or any other treasure you may possess."

Hyrcanus, smiling glassily, murmured an excuse. Then, turning away momentarily, he beckoned the clerk to him from the next room, and dispatched the man with orders to take a complete inventory of the wealth down below.

Wood shook his head impatiently at this interruption. "Depend upon it, Hyrcanus, not a gram of your metal will be missing. I am not your enemy. Rather we have enemies in common, and therefore should be allies."

The Chairman brightened a trifle. "Yes. Enemies in common. Certainly we do."

Tigris had put aside her knitting, and was now sitting with folded hands, paying close attention to the men.

Her master said to Hyrcanus: "I am thinking in particular of Prince Mark of Tasavalta. I suppose you may rejoice almost as much as I do over his recent misfortunes."

The Chairman, relaxing just a little, nodded heartily.

His formidable visitor said: "I am told that Mark is making every possible effort—so far to no avail—to heal his wife of the injuries she sustained last year."

"A pity," said Hyrcanus, and uttered a dry sound intended for a laugh.

"Indeed. My agents assure me that Princess Kristin is hopelessly crippled, and in continual pain. The only real hope of ever helping her lies in the Sword Woundhealer."

Mention of the Sword concentrated the attention of the red-faced man behind the desk. "Ah. And where is Woundhealer now?"

Wood's eyes twinkled again. "Your question brings us to the very point of my visit. The best hope of anyone's getting Woundhealer in hand lies in the Sword Wayfinder—would you not agree?"

Hyrcanus responded cautiously. "It is said that Wayfinder can guide its holder to any goal he wishes."

"Even, as has happened at least once in the past, into the deepest Blue Temple vaults of all . . . but I have no wish to remind you and your associates of past sufferings and embarrassments. Hyrcanus, I have come here to offer you a partnership."

"What sort of partnership?"

"The details can be worked out later, if you will agree with me now in principle. You were already Chairman of the Blue Temple nineteen years ago, at the time of the great robbery. I believe I am correct in thinking that you and other insiders still consider that the worst disaster that your Temple has ever suffered?"

The Chairman's face grew somewhat redder. "Let us say, for the sake of argument, that you are right—what then?"

Wood put on a sympathetic expression. "And Ben of Purkinje, the wretch who was chiefly responsible for that calamity, still lives and prospers, as the right-hand man of our mutual enemy Mark of Tasavalta."

The Chairman nodded gloomily. Ever since Mark had become Prince of that generally prosperous domain, there had been no new Blue Temple installations at all in Tasavalta—the organization maintained in that land only a single banking facility, relatively unprofitable, in the capital city of Sarykam.

Tigris so far had been maintaining a demure demeanor, so it had not become necessary for Wood to banish her, or take any steps to alter her appearance. Brightly and alertly she continued to pay attention to everything that was said and done between her master and their reluctant hosts.

Genial-sounding Wood now inquired after the health of legendary Old Benambra, founder an age ago of the Blue Temple.

Hyrcanus assured his guests that the Founder ("our Chairman Emeritus, in retirement") was still very much alive—more or less alive, by most people's standards, since he was now turned completely into a Whitehands, and lived underground somewhere, jealously counting up the bulk of his remaining treasure. Then the current Chairman, supremely stingy unless he made an effort not to be, belatedly ordered some refreshment to be served.

Presently—while the Director of Security by stirrings and mumblings gave indications that he might soon awaken—Wood smoothly returned to the subject of the Sword of Wisdom. "You, the Blue Temple authorities, have certainly known for a long time that Wayfinder was used by those daring thieves to despoil your hoard."

"Well . . . yes."

"For years you have been keeping a jealous watch for that Sword in every quarter of the world, ready to try to seize it as soon as it should appear again."

The Director of Security, had by now risen and stretched and finally re-settled himself in a chair at a little distance, much chastened in his manner. Whether he was aware of what had just happened to him or not, he was evidently grimly determined to keep an eye on Wood as long as the intruder remained.

Now the Director said: "Wayfinder's vanishing, as you probably know, was utterly mysterious. The only report we have—admittedly unconfirmed—says that the Sword of Wisdom was stolen, by some unknown agent, from the belt of the God Hermes, after he had been struck down by Farslayer."

Everyone in the room was silent for a moment, no doubt meditating on that unlikely-sounding but undeniable event.

"Yes. I know," Wood answered patiently. Though he had not been personally present at the fall of Hermes, he stood ready to accept that story as confirmed.

The slight jowls of the Chairman of the Blue Temple were quivering. "The treasure we lost at that time, including three Swords, has never been recovered."

"I know that too." The handsome, youthful-looking Wood was now doing his best to soothe his hosts. Tigris looked sympathetic too. Wood continued: "How unjust, how odious, that the robbers should have been able to prosper as they have."

"Odious is an inadequate word," said Hyrcanus fervently. "But let us get down to business."

Wood, with a smile and gesture, indicated that he was perfectly ready to do just that.

The official inquired: "What exactly do you want from the Blue Temple, that you have taken these, uh, drastic steps to bring about this conference?"

Wood smiled. His answer was straightforward, or at least it seemed to be: "I want no more than I have already indicated. A chance to use Wayfinder for my own purposes, which will in no way conflict with yours. A league of mutual assistance against Tasavalta. And against the Emperor."

Blank looks on the faces of the Blue Temple functionaries greeted Wood's last assertion. He was silently contemptuous of their ignorance, but not really surprised. The Blue Temple evidently knew little about the Emperor, and seemed to care less. Or perhaps their lack of interest was only feigned. Like the Ancient One himself, they must be aware of certain recurrent rumors, concerning the enormous treasure that potentate was reported to have stashed away.

But the problems posed by the Emperor could wait. Spelling out his proposal in a straightforward way, the wizard confirmed that he wanted to be informed as soon as any of the Blue Temple people had any knowledge, or even a clue, concerning the whereabouts of the Sword of Wisdom.

"I am aware that you have had your people on the alert, everywhere around the world, or at least across this continent, for years now, for any evidence concerning that Sword. No matter what kind of defences you devise for your vast remaining treasure, Wayfinder can probably find a way to let another bold and clever robber in."

Hyrcanus groaned audibly.

Less than half an hour later the meeting concluded, with Wood and Hyrcanus shaking hands, while their respective aides looked on watchfully. Both leaders pronounced their satisfaction with the agreement they had reached.

Outside Blue Temple Headquarters again, their removal having been effected without the use of any mundane door, Wood and Tigris strolled the streets in silence, until they were rejoined by the demon Dactylartha.

"Noble masters!" hissed the tiny voice, coming out of the barely visible disturbance in the air. "Was my performance satisfactory?"

"At least you will not be punished for it." Wood spoke abstractedly, his main thought already elsewhere.

"Madam Tigris!" Dactylartha pleaded softly. "Did I not do well?"

"As our Master has said," she responded curtly. "Did your old rulers recognize you, do you suppose, Dactylartha?"

This terrible creature, she remembered, had once been Blue Temple property, involved in the famous robbery, on which occasion the demon had failed as dismally as all the other layers of defense of the main hoard. That did not mean, of course, that Dactylartha was weak or ineffective. Against any one of the Swords, only failure could generally be expected—unless, of course, one was armed with another Sword.

A dangerous being to recruit; Tigris, though her own skills in enchantment were great, was not sure she could have controlled the thing without her Master's help.

Wood, now giving the thing its new orders, curtly dismissed it, and in a moment it was gone.

"What are you thinking about, my dear?" the Ancient One inquired. "You look pensive."

"About demons, Master."

"Ah yes—demons. Well, as a rule, one kills them, or has some firm means of control—or is as nice to them as possible. That is about all there is to know on the subject." And Wood laughed, a hissing sound that might have come from the throat of one of the very creatures he was contemplating.

Tigris changed the subject. "Which of the Twelve Swords would you most like to possess, Master?"

"Ah. Now that—that—is indeed a question." The Ancient One mused in silence for a few paces. Then he said to Tigris: "There's Soulcutter, of course. I certainly wouldn't want to draw that little toy with my own hands—having heard what has happened to others—the trick of course would be to get someone else to draw it, under the proper circumstances."

"I understand perfectly, my lord."

"Do you? Good. As for the Sword of Wisdom, I confess to you, my dear, that I nourish a certain hope—that on coming into possession of that weapon I will be able to use it to lead me to the Emperor."

Tigris wondered briefly whether she ought to pretend to be surprised. In the end she decided not to do so. She asked, instead: "What Swords does the Emperor have?"

"None, that I can determine with any certainty."

Tigris, flattering: "Then of the two greatest magicians in the world, neither now has any Sword."

It was true that her Master, Wood, at the moment had not a single Sword to call his own—while Prince Mark of Tasavalta, gallingly, had no less than four.

Tigris was taking great care not to remind her Master directly of this latter fact.

He grunted something, for the moment sounding completely human—a mode of existence he did not always appear to favor.

"Where to now, Master?"

"To a place where I trust we will not be interrupted, Tigris. We have work to do."

THREE

MORNING had arrived, and Ben of Purkinje was enduring an enormous headache.

He sat up slowly, further tormented by a fierce itching. Particles of the hay in which he had been sleeping had worked their way into his clothing. According to the feeling in his head, the hour ought not to be much past midnight, but the exterior world ruthlessly assured him that a new day had indeed begun. The cavernous interior of the barn in which he had sought shelter was now becoming faintly visible, venerable roughhewn beams and gray wall planks bathed in an illumination that could only be that of dawn. Intermittent crowing noises now issuing from the adjacent barnyard offered confirming evidence.

The noises were there, but Ben was reasonably sure that they had not awakened him; they were completely routine, and he had been too deeply asleep to be roused by anything so ordinary.

Too deeply asleep indeed. Unconscious, he thought, would be a better word for it. Recalling some of last night's adventures in the local tavern, he wondered if the second or third girl to sit on his lap might have put something unfriendly in his ale. The first, as Ben recalled, had been almost unconscious herself at the time, and he thought he could exclude her from the list of suspects.

He doubted that any of last night's girls would have played a dirty trick like that on her own accord. Someone would have put her up to it.

Ben clenched his eyelids shut again. His memories of last night were somewhat hazed. He went prowling through that fog, in search of his newly-met drinking companions. They had been three or four youngish men, who had had the look of bandits—or, if not bandits, of people who had no higher moral standard than they found absolutely necessary for survival. A couple of them, perhaps not realizing what a formidable opponent they had encountered, had challenged Ben to a drinking contest. Before that had been carried to a conclusion, the tavern girls had taken a notion to sit on his lap, first in sequence, then together . . . or had that been his own suggestion?

. . . but of course nothing could be done about any of that now. If in fact someone had tried to drug his drink, he had survived the effort. This was morning, and at least it wasn't raining—he would have heard that on the barn roof. Trouble was, the first subtle indications of this fine spring morning were that things were not going to go well today for Ben of Purkinje, known in recent years as Ben of Sarykam. Right now he feared that his headache might be the least of today's problems, because certain sounds outside this borrowed barn were like those of no ordinary farmyard in the early morning. These were the noises, he now felt sure, which had awakened him.

These ominous mutterings and footfalls evoked for Ben the presence of a number of men, maybe half a dozen or even more, clumsily exchanging low-voiced words with undertones of urgency. Muttering, and then separating, spreading out, moving quickly but quietly as if they meant to get the barn surrounded.

That was not at all a reassuring image.

Getting off to a bad start as he seemed to be this morning, Ben hoped that no one today was going to call him by any name that mentioned either Purkinje or Sarykam. As soon as anyone did that, he would know that the false identity under which he was currently traveling had been penetrated. Not that he had much hope for the false identity anyway. It had been a resort of desperation, conceived on the spur of the moment several days ago, when other plans had at last gone desperately and completely wrong. A man who weighed close to a hundred and forty kilos, and looked capable—and was—of twisting a riding-beast's iron shoe into scrap with his bare hands, tended to attract attention. For such a man, ordinary disguises were seldom of much avail.

Ben's worst suspicions were presently nourished by new evidence. If he had been in the least danger of drifting back to sleep—and with a start he realized that he just might have been—that peril was destroyed by a loud call in a hoarse male voice, coming from somewhere not far outside the barn. The words were meant for him. The man outside was threatening to fire the wooden structure if he didn't immediately come out and surrender.

The bass roar was almost instantly repeated: "Ben of Purkinje! We know yer in there!"

Despite the beseiged man's huge size, he came up to his feet softly and promptly amid the hay, the wooden floor of the hayloft creaking under the shift of weight. At the same time he took a quick inventory of assets. Through recent misfortunes his personal weaponry, apart from his own mind and body, had been reduced to one middle-sized dagger. Leaving the dagger at his belt, he caught sight of a pitchfork not far away, and swiftly and softly took possession of it.

A certain urgency within his bladder next demanded his attention, all the more so with impending combat probable. Relieving himself quietly into the hay, regretting the lack of heroic capacity that might have served to put out a fire, Ben listened for more shouts but for the moment could hear only the throbbing of his aching head.

Doing his best to give the situation careful thought, he decided that allowing or encouraging the barn to burn down around him would be a waste of time for all concerned, and a waste of some perhaps innocent farmer's property as well. Ben had no real idea how many of last night's companions and their friends might be outside. What sounded like the clumsy muttering of six or eight might instead be a much cleverer attempt by two or three men to suggest greater numbers.

Well, he would soon find out how many men were outside, and whether they were bluffing. He would go out and see. But he would do so without announcing his real intention first.

Ready for action now, he bellowed a defiant challenge, to the effect that if they wanted him, they were going to have to come in and get him.

Then, as quietly as possible, he slid down the ladder from the hayloft to the dirt floor of the barn. And then, pitchfork in hand, he came out fighting.

Ben's youth was behind him, but he could still run faster than anyone would be likely to expect from a man of his size. He went out, moving fast and hard, through a small door in what he would have called the rear of the barn. The suggestion of numbers, he saw with a sinking feeling, had been no bluff. At least five armed men were waiting for him among the manure piles the back, but at first they recoiled from him and his pitchfork, yelling.

The bass voice that had commanded Ben to give up now shouted orders meant for other ears, screaming hoarsely that if they wanted to survive this day themselves, they had better take this fellow alive. These commands and threats were issuing from a squat oaken hogshead of a man, somewhat shorter than Ben himself, but apparently little if any lighter. Not one of last night's tavern companions. Ben would have remembered this one.

Ben now had his back against the barn wall, hemmed in by a semicircle of lesser men, most of them fierce-looking enough to inspire some measure of respect. They kept him at bay, turning this way and that. While feints came at Ben from right and left at the same time, one of them got almost behind him with a clever rope. A moment later Ben's pitchfork had been lassoed, and a few moments after that several strong hands had fastened on him, and his dagger was plucked from his belt.

"We got him, Sarge!"

But in the next instant Ben proved to those who grasped his arms and legs that they really hadn't. Not quite, not yet. He used his arms to crack a pair of heads together with great energy.

The blade of a very keen-looking knife, coming up under his throat, stopped this effort.

One of the Sarge's wrists, prodigiously thick and hairy, came into Ben's field of vision. The enemy leader, striking out at his own knife-wielding man, seemed to have suddenly become Ben's ally. "*Alive,* I says! He's the one Blue Temple wants!"

That name made Ben redouble his efforts to break loose. It was useless, though. He might have been able to fight off two or three of the ill-clad, ill-equipped bandits at a time, and the remainder of them might have been poorly coordinated or plain cowardly enough to stay at a safe distance. But when the Sarge himself jumped in and grabbed him, using the biggest hands that Ben had ever seen or felt, while two of his more stubborn minions still clung on, Ben no longer had any chance of wrestling free.

This time he was down flat on his back. Raising his head as well as he was able, he peered through a drifting haze of dust and barnyard chaff to take a count. There were six or eight of them altogether, and two of them at least, the ones whose heads he'd banged, were just as flat as he was. He hadn't done so badly at that.

Now, though, four or five held Ben more or less in position, and another was commencing operations with a coil of thin rope brought from the barn, tying his wrists skillfully behind his back.

Ben, looking at the world through a reddish haze of exhaustion, his chest heaving, his pulse thudding in his ears, had the sudden notion that at forty-two, give or take a year or so, he was definitely getting too old for this kind of thing.

Now, Ben's arms immobilized, a couple of his stronger captors took him by the arms and heaved him to his feet.

It seemed there were going to be formal introductions.

"Sergeant Brod," growled the walking hogshead, standing directly in front of Ben, and extending one enormous hand as if Ben ought to be able to snap free of his bonds and shake it. "Better known to some of me own followers as the Sarge. I am the leader of this small but efficient band."

"Pleased to meet you," said Ben. Squinting at Brod and the men who surrounded him, Ben decided that Brod's men all appeared to be more or less afraid of him, and with some cause.

Brod's coloring was fair, right now still red-faced from his recent efforts. His features were fairly regular except for a nose that approached the size to qualify as a disfiguring defect.

Fancy tattoos adorned the Sarge's massive shoulders, which bulged out of a sleeveless leather vest. His dirty hair, some indeterminate shade between blond and red, was tied in long pigtails.

From inside his vault of a chest, his bass voice rasped out what sounded like an accusation: "You're Ben of Purkinje."

Ben blew a tickle of straw free of his upper lip. Trying to get his breathing back to normal, he replied as nonchalantly as he could: "You have the wrong man. My name is Charles, and I'm a blacksmith."

The Sarge had a good laugh. He really enjoyed that one.

"Aye, and my name's really Buttercup, and I sell cobwebs for a living!" Fists on hips, he sized up his prisoner's size and shape, and appeared delighted with what he saw. He clouted Ben a friendly buffet on the shoulder, rocking him on his planted feet.

In another minute the little gang was on the march, away from barn and farmyard. Ben, arms bound, marched in the middle of the group. No one bothered to grip his arms now; he wasn't going to run away. From snatches of conversation between Sergeant Brod and his followers, he gathered that he was being held for delivery to certain representatives of the Blue Temple, who had a standing offer of a great reward for the live body of Ben of Purkinje, or some lesser amount for that body dead. To Ben the proposed transaction sounded all too convincing.

That the Blue Temple wanted him was easy to believe. But that those notorious skinflints would consider paying any reward at all was frightening. It showed how badly they craved getting their hands on him.

The little band of freebooters, Ben still with his arms tied in their midst, were angling downhill, approaching the good-sized river which ran only a couple of hundred meters from the barn. On the near bank Ben saw a flatboat tied up. It was a crudely constructed craft, a score of paces long, half that distance wide, fashioned mostly of unpeeled logs.

As soon as it became obvious that he was being escorted right to the boat, Ben stumbled. Then he dug in his feet. Or gave the impression of trying to do so.

"Where are we going?" he demanded.

"Just a little cruise." Roughly he was pushed along.

On being taken aboard the flatboat, the prisoner gave every indication of trying to disguise a deep distrust of water, edging reflexively toward the center of the crude plank deck.

One of the gang, watching him with shrewd malice, probing for a weakness, smiling slyly, asked him: "Don't care for the water?"

Ben, a nervous expression on his ugly face, turned to his questioner. "Not much of a swimmer," he admitted.

They were willing to let him sit down approximately amidships. There was a little freight on board as well, a couple of barrow-loads of unidentifiable cargo tied down under a tarpaulin. From where Ben was sitting, he could see one small rowboat, stowed bottom-up on the broad deck. It looked serviceable. He couldn't see any oars.

Ben considered making a serious effort to break his bonds. Having got a look at the old rope before they used it, he thought that doing so would not be completely beyond the bounds of possibility. But any such effort would have to wait until he was unwatched.

While the men began what seemed an unfamiliar process of casting off, the Sarge, as if he wanted to talk, came to sit on a small box facing Ben.

Any effort at breaking ropes would have to be postponed. Ben, ready to try a different tactic, announced: "If I *were* this fellow from Purkinje, or wherever, why my friends might pay a better price for me even than my enemies."

"Maybe." Brod sounded doubtful of that proposition, to say the least.

"Did you ever try to get money for *anything* out of the Blue Temple?"

The other looked at his prisoner thoughtfully. "I know what you mean, friend. But they'll pay this time, in advance, or they won't get you. 'Sides, we've contracted to do another little job for them."

"What's that?"

The answer had to be postponed. Brod rose to supervise his unskilled crew's efforts to get the boat free of the shore.

By dint of much poling, and the blaspheming of many gods, along with energetic sweeps of the four long steering oars, the flatboat was at last dislodged from the riverbank and under way downstream. Ben was no great expert in these matters, but in his judgment the men manning the sweeps and poles were being pretty clumsy about it. The difficulty wasn't entirely their fault, though. Obviously this craft had been designed for use somewhere upriver, maybe for ferrying livestock about, and had somehow been taken over by these goons, who were riding it downriver into waters somewhat rougher than those for which it had been built.

At about this time Ben noticed a distracting presence, one he certainly didn't need just now, maneuvering on the outskirts of the scene. This was a large, gray-feathered bird, and with a sinking feeling he recognized it as a winged messenger from Sarykam. At any other time he would have been pleased to get some word from home, and to have an opportunity to send word back. Just now, though, the hovering presence of the courier threatened the last faint credibility of his pose as Charles the Smith.

Perhaps the creature was bright enough to understand

this in some dim way; as if unable to make up its small mind whether or not to communicate with Ben, the bird came no nearer than the bottom of the upended rowboat, where it perched uncertainly and cocked its small-brained head at him. Presently one of the bandits threw a chip of wood at it, causing it to take wing for the shore. But after being driven from the boat, the messenger just flew along the shore from tree to tree, at a little distance.

Brod had noted the bird's presence, and was evidently shrewd enough to understand what it signified.

"Reckon maybe it wants some blacksmithin' done? New shoes, maybe, so it can run like a riding'-beast?" The Sarge enjoyed another laugh.

Ben did his best to pretend he didn't know what bird Brod was talking about.

Several hours passed in uneventful voyaging, with the current bearing the clumsy craft downstream at a good pace. A tributary came in on the east bank, and the river—Ben had never learned its name—broadened appreciably. Rocky hills on the horizon ahead suggested that the water might get rougher there, when this river became narrower and swifter, forcing itself between them.

Still the gray-feathered messenger effortlessly kept pace, darting from tree to tree along the shore. Trying to put that problem out of his thoughts for the time being, Ben considered Sergeant Brod. The brawny Sergeant was still smiling at his prisoner from time to time, nodding, appraising him. He seemed to have a more than commercial interest in the famous—well, semi-famous—Ben of Purkinje as well. Ben was vaguely aware that he enjoyed an almost legendary reputation for strength, among people who were interested in keeping track of such things.

The Sarge came to stand in front of Ben. This time he

put his foot on the box. At length he remarked: "They say you're a pretty good wrestler."

"Me? No. This Ben of Purkinje maybe is. I don't bother with that kind of thing."

"Don't bother with it?" Brod screwed his eyes almost shut in puzzlement.

"No." Ben shook his head. "What's there to know about wrestling? It all comes down to who is stronger, and there I always have the edge. Nothing like blacksmithing to build the muscles. Lucky for you you had six men to help you tie me up."

The redness of the Sarge's face seemed to be deepening. "Lucky for me? What by all the gods' elbows can you mean?"

Ben shrugged.

By now a couple of Brod's followers were starting to take an interest. Obviously they were fascinated by the prospect of watching a wrestling match between these two titans.

Afterward, Ben was never quite sure just how the first specific proposal had been made, or by whom.

"Think you could take him, Sarge?"

"Gwan! Sure, our Sarge could take 'im. Could take anyone!"

"Wrestling on a boat?" Ben, glancing nervously at the surface of the river so perilously near at hand, displayed apprehension at the mere idea.

Either Brod was supremely confident in his own strength and skill or he was shrewd enough to realize that his authority might be adversely affected if he failed to meet this adversary fairly. For whatever reason, he made no objection when someone started to untie the old rope with which Ben's arms were bound.

Someone else suggested they tie a rope around Ben before the bout, so they could pull back their valuable prisoner in case he tried to swim away. Ben for a moment considered seconding the request for such a safety measure, confident that it would be denied. And sure enough the scheme was hooted down. No one could wrestle with a rope tied round them, could they?

The rocky hills ahead were somewhat closer now, and the river was gradually becoming swifter and rougher here, with traces of white water ahead. Just a few such traces, along both banks, which were growing steeper, so that the passage between increasingly rocky shores, Ben thought, might at some point require careful steering. Better steering than even skilled boatmen could manage with these sweeps.

The ropes were off.

Brod was considerably younger than Ben. Ben, sizing his opponent up, was struck for the first time by the fact that this fellow was young enough to be his son.

But he couldn't *really* be . . . could he?

Ben found that an ugly suggestion, but not one that was going to cause him a whole lot of worry. Besides bulk and apparent strength, there was very little resemblance.

Ben moved out to the middle of the crude plank deck, rubbing his arms, stamping his feet to get the circulation going. Actually the blood was flowing pretty well already, but he wanted another chance to look around, getting a good view now of the stern of the boat, which had been behind him when he was tied.

Brod, doing his own muscle-flexing, was grinning at him. "You were really a good wrestler once, hey pop?"

"Did a lot better after I got my full growth." Ben considered. "You probably will, too."

There was really no problem about room. A central space was quickly cleared of a litter of odd personal possessions and miscellaneous garbage. Basically the arena was a deck of rough planks, covering the central two-thirds of the craft. The crew grinning and making almost-secret wagers—no one wanted to offend the chief by betting openly against him—arranged themselves around the rectangle, while with a minimum of preparation the two contestants moved to diagonally opposite corners of the space.

There rose a minor chorus of cheers, incoherent enough that Ben could not tell who they were meant to encourage.

The two contestants began circling, stalking each other.

Ben noted from the corners of his eyes that two of the gang who were currently supposed to be on watch, manning a couple of the large sweep oars, had abandoned their duties, preferring to keep an eye on the contest. The drifting raft was turning this way and that.

Brod growled, shuffled his feet and flexed his muscles. Both feet and muscles were really enormous.

Ben stood in one place, swaying slightly with the motion of the planks underfoot, doing his best to appear hesitant and uncertain, yet gamely determined. This was a clumsy blacksmith, wondering what to do. He looked wide-eyed, innocent in an ugly sort of way.

Brod, quicker than he looked, lunged at him. The two men grappled, grunting and straining, coming to no immediate conclusion, each testing the other's strength and skill. The watchers yelled incoherently. Ben felt sure that some of them at least were cheering for him. Not that he gave a damn.

Ben and Brod broke apart, each backing up a step or two.

"Don't know no wrestling, huh?" The Sarge shook his pigtails in what might have been admiration. Ben's fingers had left red and white imprints on his hairy arms.

Ben seemed to be wondering what all the excitement was about. "Anybody can do this."

The Sarge's face stiffened. He charged again. At the impact, a cheer went up from the onlookers; Ben, bracing his booted feet, took the charge without being driven back.

"Don't like the water, huh? 'Spect me to believe that?" Brod gasped between exertions.

Ben said nothing, saving his breath. He had the feeling he was going to need as much of it as he could get; the Sarge was just about as strong as he looked.

After the pair of them had made the round of the little arena a couple of times, struggling from fore to aft and port to starboard, Ben nodded to himself. He thought he now had his opponent pretty well figured out. Unfortunately, a real win in this situation was going to require more than putting Brod down on his back.

Before Ben could plan his next move, Brod took the initiative again, coming in a screaming, all-or-nothing charge. Ben, trying his best to sidestep, could get only partially out of the way. The two big men, arms momentarily linked like those of whirling dancers, spun out of the arranged arena, toward the edge of the raft-like deck, almost under one of the stern sweeps.

The watchers were screaming themselves hoarse. The long, unwieldy steering oars were bouncing in their locks, unmanned. The two wrestlers had come to a stop only a step from the water. Brod's wide, astonished eyes, half a dozen centimeters from Ben's stared at the unmanned oars. The little crowd of onlookers was sending up a greater roar than ever.

There came a crash, a great shuddering impact. The raftlike craft had struck a glancing blow against a rock.

Feet planted solidly, Ben kept his balance. He gulped his lungs full of air, held his breath, and strained his muscles. Lifting his opponent clean off his feet, he took him overboard. Brod's scream had something in it of the tones of a delighted child.

Cold water smote them both, the fierce current twisting their bodies even as they sank. The Sarge's grip loosened immediately as they hit the water. Ben pushed his opponent away, and let himself plummet as deep as the river would take him, trying to swim upstream. He rejoiced to find that right here, at least, the cold torrent was deep enough to offer concealment and protection.

When he had to come up for air, Ben looked back in the direction of the boat and was glad to see that half the people aboard had been knocked off their feet. No one at the moment was even thinking about pursuing Ben.

Right beside him, as in several other places in the vicinity, some rocks rose well above the surface, offering the fugitive a solid refuge while he caught his breath.

Many of the raftsmen looked terrified. Maybe they couldn't swim. They clung desperately to whatever portion of the boat they could get their hands on. Some, shrieking and cursing, went sliding helplessly overboard.

Ben couldn't wait around all day, watching the fun. Orienting himself toward the west bank, which looked to him a little more hospitable, he plunged under water again and started swimming.

Swimming with boots on was difficult indeed, but there hadn't been time to take them off. Besides, he expected that he was going to need footgear when he came ashore.

Though the river was perhaps a hundred meters broad at this point, most of its depth was concentrated in a single narrow channel. Striking for the west bank, trying to angle upstream to put more distance between himself and the flatboat, Ben soon found he could once more plant his feet on the bottom and still get his face high enough to breathe.

Fortunately the majority of his former captors still had their hands full with other problems. But a few had recovered. A few missiles—one arrow, a slung stone or two—hurtled inaccurately after him. Ben saw the arrow pierce only the current, the rocks go banging and breaking on bigger rocks.

If he lingered in the neighborhood, the next step would probably be a determined swimmer or two, blade-armed, coming after him.

Ben decided not to wait. A couple of additional missiles landed in the general neighborhood. He thought he could hear Brod, surfaced and clinging to another rock, or back on the boat, bellowing in rage. Gulping a breath, Ben went under water again, striking once more for the west bank, swimming powerfully, staying under as long as he could.

Briefly he worried that the bandits might find oars for the rowboat, and launch it successfully. But in the continuing confusion that threat now looked increasingly unlikely.

Currents and rocks grew tricky, and he endured a struggle in rough water to reach shore—but, being an excellent swimmer, he made it safely.

Definitely he was ready for a rest. But now was not the time. Stamping and squishing, he moved inland, getting Brod and all his people thoroughly out of sight and sound.

FOUR

GETTING away from the river as expeditiously as possible, Ben struggled to put distance and obstacles between himself and the bandits. Their angry yells—concerned more, he was sure, with their own plight than with his escape—were drowned by the water raging at the rocks; and then all sounds coming from the river faded altogether.

Unfortunately the messenger-bird from Sarykam had now disappeared as well. For the next half hour he concentrated on making strides inland, staying on the hardest ground he could find, just in case anyone should attempt to trail him. No doubt the Blue Temple had promised a good reward.

After half an hour it was necessary to pause for a brief rest. Once he had squeezed some residual water from his clothing, he continued west at a steady pace.

The landscape ahead of Ben spread itself out in a rugged, arid, and uninviting prospect. In several places he could observe distant hills approaching the size of mountains. There were no roads, fences, or houses to be seen. In another half hour his steady pace became hesitant. Then he began to angle to the north. Lacking anything in the way of food, or even a canteen, he was reluctant to go straight out into what looked like utter desolation.

Ben spent the night in the open, having encountered no one, and seen few signs of settlement. He lay down in the chill of early night, grateful that at least by now his clothing had dried completely, and wishing for last night's itchy hay. He breakfasted on a couple of juicy roots, and kept on going.

A full day after his escape from the flatboat, now walking almost straight north, he caught sight of three people on foot in the distance. They were approaching him from the northwest, on a course that seemed calculated to intercept his own. Ben halted, squinting with a hand raised to shade his eyes. Even at a distance it was obvious that these three were not members of Brod's cutthroat gang.

Shrugging his shoulders, he resumed his advance. As the distance between them diminished, he observed that there was something familiar about two of the approaching figures; and one of those two was holding in both hands a gleaming thing, like a long sword.

Or, rather, like a very different kind of weapon. Something much more than any ordinary sword.

A minute after making that discovery, Ben was exchanging enthusiastic greetings with two of the travelers he had so fortunately—as he thought—encountered.

One of these two old acquaintances, she who had once been the Silver Queen, was saying to Ben: "So, you are my gate to peace and truth, you man of blood? It seems unlikely. And yet the Sword of Wisdom has fastened me upon your trail."

Ben looked at the Sword, and at the woman who held it. He said: "I think I must hear some explanation."

As soon as the greetings between old friends had been concluded, Valdemar and Ben were introduced. Valdemar was certainly the taller of the two gigantic men, but

Zoltan, watching, thought it hard to judge which was the more massive. The two clasped hands, and sized each other up with quick appraising glances.

Presently Ben heard what Valdemar's request to the Sword of Wisdom had been: to be guided to some woman who would match his image of an ideal wife.

The older man sighed wearily. "Maybe I should have asked that oracle the same question, years ago."

The day had been gray ever since sunrise, and now a threat of rain was materializing. Casting about for a place of safety and reasonable comfort, the party of four took shelter from a shower under an overhang of cliff. From here it was possible to look back in the direction Ben had come from the river, so any bandits who might be after him ought to become visible in time to be avoided.

The three old friends naturally had much to talk about. Zoltan demanded of Ben: "Tell us how things are going back in Sarykam. How long ago did you leave there?"

Some of the cheerfulness so recently restored now faded swiftly from Ben's eyes. He said softly: "They are not going well."

Yambu, like Zoltan, was strongly interested in what news of Tasavalta Ben might provide. "Then tell us," she urged.

Ben drew a deep breath. "I'll try to put the worst of it in a nutshell. There was an attack on the palace last year; all of the royal family survived, but Princess Kristin was badly crippled in a fall from the roof. For a time everyone feared that she would die. Now—some say death is the happiest result that can be expected."

All of them were quick with more questions. Ben's answers offered them little or no comfort. The stones of a Palace courtyard had badly damaged Kristin's spine, had broken other bones, and crushed internal organs.

Her mind, spirit, and body had all been badly damaged.

Zoltan, who was Prince Mark's nephew, muttered blasphemies in a low voice. Yambu frowned in silence.

Valdemar, who knew next to nothing of Tasavalta or its rulers, still expressed his indignation, and his loathing of villains who could cause such pain. He then demanded to know who was guilty of launching the attack.

Ben shrugged. "Chiefly Vilkata and his demons, along with a certain Culmian prince. We're rid of them all now. Good riddance. But—too late to help our Princess."

Yambu was looking closely at her old associate. "And you, Ben? How are you, apart from this evil that has befallen those you love? How are your own wife and daughter—Barbara and Beth are their names, are they not?"

"As far as I know, my daughter and my wife are well enough in body," Ben answered shortly. "Let me put it this way. My life at home has recently been such that I do not mind spending most of my days and nights away from home."

Yambu was sympathetic. "How old is the girl?"

"Seventeen."

"That can be an age of difficulty."

Ben made a sound somewhere between a grunt and a laugh. "When I myself arrive at some age that fails to bring its troubles, lady, I will make a note of it."

Zoltan gave Ben one sympathetic look, but then the young man's thoughts quickly turned to the difficulties his aunt and uncle, and all their realm, must be experiencing.

He asked: "Tell us of my Uncle Mark."

Ben seemed glad to leave the talk of his personal affairs. "Your uncle is unhappy," he answered shortly, "as one might expect."

At that point he fell silent, staring past the lady's head. When the others turned to see what he was looking at, they saw, and Yambu and Zoltan recognized, one of the half-intelligent messenger birds of Tasavalta, sitting on a branch of the only sizable tree in the immediate vicinity.

Getting to his feet, Ben addressed the bird: "I had given you up, messenger. Well, now I am here, free to talk with you. What word have you for Ben?"

Spreading soft wings, gliding from its branch to a nearby rock, the creature chirped in its inhuman voice: "Ben, the Prince asks you for news. The Prince asks you for news."

"Well, when you reach the Prince again, tell him the news could be a lot worse; because here I am, still alive, and I have met friends who are armed with a Sword. But it could be better, because I am no closer to finding the Sword we want."

"Say message again. Say message again."

"I will, messenger, I will. But later. There's no hurry about this one." Ben spoke slowly and distinctly, as if to a child. "Rest now. Message later. Rest now."

The bird flew back to its higher perch, where it settled itself as if to rest.

"The Prince is at home, then," Zoltan commented.

Ben nodded. "Since Kristin's crippling, he's spent more time in Sarykam than he did in the past two or three years put together. No more roaming the world, trying to look out for the Emperor's business."

"And what of their sons?" Yambu wanted to know. "How old are the two princelings now?"

Ben considered. "Stephen must be twelve. He has a temper. He'll be a dangerous man in a few years."

"And Prince Adrian?"

"Two years older. Secluded, somewhere well away from home, I don't know where, perfecting his wizardry. I expect we'll not see much of him for a year or two to come." It was common for serious apprentices in the arts of magic to withdraw from the mundane world for a time of preparation.

"And nothing can be done for Kristin?"

"In the ordinary ways of healing and of magic, nothing. There is only one real hope, of course," Ben concluded shortly.

"The Sword Woundhealer." Yambu nodded, and sighed.

Ben nodded too. "Of course we had the keeping of it there in Sarykam for years, but . . . there's no use worrying over that now. Mark nowadays thinks of little else but somehow getting Woundhealer back. He stays in Sarykam himself, but he sees to it that every clue, every hint we can obtain—whether reasonable or not, I sometimes think—is followed to the end.

"That is why I am here now. There was one rumor, one hint, about Woundhealer, that we thought especially promising. It put the Sword somewhere in this area."

"And you came alone to track down this hint?" asked Valdemar, who until now had been largely silent.

Thunder grumbled overhead, and more rain was starting to come down. Ben looked at his questioner. "I was not alone when I set out. Six other people and three of the great birds came with me. I can give you the unpleasant details later, but at this point only I, out of seven humans, am still alive; as for the birds, they no longer travel with me, but one of them finds me from time to time, as you have seen. Thus I am kept somewhat in touch with Sarykam."

Ben related to Yambu, Zoltan, and Valdemar additional details of his struggle with the band of river bandits, and his escape.

Zoltan asked: "Are they seeking the Sword of Mercy too?"

"Perhaps. They had something going with the Blue

Temple, besides selling me to them—or they thought they did."

In turn, the Silver Queen and Zoltan told Ben the tale of their recent harassment by the leatherwings, of their fortunate encounter with Valdemar and the Sword he had been so strangely given, and how during the last few days the three of them, with Wayfinder's help, had managed to avoid the flying reptiles.

Ben gestured toward the Sword of Wisdom. "Speaking of your treasure there, I suppose you'll have no objection to my borrowing its powers for a while?"

Yambu smiled faintly. "I have been expecting you to ask. Let me see if I can guess for what purpose."

"No doubt a single guess will be all you'll need. I want first to locate the Sword of Healing, and then to get my hands on it."

"Have you no more selfish wants than that, big man?"

"That will do for the time being."

In unconsciously queenly fashion, Yambu raised Wayfinder in her own hands and apostrophized the Sword: "I asked you, Sword, for peace, and you have led me to this man of blood."

Zoltan saw Ben frown slightly at that.

Yambu continued: "I see my own quest must give way to one of greater urgency. But before I hand you over to him, Sword, what else do you have to tell me? Is it possible that by following him I will discover the peace that has eluded me for so long?"

The other three, watching closely, could see plainly how the Sword tugged, slowly twisting in her hands until it bent her wrists, aiming itself at the huge man.

Without further comment the Silver Queen reversed her grip on the black hilt, and handed Wayfinder over to Ben.

Reaching for the weapon eagerly, he murmured thanks. Once Wayfinder was in his grasp he wasted no time, but at once demanded of it bluntly: "Sword, lead me where I want to go!"

The Sword of Wisdom in his hands at once twisted around sharply; Zoltan, though no stranger to the Swords and their powers, felt his scalp prickle. The weapon reminded him of some intelligent animal, responding differently as soon as it came under the control of a different master, perhaps a warbeast roused from sleep and scenting blood. Zoltan thought that this time he saw the blade actually bend, until the tip pointed somewhere to the northeast. That direction, he thought, was close to, though it did not exactly coincide with, the bearing of Sarykam.

Still holding the Sword leveled, Ben shuffled his feet, as if getting his weary legs ready to move again. He asked his companions: "Are all of you ready to move?" It did not appear to have entered his thoughts that any of the three might choose not to accompany him.

Valdemar stood up, towering over everyone else. He said slowly: "I began my journey holding in my hands that Sword you now have, and with my own goal, not yours, in mind. And so now I have my doubts about going with you."

At that Zoltan turned on him sharply: "I suppose you think your quest is more important than this one?"

Valdemar raised his eyebrows. He said mildly: "It is important to me."

The two young men were of the same age, or very nearly so; but Valdemar—only partially because of his size—generally gave the impression of being older.

"Well, perhaps you can manage to locate a wife without the help of Wayfinder," said Zoltan. "Or—who knows?—if you come with us you might discover one to your liking in Sarykam."

The other shrugged. "Perhaps, friend Zoltan. Anyway, you should remember that I am not ready to abandon my purpose. But I have already given the Sword to Lady Yambu, given it freely, and so I have no claim on it any longer."

"You are welcome to take it back, long enough to ask a question," the lady assured him.

Ben nodded. "Just don't be all day about it."

The lady paused in the act of handing Wayfinder back to Valdemar. Frowning, she said to him: "You are something of a magician, are you not?"

The tall youth blinked at her as if the question had surprised him. "I have a certain knack for doing tricks with light, and mirrors, and sand and water," he admitted. "No more than that. Depending on the company in which I find myself, I sometimes claim to know a little magic. But how did you know?"

"I have known another magician or two in my time. The art is wont to leave its traces." Yambu shrugged. "In this company you may freely claim competence," she told Valdemar. "I doubt that any of us are able to surpass you, in whatever it is you do with light and mirrors."

Valdemar received the Sword from her, and held it steadily. "I ask—" he began firmly, then hesitated, looking at the others. "I suppose there is no preferred formula of words?"

"None I know of," said Ben impatiently. "Just ask your question." The rain was falling harder now, though so far the the overhang of cliff had kept them almost dry.

"Then I ask," said Valdemar, with perhaps a hint of embarrassment in his voice, "the same question as before. When I spoke to this Sword in my own house."

Wayfinder pointed straight in the direction of the Silver Queen.

The rain slackened somewhat. Ben, though tired, was eager to get moving, and none of the others insisted on a chance to rest. All four set out together, in the direction indicated by Wayfinder.

Ben, who walked with Zoltan in the lead, now wore the Sword of Wisdom at his belt—drawing and using it occasionally, to confirm that they remained on the proper course—while Lady Yambu walked at Valdemar's side.

They had been hiking for a quarter of an hour when Valdemar asked: "What lies ahead of us?"

"Not much but desert," Ben returned shortly. "And somewhere in it, I suppose, the river I went boating on yesterday."

"A wasteland," said Yambu. "One that will take us days to cross."

FIVE

ONCE Wood decided to depart the city where he and Tigris had visited the Blue Temple headquarters, he summoned up his preferred form of rapid transportation. He and his young lieutenant were soon mounted upon a griffin, riding the wind a kilometer above the land. The Ancient One's chosen destination was one of his remoter strongholds. He and Tigris were bringing with them only a few assistants, chosen from those of his people he least mistrusted, who rode clinging for their lives on the backs of similar steeds.

As soon as the Ancient One and his party had reached their goal, all of his helpers, including Tigris, were promptly assigned their tasks of magic, and set to work.

Some hours later, laboring inside a stone-vaulted chamber enclosed by many barriers of matter and of magic, the master of the establishment raised his head over a massive wooden workbench lighted by Old World globes and marked with an intricacy of carven diagrams.

He asked: "Tigris, are we completely secure against unfriendly observation?"

"Master?" Across the room the young woman, startled, looked up from her own work.

"I mean observation from outside. Are there spies,

human or otherwise, anywhere in sight of our walls? Do you make sure that there are none. I would attend to the matter myself, but I am otherwise engaged at the moment."

"Now, Master?"

"Now."

Suffering in silence the interruption of her own work, the young woman methodically disengaged herself from her current task. Then she employed her considerable powers to satisfy her Master's latest wish, sending her perception outwards, while her body remained standing beside the bench.

Outside the stronghold, not many meters distant and yet a world away, behind grim walls of heavy rock and curtains of dark magic, some trees and other vegetation grew naturally. There a handful of birds were singing. Not messengers, these. These birds were wild and small and totally unintelligent.

Of unfriendly observation there was not a trace. Unless the small birds could be counted as unfriendly to the Master and his cause.

For another moment, a moment longer than was really necessary, Tigris harkened carefully. Her body standing indoors did not move, except that her red lips parted.

"Well?"

The young woman returned fully to her body. "Nothing, Master. Nothing and no one out there now."

"You sense nothing?"

Again Tigris employed the full range of her trained perceptions. Again she came back. "Only songbirds."

The Ancient One grunted something, a sound of grudging satisfaction, and returned to his powerful ritual, whose goal, his assistant knew, was the discovery of information about certain of Wood's enemies, notably the Emperor, and the Emperor's son, Mark of Tasavalta.

Tigris, aware of a strange reluctance to do so, firmly

put from her thoughts her memory of the outside world. She also returned, but more slowly, to her tasks.

At odd moments during the next few hours, she pondered her own reactions. She had been somewhat surprised—though not entirely—to find herself prolonging the reconnaissance unnecessarily, simply to harken to the songbirds for one moment more.

The hours passed. Lesser aides, bringing messages, were intercepted by Tigris, so that her Master should not be disturbed. The great magician had been isolated at his workbench for some time with certain half-material, semi-animate powers, and his own thoughts.

At length, when it seemed a safe moment to interrupt her lord, Tigris approached him.

His eyes, coming back from a great distance, at length focused on hers. "Well?"

"Master, a reptile scout has just arrived at the stronghold, carrying intelligence." She named a region that was many kilometers away.

"So? What word, then?"

"Sire, some Blue Temple people in that area have very recently acquired the Sword of Mercy."

Now the man's beautiful blue eyes were truly focused. "Woundhealer." He breathed the name in a hoarse whisper. "We know just where it is? There is no mistake?"

"The location is only approximate. But I believe the report."

In excitement he seized her arm. His grip for some reason felt icy cold. "Tigris, my plans bear fruit!"

"Master, we all expected nothing less."

Wood paused in thought, clasping his hands in front of him, smiling and nodding with satisfaction. "Woundhealer, my dear," he remarked to his young associate, "is perhaps the only Sword that I would be willing to trust in the hands of a subordinate.

"Therefore I am not rushing out into the field to take it away from those Blue Temple fools—I may decide to send you. When you have completed your present tasks."

The blond head bowed deeply. "I will of course be honored, Master."

"We shall see. As usual, I have other important tasks to perform. Though I must admit that, in a way, there is no other Sword that I am more anxious to possess."

Tigris allowed herself a display of mild surprise. "Master, the Sword of Mercy is certainly a tool of great value. We are, any and all of us, subject to injury sooner or later."

"Obviously. But I think you miss my point."

"Master?"

"Certainly, when one is badly hurt, healing is priceless. But surely you cannot fail to see that Woundhealer will also be of exquisite value in the torture chamber."

"Ah."

"Yes, 'Ah' indeed. Just consider the possibilities, when the occupant of the rack or of the boot can be revived over and over, times without number. When one is entertaining one's enemy under such favorable conditions, one always hates to say a permanent goodbye. Imagine the guest, just as final unconsciousness is about to overtake him—or her—being restored to perfect physical health and strength, every nerve and every blood vessel intact again. And restored quickly, almost instantly! No need even to remove him—or her—from the rack for a period of recuperation."

Wood sighed faintly. "I tell you, Tigris, I would give a great deal to be able to take the Sword of Love—and a few well-chosen guests, of course—and retire to one of my fortresses for a few years of well-earned rest and entertainment."

"My Master, I look forward to making such a retreat

with you. What pleasures could we not devise?" The blond young woman giggled, a delicious sound.

"Yes." Wood stroked her hair, and his features softened momentarily. "You are a beautiful creature."

"Thank you."

"And loyal to me."

"Naturally, Master."

"Naturally." The stroking hand moved on. "Really beautiful. And, of course, still really young. That is a rare quality among my close associates, and one I value. Yes my dear, you are precious to me."

The head of yellow curls bowed humbly.

But Wood's expression was hardening again. His fondling hand fell to his side. "Unfortunately, we can spare no time for any prolonged diversion now."

"No, Master."

Standing with hands braced on his workbench, issuing brisk commands, the Ancient One dictated the reply he wanted sent back to his people in the field.

The necessary materials were readily at hand. Tigris wrote what she was ordered to write. The message was short and to the point; the written words glowed briefly, then disappeared from the thin parchment, not to regain their visibility until the proper spell should be recited over them.

Now the wizard paced as he completed the dictation. "Tell my people that they are graciously granted permission to use Woundhealer to cure whatever wounds they may have suffered."

"Yes, Master."

"As for healing anyone else, if the question should come up . . . I think not." The handsome man smiled his youthful smile.

A few minutes later, standing on the battlements to make sure that the winged messenger was properly dispatched, she gazed upon the open sky, and heard bird-song again.

This time, as she listened, the faint crease of a frown appeared above her eyes. There was something she did not understand. Something that bothered her.

Something those cheerful voices not only symbolized, but actively conveyed. A plea, or a warning, that she ought to, but still did not, understand.

The singers of course were only birds, nothing more than they seemed to be, she was very sure of that. And that point perhaps had meaning. Small and mindless and meaningless animals. Perhaps, though, simplicity, an absence of trickery, was not altogether meaningless.

Tigris had the irrational feeling that, years ago, when she was only a child, she might have been able to comprehend the birds . . . though the child she had been of course had not begun to understand the world as it really was.

Yet recently—today was not the first experience—she had been nagged by the notion that in childhood she must have known something of great importance, something essential, which she had since utterly forgotten. Recently there came moments when it seemed to her that the thing forgotten had once been, might still be, of overriding importance in her life.

It was unsettling.

Tigris closed her eyes, long enough to draw a breath and let it go. For no longer than that did she allow herself to waste the Master's time. Here in the stronghold of the Ancient One, one had to guard one's very thoughts with extreme care.

At that same hour, the Sword of Wisdom gripped in the huge right hand of Ben of Sarykam was guiding four people across an extensive wasteland.

They were making good time for travelers on foot, and

Zoltan, the most impetuous of the four if not precisely the youngest, did a good job of restraining his impatience with the comparative slowness of his elders. But he kept wanting to hurry them along. As soon as Zoltan had heard of his Aunt Kristin's horrible injury and desperate need, he had become wholeheartedly committed, perhaps even more than Ben, to the search for Woundhealer.

Their march across what was basically an uninhabited plain had gone on for two days now. In the afternoons the spring sun grew uncomfortably warm. Shade was scarce in this wasteland, and the walkers were all thankful that summer was yet to come.

Now and then Ben grumbled that if they kept on much longer in this direction, they were bound to come back to the river on which he had left the bandit boat, though at a point considerably downstream from that where he had made his escape.

"You are reluctant to reach a river?" Valdemar asked him. "I think it would be a refreshing change."

"This one has bandits on it. I'll tell them you're the real Ben of Purkinje."

As the day drew toward its close, the four, led to water by the sight of thriving vegetation, came upon a small stream that issued from a spring at the root of a rocky outcrop. Ben consulted with the lady, and by agreement they called a halt for food and rest.

Shrugging out of his small pack, Valdemar remarked: "I have no doubt that we are being led toward Woundhealer. But I wonder how far we have to go."

Zoltan, shedding his own pack, answered: "No telling. We may not even be going straight toward the Sword itself."

"Ah. It has already been explained to me that I may not be going directly toward my bride. Whoever she may be."

"Right," Ben grunted abstractedly.

"My purpose then may well be twice delayed." For the first time since he had joined the others, the young vineyardist sounded faintly discouraged.

As the simple process of making camp got under way, Ben began to reminisce about another journey once taken under the guidance of the Sword of Wisdom. That had been nineteen years ago, and Wayfinder had been then in the hands of the vengeful Baron Doon, who had used the powers of the Sword to guide himself and his band of plunderers to the main hoard of the Blue Temple's treasure.

"You speak as if you were there," commented Valdemar.

"I was," Ben answered shortly.

"I have heard some version of the story."

"Would you like to hear the truth?"

"Of course."

"Maybe one of these nights, when we are resting."

The four had pooled their food supplies, but the total was quickly becoming ominously low. Zoltan expressed a hope of being able to find game in this country, despite its barrenness. He had with him a sling, a weapon with which he had gained some proficiency over the last few years. Zoltan went away to hunt.

At least two kinds of wild spring berries were ripening in this otherwise harsh land. And edible mushrooms were also coming up after recent heavy showers. Yambu and Valdemar were able to gather a useful amount of food within a short distance of the camp.

Meanwhile Ben was building a fire of dried brush and twigs. In anticipation of making a stew of small game and vegetables, he also cut a large gourd from a last year's groundvine. This receptacle he hollowed out with a skillful knife, to serve as a cooking pot. A couple of hot stones dropped in would boil the water nicely.

Once darkness had fallen, and the rabbit stew had been cooked and consumed, Ben and Yambu drifted into serious talk beside the small campfire.

Their conversation acquired an earnest tone when Ben began to reminisce about that last time, nineteen years ago, he had taken part in an expedition guided by Wayfinder.

"Oh, I trust our guide, all right." He patted the black hilt as if it might have been a favorite riding-beast. "As some of you well know, this is not the first time I have held this Sword, and followed it."

Zoltan and Yambu nodded.

Ben was coming to the point now. He turned his ugly face toward Yambu. "Ariane too was a member of that party."

She returned his meaningful gaze with an intent look of her own. "I know that."

Valdemar, looking from one of the two older people to the other, asked innocently and idly: "Who is Ariane?" There was not much hope in his voice; doubtless he thought it unlikely that any woman who had been robbing the Blue Temple nineteen years ago would qualify now as a good wife for a man of twenty.

Yambu answered without looking at him. "She was my daughter, and the Emperor's. And she died, nineteen years ago, in that damned Blue Temple treasure-dungeon."

"I am sorry to hear it," said Valdemar after a moment. He sounded as if he truly was.

Keeping his gaze fixed on Ariane's mother, Ben said: "Four years ago, you and I had a chance to discuss what happened in that treasure-dungeon, as you aptly call it. Four years ago we started to talk of Ariane, but it seems to me that, for whatever reason, we said nothing important. Now I want to talk with you about her, whom we both loved. And about the Emperor."

Silence held. Yambu was not looking at Ben, but no one doubted that she was listening.

"Because there is something I did not tell you when we met four years ago," Ben continued, frowning.

"Yes?" Yambu's tone was noncommittal. She tossed a handful of fresh fuel on the fire.

"A few years before our last meeting I encountered Ariane's father. The Emperor told me that she was still alive. That she had been living with him."

Ben's words hung in the air. Meanwhile the small campfire went on about its business, snapping with brisk hunger at its latest allotment of twigs. In the infinite darkness beyond the firelight wild creatures prowled, not always silent. Yambu was looking at Ben now. She stared at him in silence for what seemed a long time.

At last she asked: "Where, under what circumstances, did you have this conversation with the Emperor?"

"On the shore of Lake Alkmaar. I was pretending to be a carnival strongman, he was pretending to be a clown. You, as I recall, were not far away, nor was Zoltan; you must both remember our situation."

Zoltan nodded thoughtfully.

Ben went on: "Understand, at the time my mind was on other things entirely. I was afraid Mark might be dead, and I said something about that. He said no, Mark was alive, it was hard to kill one of his—the Emperor's—children. And then he said to me something I have never forgotten: 'My daughter Ariane lives also. You may see her one day.' At the time I could not even begin to think about Ariane again. But her father's words have kept—coming back to me. Though I've never allowed myself to believe them."

"How . . . strange." Yambu was staring into some

distance where none of her companions' thoughts or even imaginations were able to follow.

Ben's eyes remained fixed on the Silver Queen. His voice was urgent: "You know him better than I do. You tell me how likely he is to be truthful in such a matter."

"I, know him?" The Silver Queen, shaking her head, gave a kind of laugh. "I've shared his bed, and borne his child. But I don't even know his true name—assuming that he has one. Know him? You'll have to seek out someone else for that."

"But does he tell the truth?"

The gray-haired woman was silent for what seemed to Ben a long time. At last she said: "More than anyone else I've ever known, I think. One reason, perhaps, why he's so impossible to live with."

No one said anything for a time. Then Valdemar, yawning, announced that he intended to get some sleep.

Conversation immediately turned to the practical business of standing guard—whoever was standing watch would of course be armed for the job with the Sword of Wisdom.

Zoltan, having by lot been given the honor of standing the first watch, paced in random fashion for a time, his worn boots making little sound in the sandy soil. Slowly he looped round the still-smoldering fire in an irregular pattern, remaining at a considerate distance from the three blanket-wrapped forms of his companions.

Now and again the young man, his face vaguely troubled, stopped to gaze at the naked weapon he was carrying. Then he silently and deliberately paced on.

During one of these pauses, as Zoltan stared at the Sword of Wisdom, his lips moved, as if he might be silently formulating a new question.

Even in the night's near-silence, the words were far too soft for anyone else to hear: "If I were—*if* I, like Valdemar, were seeking the right woman for myself—which way would I go?"

If the Sword reacted at all to this hypothetical new command, the turning of its point, the twisting of its black hilt in Zoltan's grasp, must surely have been very subtle, a movement right at the limit of his perception.

But probably, he thought, the Sword would not answer such a conditional question at all.

Ought he to make the query definite? No, That part of his life he ought to be able to manage for himself.

But it did cross Zoltan's mind that perhaps it would be wise for him to ask, now when the Lady Yambu could not hear him, whether he should remain with the Lady Yambu any longer or not.

In response to this question—if it was indeed a real question—the reactions of Wayfinder in Zoltan's hands were very tentative, indicating first one direction and then another.

Or was he only imagining now that the Sword responded at all?

Frowning with dissatisfaction, Zoltan sat down for a time, his back to the dying fire, the weight of the drawn Sword resting on the sand in front of him, faint stars and sparks of firelight reflecting in the blade.

When the stars in their turning informed the young man that his watch had passed, he crawled softly to Valdemar's side and woke him with a gentle shaking.

"All quiet?"

"All quiet."

Moments later, Zoltan was wrapped in his own blanket and snoring faintly.

Now Valdemar was the one holding Wayfinder, and pacing. Presently, like Zoltan, he sat down for a time, and like the smaller youth he found another question to whisper to the oracle.

"Sword, how soon will you bring me to the goal I have asked for? Another day? A month? A year?"

There was no reply.

Softly he pounded his great fist on the ground. He breathed: "But of course, how can you answer such a question? It is only *Where* that you must tell, never When or Why or How—or Who. So *Where* must be enough for me."

Ben's turn on watch followed in due course. The older man did little pacing—his legs felt that they had accomplished quite enough of that during the day just past. But he moved around enough to be an effective sentry. And he stayed creditably alert.

Ben too, found some serious personal thoughts and questions that he wished to put to the Sword. But none of these queries were voiced loudly enough for anyone else to hear.

He did not fail to keep track of time, or neglect to wake the Lady Yambu when her turn came around, well before the sky had begun seriously to lighten in the east.

Yambu took advantage of the opportunity to have a word or two with Ben.

"What do you think of him?" she whispered, nodding in the direction of the sleeping Valdemar.

Ben shrugged. "Nothing in particular. I doubt he's much more than he seems to be. What I do wonder . . . "

"Yes?"

"How it is that the Sword will satisfy his wish, and yours, and mine, by leading us all together in the same direction."

If the Silver Queen nursed private thoughts during the hours she spent alone with Wayfinder she was not inclined to share them, even with the Sword. Her watch passed uneventfully.

When the sun was up the party of four adventurers broke camp and moved on, following the guidance of the Sword of Wisdom, once more in the hands of Ben.

For another day or two the Sword continued to lead them steadily northeast. Foraging and hunting kept them tolerably well fed. At night they camped by water when it was available, and made dry camps when it was not, and in either case stood watch in turn, in turn armed with the Sword of Wisdom.

Still there was no sign of the river Ben said they must inevitably encounter; evidently its winding course was carrying it also farther to the east.

Progressively the country surrounding the four seekers became more and more a desert. And then one day the river, of which Ben had been so wary, was again in sight.

SIX

THE course of the rediscovered river, as indicated by the vegetation growing thickly along its banks, ran ahead of the travelers and somewhat to the east. A kilometer or so after slicing its way into view between hills to the north, the watercourse emerged from a rocky gorge onto relatively flat land. Becoming visible at approximately the same time was a faint road or track, the first sign of human endeavor the travelers had seen for days. This came gently curving toward the river from the west, with a directness suggesting that the point of intersection would provide a ford.

Shortly after this road came into their view, the sight of half a dozen scavenger birds, circling low in several places above the near bank of the river, alerted the four travelers to the presence of death. The number and position of the gliding birds suggested that destruction of animal or human life might recently have occurred on a substantial scale.

Less than an hour after first sighting the birds, the four seekers, advancing steadily but cautiously, their afternoon shadows now gliding far ahead of them, reached the place where the sketchy road descended a shallow bank to ford the river.

Mounting a slight rise, Ben, who was a little ahead of

the others, came to a stop, grunting. The bandits' flatboat had survived, substantially intact, its encounter with the rapids. It now lay run aground several hundred meters away, a little downstream from the ford.

Ben pointed, and said to his three companions: "That's the boat I swam away from."

The flatboat's sweeps and poles, or most of them, were missing, as was the covered cargo, whatever that had been. There was no human presence, living or dead, on the boat or near it.

Some small four-legged scavengers, whose presence had evidently been keeping the hungry birds aloft, slunk away along the shoreline as the four humans approached. One of the scampering little beasts turned to bare its fangs, until Zoltan slung a stone at it, scoring only a near miss, the missile kicking up a spurt of sand.

"I think I see a dead man," said Valdemar in a strained voice, standing as tall as he could and squinting ahead from his great height. "There. Just upstream from the ford."

The four advanced, still cautiously, the three who were armed with hands on weapons. It was soon possible to confirm Valdemar's sighting. Then almost at once they came in sight of another fallen body, lying nearer to them, motionless beside a slaughtered riding-beast. And then a third man, this one obviously dead, his skull crushed in.

"No more than a day ago," Zoltan muttered, looking closely at the handiest corpse and sniffing.

Soon the total of human dead discovered had reached approximately a dozen, all within a stone's throw of the ford.

Ben, peering closely now at the bodies, announced that he could recognize some of the bandits from whom he had so recently escaped. He confirmed that this definitely was—or had been—Brod's band, though the Sarge himself had not yet been found.

"Some of them are wearing blue and gold," Valdemar commented in a subdued voice. "That has to mean Blue Temple, doesn't it?"

Ben nodded. "Brod kept his rendezvous with them," he mused. "Can't say I'm surprised that a fight started—but over what?" He drew Wayfinder, which he had momentarily put away, muttered over the Sword, turned it this way and that.

Signs on the ground indicated that riding-beasts, and perhaps loadbeasts too, had galloped here, had run in panicked circles on the flat land where the stream widened and smoothed into the ford. All this could be read according to the tracks, which were quite plain in the moist sand of the riverbank. The imprints were a day old, or not much more than that, drying and crumbling around the edges. But no running animals were now in evidence; whatever mounts and loadbeasts might have survived the fight had evidently scattered.

Zoltan, darting about on the field of combat more energetically than any of his companions, was seeking among bushes and boulders, bending over bodies, examining one after another in rapid succession.

The four, exchanging comments, reached a consensus: One side, either Blue Temple or bandits, had tried to cheat the other. Or perhaps both had simultaneously attempted some kind of treachery. Then they had efficiently killed each other off.

Ben was still leveling his Sword, turning it this way and that, frowning, trying to interpret what the bright blade told him now. Wayfinder's point was twitching.

Violent death was nothing new to any of the travelers, except perhaps to Valdemar.

"Have you seen this kind of thing before?" the Silver Queen inquired of him.

The towering youth replied with a shake of his head. He appeared to be repelled, and somewhat upset by the unpleasant sights.

He muttered: "Foolishness, foolishness. Why are folk determined to kill each other? It's as if they looked forward to their own dying."

"I have no doubt some do," Yambu assured him.

Now Zoltan, who with a veteran's callous practicality had begun rifling the packs of the fallen, announced with a cheerful cry the discovery of food.

The provisions were mostly dried meat and hard biscuit. He began to share them out with his companions. He came upon spare clothing, too, and announced the welcome find.

Zoltan compared his own right foot with that of a corpse. "I think this one's shoes may fit me. Just in time, mine are wearing through."

There was a cry—really more a grunt—of excitement, from Ben. Not long distracted from his quest by a mere battlefield, he had been guided by Wayfinder to a wounded loadbeast.

The others saw him pointing the Sword at the animal where it stood amid some scrubby bushes, which until now had screened it from their observation. The loadbeast's harness was marked with the Blue Temple insignia of gold and blue, and it carried a full load on its back. The beast was favoring its right foreleg, streaked with dried blood. There was water here, and some good grazing along the river, so the animal must have been disinclined to wander far.

No doubt, thought Zoltan, the scavengers had so far let the loadbeast live because there was easier meat on hand for the taking.

In Ben's hands the Sword of Wisdom was pointing straight at the trembling, braying animal.

Valdemar said: "Put the poor creature out of its misery, at least."

But Ben had already sheathed the Sword of Wisdom, seized the animal by its bridle, and pulled it out of the bushes so he could get at its burdens more easily. In another moment Ben was unfastening panniers from the loadbeast's back and dumping their contents on the ground.

His companions, alerted now, scarcely breathing, were all watching him in silence.

Of all the bundles that had been strapped to the back of the burdened animal, only one was long and narrow enough.

When the coverings of this package were ripped away by Ben's powerful hands, it proved indeed to contain a Sword, black-hilted and elegantly sheathed.

"Wait! Before you draw. That could be Soulcutter . . ." Valdemar fell silent.

Ben was holding the sheathed and belted Sword up for the others to see. A single look at the white symbol on the hilt, depicting an open human hand, allayed whatever fears they might have had. Here was Woundhealer, the very Sword they had come looking for.

Ben, with grim satisfaction, strapped on the Sword of Mercy. Then he turned, his eyes sweeping the horizon, warily ready for someone to challenge him for his prize.

Valdemar studied him for a moment, then turned away, once more examining the fallen on the field.

"What are you looking for?" asked Yambu.

"I want to see if any of them are still alive."

Indeed one of the fallen, and only one, still breathed. Evidently he had managed to drag himself under a bush, and so lay relatively protected from the sun, the scavengers, and discovery.

Ben on getting a look at the fallen man at once recognized Sergeant Brod. "This is the very one I wrestled with."

The squat leader of the bandits, his chest rising and falling laboriously under his leather vest, lay in a welter of his own dried blood, dagger still clutched in his right hand, not many meters from the treasure the two armed factions must have been struggling to possess. Either he had not known Woundhealer was there, or he had been too badly hurt to reach it.

Valdemar cried out suddenly, his voice for no apparent reason argumentative: "Ben! If that's really the Sword of Healing, you'd better use it!"

Ben, faintly puzzled, looked at the young giant in wary silence.

"Use it, I say!" Valdemar sounded angry. "The man is dying. Even if he was your enemy."

"Did you think I wouldn't use it?" Ben asked mildly. Stooping, he grabbed Sergeant Brod by both ankles and pulled his inert weight roughly straight out from under the bush, evoking a noisy breath that might have been a gasp of pain, had the victim been fully conscious.

Valdemar looked slightly surprised and vaguely disappointed, as if he had been ready for a confrontation with Ben.

Bending over the fallen man once more, Ben pulled the dagger from Brod's hand, and took the added precaution of kicking out of his reach another weapon which had fallen nearby.

"Just in case," he muttered. "Actually, I look forward to speaking with an eyewitness of this skirmish. Might be a help, even if we can't believe much of what he says."

Once more Ben delayed briefly, this time to search the pockets of the fallen man, and his belt pouch. Evidently the search turned up nothing of any particular interest.

Then Ben, who was no stranger to the Sword of Mercy and its powers, postponed the act no longer, but employed Woundhealer boldly, thrusting the broad blade squarely and deeply into the victim's chest.

Valdemar flinched involuntarily at the sight. Zoltan and Yambu, more experienced observers of Swords' powers, watched calmly.

The bright Sword's entry into flesh was bloodless—though it cut a broad hole in the Sarge's leather vest, which Ben had not bothered to open—and the application of healing power was accompanied by a sound like soft human breath.

Recovery, as usual when accomplished through the agency of Woundhealer, was miraculously speedy and complete. The man, his color and energy restored, sat up a moment after the Sword had been withdrawn from his body. He looked down at his pierced and bloodied garments, then thrust a huge hand inside his vest and shirt and felt of his own skin, whole again.

A moment later Brod, now staring suspiciously at Ben, got his legs under him and sprang to his feet with an oath. "What in all the hells do ye think yer doing?"

Ben stared at him with distaste. "What *am* I doing?" he rumbled. "I may have just made a serious mistake."

The Sarge was scowling now at the Sword in the other's hand. "Reckon you know that's my proppity you got there?"

No one answered him. Ben slowly resheathed Woundhealer at his belt. He grunted: "You might express your thanks."

Brod turned slowly, confronting each of his four rescuers in turn. When he found himself facing the lady, he introduced himself to her, using some extravagant gestures and words.

Yambu was neither much impressed nor much amused. "I am not the one who healed you, fellow."

Brod finally, reluctantly, awkwardly, thanked Ben.

"I had a reason." Ben gestured at the field of death by

which they were surrounded. "Now entertain us with a story about your little skirmish here. And you might as well tell the truth for once."

"You think I'd *lie?*"

"The possibility had crossed my mind."

Protesting his invariable truthfulness, Brod began to talk. He told his rescuers that his worst problem had been surviving the scavengers, having half a dozen times come close, he thought, to being eaten alive. He said that whenever he had regained consciousness he had waved his dagger at the predators, and by that means managed to keep them at bay.

Moving about a little, surveying the field, he grimaced at the sight of his fallen comrades, their bodies stabbed by Blue Temple blades and gnawed by scavengers. But the Sarge was able to be philosophical about their loss. "The magic hasn't been made yet that'll do any of these a bit of good."

Meanwhile Zoltan had quietly borrowed the Sword of Mercy from Ben, approached the injured loadbeast, and tried Woundhealer on the leg which it kept favoring, listening meanwhile to Ben's ongoing interrogation of Sergeant Brod. It did not sound like Ben was managing to learn anything of importance.

Almost at the Sword's first touch, the animal's braying ceased, and the wound disappeared from its leg. It looked at Zoltan in mild satisfaction, accepting with inhuman complacency its miraculous return to health. The young man rubbed its head before it turned aside to graze along the riverbank.

By now the Sarge, in response to insistent, probing questions from Ben and the Silver Queen, had launched upon a rambling and at least generally plausible explanation of just how the fight for Woundhealer had come about between his gang and the Blue Temple people. The latter, Brod said, had been in the process of escorting the Sword of Healing back to their headquarters, and had hoped to engage the bandits—at a ridiculously low fee, according to Brod—as additional guards.

He complained bitterly about Blue Temple stinginess, which he said he was sure lay at the root of their treacherous behavior.

Zoltan, his cynical amusement growing as he listened, thought that this Sarge was not so much a dedicated enemy of truth and Tasavalta, as a complete opportunist.

Brod, his imagination now warmed by the fact that his audience so far seemed to believe him, began to stretch his story. Now, it seemed, the Sarge had been trying for some time to get the Sword of Healing for the noble Prince Mark of Tasavalta.

Ben and Zoltan exchanged glances in which amusement and outrage were mingled.

Yambu appeared to share their sentiments. But by now she had moved a little apart from the others, and, sitting on a rock in deep thought, did not seem to be giving much thought to the Sarge and his tall tales.

Valdemar now was looking with distrust and disgust at the man whose rescue he had insisted upon.

Brod returned Valdemar's gaze with some curiosity, and demanded to know this young giant's name. When he had been told, his next question was: "Ever do any wrestling?"

"Some."

"Ah. Aha! Maybe you and I should try a fall or two one day."

"I don't know why." Valdemar did not appear at all interested in the challenge.

Brod shrugged. "Have it your way." He squinted once

more at Ben and Zoltan. "Atmosphere's a little chilly in these parts. Guess maybe I'll be on my way."

"An excellent idea," said Ben shortly, standing with his powerful arms folded.

Brod made a casual move to rearm himself, bending as if to pick up a fallen weapon or two from the field, but this action was cut short by a sharp "No" from Ben.

Brod straightened. "What?"

"Don't pick up any tools. Just start walking." Zoltan too was watching Brod closely, and Zoltan's hand was on the hilt of his own serviceable sword.

The bandit leader, all injured innocence, loudly protested, "You'd send me away as nekkid as a babe? Man's got a right to protect himself, don't he? There's wild animals in these parts." He paused, as if gathering breath to deliver the ultimate argument, then spat: "There's *bandits!*"

"Get walking," said Ben quietly. "Before I change my mind."

Brod turned. "Lady Yambu? A high-born lady like you wouldn't . . . " His voice died, withered by the expression on Yambu's face.

Ben, his right hand on the hilt of one of his two belted Swords—the one devoid of healing power—continued to consider the Sergeant thoughtfully.

Brod fidgeted uncomfortably under this inspection. He glowered, but then with an obvious effort, he smiled, achieving at least a pretense of gratitude and co-operation. "All right. All right. Maybe you're right. I'm going, just the way you want."

The others, remaining more or less suspicious, watched him walk a semicircle, first, as if completely undecided as to which way he wanted to go. Then the Sarge moved in the direction of the ford, and went downstream along the near bank of the river. On reaching the grounded flatboat, a hundred meters or so from where his watchers stood, Brod waded to it and climbed aboard. There he helped himself to the small boat that still was lashed to the deck, loosing the lashings, and manhandling the small craft into the water.

Zoltan, idly pulling the long thongs of his hunting sling through his free hand, commented: "Might be some weapons there."

Ben shrugged. "Let him help himself; as long as he keeps moving, away from us."

Now that Ben had the Sword of Healing securely at his belt, he had only one thought: to be done with worrying about Brod and other unimportant matters, and convey his new treasure quickly back to Sarykam.

Another gray Tasavaltan messenger-bird arrived at this point, as if it had been waiting for the Sarge, antagonistic as he was to Ben, to take himself away. Ben made welcome use of the opportunity to dispatch a written note to Mark, informing the Prince that his friends had now acquired the long-desired Sword.

Then Ben, Valdemar, Yambu, and Zoltan all availed themselves of Woundhealer, clearing up all of their own hurts, old and new; the most recent of these being a couple of minor injuries sustained by Ben in the course of his wrestling bout and subsequent escape from the flatboat.

Accepting the Sword of Mercy, Yambu murmured: "This knee is wont to give me problems . . . " And with a surgeon's steady hand, she pulled up one leg of her gray trousers, and thrust the hurtless Blade straight into the pale skin . . .

There was no pain, and of course she had not thought there would be any. But the shock was unexpected, and tremendous, far greater than she had anticipated. In the instant when Woundhealer entered Yambu's body the world changed, subtly but powerfully. Her chronically sore knee was healed, but the nagging pain and its relief were alike forgotten, in the simultaneous curing of a greater, deeper anguish, so long endured that the Silver Queen had ceased to be consciously aware of it at all.

So long endured . . . ever since that day of evil memory, almost a score of years ago, when she had overcome the Dark King's army with Soulcutter in her hands.

"Ah . . . " said she who had once been the Silver Queen, and let the black hilt of this far different blade slide from her grip. The Sword of Love fell to the earth. She stood for a moment with head thrown back, a woman overtaken by some sudden fundamental pain, or ecstasy—no human, watching, could have said, in that first moment, which . . .

The paroxysm shook her for no more than a handful of heartbeats. Then Yambu could move again.

There were no mirrors at hand, and for long moments she could only marvel silently at the way her companions, open-mouthed, were staring at her now.

And even more strongly did the Silver Queen wonder at her own internal sensations, when she paused to savor them. This, this, she could remember now, was what it felt like to be fully alive.

At last she demanded: "What is it? Why do you all stare at me?" But in her heart she thought that she already knew the important part of the answer.

"My lady . . . " This was Zoltan, her traveling companion for several years, now suddenly hushed and reverent. "My lady, you have grown young again."

Ben, his ugly countenance a study in awe, was nodding soberly. Valdemar stood gaping.

"Young again? Nonsense!" And to confirm that it was nonsense the Silver Queen could see strands of her own long hair, still gray, drifting before her eyes. She could clearly see her own hands, weathered and worn, not at all the hands of a young girl.

Yet even as Yambu contradicted Zoltan, she felt that he must be speaking some fundamental truth.

"You are all looking at me so . . . has anyone a mirror?"

What had seemed almost a spell was broken. Zoltan's thought was that there might possibly be a mirror in one of the Blue Temple or bandit packs that now lay scattered about. He went to look.

Ben agreed, and joined the search. But he failed to prosecute this effort vigorously, stopping every few seconds to turn and look back at the Silver Queen.

Valdemar was in this case the most practical of the four. He said nothing, but went a little apart to squat on the very shoreline of the river, where he scooped up sand with his huge hands, and splashed and puddled water into a concave excavation, muttering the while. When his efforts at magic had born fruit, he lifted from the bank a kind of reflective glass, as broad as a human countenance, formed by the solidification of warm river water.

The object he handed to Yambu was as heavy as liquid water but no heavier or colder, flat and mirror-smooth on one face, rough as stone on its round edge and convex back. "My lady, be assured that the glass as I give it to you is completely honest."

Accepting the gift, Lady Yambu stared into the brilliant surface. There was no denying it, she now looked forty again, or even slightly younger, instead of the sixty she had appeared to be before Woundhealer touched her—or her true age of fifty-one.

Her hair was still white, or nearly so; but this alteration in color now appeared premature. Lines of tension and weariness, so long-engraved she had forgotten they were there, had been expunged from the face which now looked back at her, in which a long-vanished light and beauty had now been re-established. This was the countenance of no mere girl, but neither was it any longer old.

Zoltan, who had been her fellow pilgrim for several years, continued to stare at Yambu in timid awe, as if she were a stranger.

It was time now for the others to enjoy their turns at gaining what benefit they might from the Sword of Mercy's power. None of the three underwent any visible transformation. Ben stretched and groaned with the enjoyment of having several minor aches and pains removed, as a tired man might luxuriate in a massage. Valdemar was silent and thoughtful as Woundhealer's blade searched his flesh for damage; the youth had evidently not accumulated much.

When Zoltan had had his turn, it was time to make camp for the night. Even freshly healed, they were tired enough to camp where they were, right by the ford, with water readily available. But the dozen dead still held that field, and none of the four were minded to spend their own time and energy as a burial or cremation detail.

Another problem with this location lay in the fact that Brod would be able to find them easily should he return with some mischief in mind. But these were minor considerations beside the counsel of the Sword of Wisdom.

It was Yambu who at last put the question directly to Wayfinder: "Where is our safest place to camp tonight?" And the Sword promptly pointed them across the ford, away from the field of death.

Before leaving the battlefield, Valdemar did as Brod had been forbidden to do. He armed himself with two of the many weapons, now ownerless, that lay about for the taking.

From one fallen soldier Valdemar chose a battle-hatchet, and from another one a dagger, with its sheath. He had to unbuckle this last tool from its owner's stiffened corpse. The business was unpleasant, but still he did it without hesitating.

He muttered to himself: "If I am to be a warrior, I am going to need a warrior's tools."

Zoltan asked him: "Have you any skill with those?"

"Not with weapons. But knives and hatchets are familiar implements enough."

"Then I suppose you've chosen well."

Having forded the river, the four headed northeast by north, still following the Sword of Wisdom in Ben's hands.

Following them, for a short distance only, came the healed loadbeast.

The creature paused, watching them depart. Then it shook its head and went back to where grass grew along the river.

SEVEN

ATOP the highest tower of the sprawling white stone Palace in Sarykam, standing on a paved rooftop that overlooked the red-roofed city, the placid harbor, and the Eastern Sea red-rimmed with dawn, Prince Mark of Tasavalta, wearing nightshirt and slippers, wrapped in a robe against the morning chill, was leaning on a railing, gazing to the south and west, waiting and hoping for the arrival of one of his numerous winged messengers or scouts.

Dawn was a good time, the most likely time in all the day, for certain birds, the night-flying class of owl-like scouts and messengers, to come home.

The Prince of Tasavalta was a tall man, strongly built, his face worn by weather and by care, his age just under forty, his hair and eyes brown, his manner distracted.

The semi-intelligent creature whose arrival Mark was anticipating presently became visible in the dawn sky as a faraway dot that in time grew into a pair of laboring wings.

Twelve-year-old Stephen, Mark's younger son, already fully dressed, joined his father on the rooftop, as he did on many mornings, to see whether any messengers might arrive.

The boy was sturdily built, his hair darkening to the

medium-brown of his father's. The facial resemblance between father and son was growing stronger year by year.

The beastmaster attending the eyrie this morning was a man of exceptionally keen vision. He was the first to confirm the distant wings, now laboring in from the southwest, as those of a particular messenger-bird, whose arrival had been expected for more than a day.

The beastmaster climbed up on a perch to meet and care for the animal, which on landing turned out to have suffered some slight injury from the claws of a leather-wing. The Prince and his son, climbing also, were first to touch the large owl-like creature. Mark gently took from around its neck the small flat pouch of thin leather.

The great bird, its huge eyes narrowed to slits against the early daylight, hooted and whistled out a few words indicating that it had been delayed for some hours by storms as well as reptiles.

Leaving the bird to the beastmaster's professional care, Mark carried the pouch down from the perch. After hastily performing a magical test for safety, he snapped open the container and extracted the single piece of paper which lay inside.

Unfolding the note, Mark read, silently the first time through. The message had been sent by Ben of Purkinje.

"Is it from Ben, Father?"

"Yes. He's several days away from Sarykam, or he was when he wrote this . . . " The Prince read on, skimming bad news, not wishing to contemplate any more of that than absolutely necessary.

"Ben's coming home?"

Mark's face altered. He stared at the note, his mind almost numbed by the two code words that leapt out at him from near the end. Almost he feared to allow himself to hope, let alone to triumph.

Putting down the paper for the moment, he looked around to make sure that no one but his son was close enough to hear him.

"Ben mentions an earlier message," he announced softly, "and repeats it here, to the effect that he has found Wayfinder. We never got that message. Some are bound to go astray."

"Dad! That means—if we've got Wayfinder—that means we can use it to find Woundhealer. Doesn't it?"

Mark held up the note. "We could, but there's more. He already has Woundhealer too."

"Dad!"

"He also says here that he's encountered old friends, your cousin Zoltan, and the Lady Yambu. I don't know if you remember her."

"What are we going to do?"

Mark grinned. "What would you do if you were in command?"

"Go get those Swords at once!"

"Not a very difficult decision, hey?"

But there was a considerably harder choice to be made immediately: Whether to let the news of Ben's evident success spread through the Palace, and thence inevitably, before long, into the ears of enemy agents. The boost in home morale that this news should produce would be welcome, but if the effort to bring Woundhealer home came to nothing, a corresponding letdown would ensue.

Stephen was staring anxiously at his father. Mark commanded the boy to tell no one else the content of Ben's message for the time being. The Sword was not yet safely home.

When Stephen had been given a chance to read the note for himself, father and son, teasing and challenging each other like two twelve-year-olds, went skipping and jumping down a set of ladders to the next lowest level of the tower, and thence down several levels to the broader roof of the keep below.

There, moving decisively, the Prince quietly began to set in motion preparations for an expedition to reclaim Woundhealer.

Stephen, as his father had expected, wanted to come along.

"Father, will you be leaving right away?"

"Within a few hours."

"Can I come with you?"

Mark made quick calculations. "No, you'll be needed here."

The refusal sent Stephen into a silent rage; he asked no questions, said nothing at all, but his face reddened and his jaw set.

Mark sighed; knowing his son, he was not surprised. He had no reason to expect or hope that this boy might be sheltered from danger all his life, and every reason to believe that the lad had better be hardened to it. The Prince would probably have acceded to his son's request to join the expedition but for one fact: Stephen seemed to be the only person capable of brightening his mother's countenance or manner in the least.

Mark explained this point. Then he repeated his refusal, couching it this time in terms of military orders, which made the pill somewhat easier to swallow.

When Stephen choked on another protest, his father ordered briskly: "Get control of yourself and speak coherently."

"Yes, Father." And the boy managed. He was learning.

"Now. This is an order . . . "

With Stephen under control, for the time being at least, the Prince's next impulse was to rush to Kristin with the good news.

But then on thinking the matter over, he was not sure how much he ought to tell his wife.

Catching sight of a junior officer going about some other errand, Mark hailed the man and dispatched him to find General Rostov.

Proceeding in the direction of his wife's room, Mark encountered the chief physician of the Palace, a tall woman with a dark, forbidding, ageless face and kindly voice.

This lady inquired: "Good news, Highness?"

"Yes. Or the possibility of good news, at least. I will be making an announcement presently." Yet Mark hesitated; it would be terrible, he thought again, to raise hopes that might in a few days be dashed.

Since Kristin's fall, neither physicians nor wizards had ever been sanguine about her prospects for recovery. None of the experts saw any real hope, unless the Sword of Healing could somehow be obtained.

The physician said: "I have just come from Her Highness's room."

"What word today?"

She bowed slightly. "Your Highness, I have no good words to say to you."

Mark interrupted the doctor at that point, and dispatched Stephen to look for Uncle Karel. "And when you have found him, I expect it will be time you are about your regular morning tasks."

"Yes, Father."

When Prince and physician were alone, the healer went on gloomily to explain that she had quietly alerted the attendants to maintain a watch against a possible suicide attempt on the part of the long-suffering patient.

"As bad as that." Mark was not really surprised; but no mental preparation could shield him from the chill brought by those words.

"I fear so, Prince."

"Well, well." He could still force his voice to be calm. "Carry on. We will do what we can."

The doctor bowed again, and moved away.

Mark had not progressed a dozen paces farther in the direction of his wife's room before he encountered General Rostov, who seemed already to have learned somehow that important matters were to be decided.

Rostov was as tall as Mark, but the general's barrel-chested frame was even broader. He had black skin, with an old scar on the right cheek. His curly hair had once been black, but was now almost entirely gray.

Drawing Rostov aside, Mark quietly outlined for him the expedition he wanted to lead out to gain possession of both Swords.

"Karel will be going with you?" Rostov asked.

"He will." Mark considered that Kristin's uncle, the chief wizard of the royal family and of the nation, would be indispensable on such an expedition. "Therefore you will be left in charge here at the Palace."

After providing the Prince with requested advice on several points, and receiving a few detailed orders, Rostov saluted and moved away, going about his business with his usual efficiency.

The Prince at last reached his wife's room and entered.

The Princess was occupying the same chamber as before her injury, though now the room was even more brightly decorated. Cheerful paintings, some of Kristin's favorites in her days of health, hung on the walls, and her favorite flowers stood in vases, or grew in pots. Everything about the place was joyous, airy, lightsome, and pleasant—everything except for its occupant, who lay garbed in a plain white gown, her countenance like a mask of clay.

Originally the nurses and other attendants assigned to care for the crippled Princess had been chosen as much for their cheerful attitude as for their professional ability.

But those people had been replaced, when Kristin, complaining bitterly to her husband, had said she could not stand having such laughing fools around her.

This morning Kristin was in her bed as usual. She was capable of leaving it only seldom and briefly. Her body, always slender, was twisted now by broken bones that had healed only poorly, and by spasmed muscles. Her face, once beautiful, had been eroded from within by pain and loss of weight. Indoor pallor had replaced her tan.

Other than to utter an occasional grim comment on her own future, or lack of one, Kristin now rarely spoke.

Pulling a chair close to the bed, Mark sat down and gave his wife a partial report on the information that had just arrived by courier. Mark said only that there was new hope now, and that he would soon be leaving town in search of Woundhealer.

The Prince took this precaution against raising hopes that might be dashed, though in the bleak silence of his own thoughts he felt sure that the problem with Kristin was really the absence of any hope at all.

Mark took his wife's hand, but then let it go when the touch seemed to cause her some new discomfort.

Kristin appeared to listen to what her husband had to say, but she made no comment. Obviously her attitude regarding the news was one of bitter pessimism.

Her husband was saddened but not surprised by this reaction. That, he had learned, was consistently the disposition of his wife's mind whatever news he brought, or when, as was more usual, he had none to bring.

After leaving the sickroom, Mark found the old wizard Karel waiting for him, a fat old man with puffing breath and a rich, soft voice.

Karel, on learning of the morning's message, was in a hopeful mood.

"I might suggest, Prince, that you send a strong flying squadron to pick up the prize and carry it back to us, as we ride south. If this plan is successful, it would speed up your gaining possession of the Sword by a day or two at least."

Mark was impressed favorably by the old man's suggestion, but he postponed making a final decision on it. If he were eventually to decide in favor of such a maneuver, there would be no need to tell Ben about it in advance. So the Prince omitted any mention of the scheme in the message he now began drafting to be carried back to Ben.

As Mark considered it, strong arguments took shape in his mind against sending such a flying squad. Chief among these was the fact that any such half-intelligent flying force would run the risk of being detected, and then ambushed, by enemy magic, flying reptiles, or griffins. No birds were strong enough to stand against such an attack.

Wood himself, who Mark loathed as one of his great antagonists, was known to travel airborne on a griffin, or sometimes even on a demon's back.

The danger presented by the possibility of ambush eventually came to seem too great. By the time he had dispatched the message to Ben, Mark had all but finally decided not to take the risk.

Shortly after sunset the Lady Yambu, her new reserves of energy not fully depleted by a long day's hike, was pacing restlessly about the simple camp she shared with her three companions. The conversation that had begun a quarter of an hour ago had gradually died out, and the three were now all watching her in vague apprehension.

Suddenly she stopped her pacing, and declared: "I think I must consult our Sword again. I grow doubtful that the road I must follow to the truth lies through Tasavalta."

Ben looked at her, grunted, then wordlessly detached Wayfinder in its sheath from his belt, and held the weapon out to her.

Valdemar's expression suggested that he was surprised. He said to Yambu: "If you are having doubts, then I must have doubts also."

For several days now, the four had been slogging steadily northeast, in the general direction of Tasavalta. The land through which they traveled had gradually grown more rugged, and their progress had become correspondingly slower.

Now and then the Sword they followed decreed some slight variation in their course toward Sarykam. When this happened, the four travelers sometimes speculated about the possible cause of this deflection. But none of the three who had considerable experience with the awesome power of Swords suggested doing anything but going along with Wayfinder. And the detours, whatever their cause, had proven short. At the moment the four were once more, as nearly as they could estimate in this almost roadless waste, on or near a straight-line path toward the Tasavaltan capital.

Over the last few days and hours, Yambu had started several times to ask Ben more about what the Emperor had said to him regarding Ariane. But Ben, who had suggested such a conversation, no longer seemed to know what else he wanted to say, or hear, on that subject.

The lady was about to raise the matter with Ben again. But before she could do so, the travelers were excited by the arrival of a winged messenger.

Eagerly Ben unfastened the pouch from the great bird, and fumbled it open. Intently he scanned the note inside.

Zoltan read it over his shoulder. "Nothing of importance," the young man complained.

"Better than it looks," Ben assured him. "There are a couple of code words. First, congratulations—that'll be for our getting Woundhealer. And second, help is on the way."

Their spirits considerably lightened, the four pushed on.

Within an hour, they had became aware that someone was following them, maintaining a careful distance.

"Your old friend Brod," Zoltan decided, squinting at the distant, barely visible man who doubtless thought himself adequately concealed. "We should have finished him when we had the chance. I suppose he went off in the little boat just to be deceptive."

"Why should he be following us?" Valdemar wondered.

Ben shrugged. "His gang's been wiped out, and he's going to have to find some other way to make a living."

The Silver Queen had no comment; her thoughts were evidently elsewhere.

That evening, she spoke confidingly to her old friends Ben and Zoltan, and her new follower Valdemar.

"I am almost a girl again . . . no, I don't mean that. What foolishness! I am fifty-one years old, and healing will not turn back the years; age in itself is not an illness or an injury. But in a way I *feel* like a girl. The horrible burden that Soulcutter put on me so many years ago has at last been lifted. Can you understand what that means? No, there is no way you could understand."

And in her emotion the lady laughed and cried, in a mixture of joy and confusion; the emotional reaction which had come upon her when she was healed was now repeated, even more strongly than before.

"Can you understand? I can no longer be certain what my purpose in life is, or ought to be."

"I think I can understand, my lady." Ben's large hand

pulled the Sword she had given them out of its sheath; he held the black hilt out toward her.

Zoltan nodded; it was a slow, uncertain gesture, as if he had trouble comprehending the Lady's difficulty, but considered that Wayfinder's powerful medicine ought to be worth a try in any case.

Once more gripping Wayfinder, Lady Yambu posed a new question.

"Blade, once more I seek your guidance. Was I speaking only foolishness when I asked you to find eternal truth for me? You answered me, I know, but . . . I am no longer sure what I was thinking two days ago. It is almost as if I have been reborn."

The Sword of Wisdom hung inert in her grasp. Of course. The question she had just asked, as Yambu understood full well, was not the kind Wayfinder could be expected to answer.

"Take your time, my lady." Ben was respectfully concerned.

The trouble, Yambu was discovering, was that she now found herself unable to formulate any inquiry to her own satisfaction. Indecisively she raised the Sword, and lowered it, and raised it up again.

At last, words burst forth: "Was my healing the only truth I needed? I have been granted the touch of the Sword of Mercy . . . but again, that is not the kind of question any Sword can answer for me, is it?"

Even as she spoke, Yambu was wishing that she had gone off by herself to so apostrophize Wayfinder. Certainly the others were watching and listening with intense interest. But now, as if he were embarrassed, Ben motioned to the two younger men, and all of them moved away, leaving the Lady alone with Wayfinder.

The mute Sword only quivered uncertainly, in response to the questioner's uncertainty.

"Changeable, are you? At least you are a silent counselor, and there's wisdom to be found in that."

Rejoining the others, she sought out Valdemar, and held out the black hilt of the sheathed Sword. Yambu said: "I am having but poor success. Will you try it for yourself once more?"

The young man in farmer's clothing hesitated, then shook his head doggedly. "No, I have already used Wayfinder more than once, and each time it has led me to you. My purpose has not changed. So, for now, let me continue as I am."

"Even if I have changed? If I no longer know where I am going?"

The young man smiled faintly. "Very well then, let me try the Sword once more."

As steadily as ever, the Sword of Wisdom with its black hilt once more in the huge hands of Valdemar, pointed straight toward the Silver Queen.

He returned the weapon to her hilt-first, making an almost courtly flourish. He said: "I am content to follow, Lady, whatever you decide to do."

She sighed. "Then let your fate be on your own head."

EIGHT

THIS night it was Valdemar's turn to stand the last watch, the hours just before dawn.

At the proper time Ben woke him, and silently held out to him the black hilt of the Sword of Wisdom, with which his comrades were to be protected as they slept.

The young man sat up, the folds of his blanket falling from around his massive shoulders, and held both hands to his head for a long moment before he accepted Wayfinder.

"Bad dreams?" Ben inquired in a low voice.

"No. Yes, I think so, but I don't remember." Valdemar shook his head. "I keep worrying about my vineyard."

"Once upon a time," said Ben, "when I was very young, all I wanted out of life was to be a minstrel. I really thought that I could be one, too. Carried a lute around with me everywhere. Can you believe that?"

"Yes, I can," said the other after a moment's thought. "Were you any good?" he asked with interest.

Ben appeared to consider the question seriously. "No," he said at last, and turned away. "Me for my own blanket."

Valdemar began his watch in routine fashion, by asking the Sword of Wisdom a question concerning the safety of the camp. Testing the limits on the kind of question the Sword would answer, he tended to keep trying new variations. Tonight's first variant was: "Will we be safer if we move?"

To this query the Sword in Valdemar's hands returned him no detectable answer; he presumed that Wayfinder would have pointed in the proper direction had its powers decided that the camp would indeed be more secure somewhere else.

The general safety assured, for the moment at least, to the sentry's satisfaction, he asked his second question of this watch. This one was whispered so softly that he could not hear his own words. "Where is the nearest person present whose advice I should be following?"

The Sword of Wisdom indicated Yambu, who appeared to be fast asleep.

Valdemar nodded. Carrying Wayfinder drawn and ready, he paced the vicinity of the small camp, applying the good sentry's technique he had learned from his new friends. He varied his route and pace, turning sharply at irregular intervals, eyes and ears alert to the surrounding darkness. He kept his eyes averted from the small fire's brightness to preserve their sensitivity in the dark.

Meanwhile his routine worries returned. Counting the days he had already been away from home, confirming his estimate of the advancing season by the current phase of the Moon, Valdemar knew with certainty that his vines would soon be leafing out, and would need care. He had done all he could for the plants before he left, but they would soon be growing wild, and insects would attack them.

He lacked the skills of magic necessary to do anything effective about these problems at a distance, though of course he could try. Valdemar doubted whether he could project any potent spells against insects, at least not over more than a few meters. He'd make the effort, of course, but not now. Right now he had to concentrate upon his duties as a guard.

Once more he put a safety question to the Sword, on the chance that circumstances had changed adversely in the past few minutes. Once more Wayfinder seemed to assure him that all was well.

Time continued to pass uneventfully. Ben had hardly hit the ground before falling fast asleep, as a faint rumble of snoring testified. The night wind ghosted past Valdemar's ears, and the moon and the familiar stars, though only intermittently visible through a patchwork of clouds, moved in their familiar paths above his head.

Where, he wondered suddenly, was Woundhealer resting at this moment? He tried to remember who had been carrying the Sword of Mercy. Then, in the course of his next sharp turn as he patrolled, the young man, peering intently by the vague light of stars and moon, caught a glimpse of the black hilt. The Sword was currently in Zoltan's custody, its shape unmistakable within its wrappings, lying in contact with his sleeping body.

All was well, then. Valdemar relaxed though he reminded himself sternly to remain alert. But as his watch dragged on, he strayed into asking Wayfinder one private question after another, only to realize guiltily once more that long moments had passed in which the Sword of Wisdom was no longer really charged with protecting the camp.

Tonight he was not only worried about his vineyard, but also bothered by particular concerns about his bride-to-be. As pictured in his imagination, she was a creature of unsurpassed loveliness. But her existence, as anything but a creation of his own imagination, he had begun to doubt.

Lost intermittently in these problems, Valdemar continued his pacing, circling the small campfire on an irregular path, the Sword of Wisdom naked in his right hand, a battle-hatchet belonging to some fallen warrior stuck in his farmer's belt.

At the moment his half-distracted mind presented Wayfinder with a new inquiry for the benefit of himself and the sleeping three: "Which way to go to foil our enemies? Which way to go—"

This time the Sword returned him a firm answer; generally northeast, the direction of their daytime travel.

Then Valdemar stopped, listening to himself. Actually, of course, neither he nor any of his three companions wanted to *go* anywhere at the moment—right now they all wanted to get some rest.

But how hard it was, thought Valdemar as he paced on again, for a man to know consistently what, beyond the physical necessities of the moment, he really wanted to do, to achieve. The world held so many kinds of things to want.

Anticipating the first rays of dawn, the young man found it impossible to keep his mind with absolute consistency upon the camp's defense. Then he would silently upbraid himself, and once more stalk about in his random pattern holding the Sword, and murmur: "I seek the safety of this camp. I seek the safety of this—"

Receiving no answer to what was not really a question, he would shake his head and mutter: "No need to keep repeating things like that. No need to keep repeating things . . . "

An hour passed. All continued quiet, and nothing untoward occurred.

And, as nothing in particular seemed to be happening, other questions, other urges, drifted as subtly as growing vines into control of Valdemar's mind.

Thus it was that the pacing, dreaming sentry was granted no warning whatsoever. One moment he and his sleeping companions were, as far as he knew, all safe, all at peace, save for the faint animal noises of the nocturnal wasteland, sounds more reassuring than disturbing.

And in the next moment they were being overwhelmed.

The onslaught, as Valdemar came later to understand, was well-coordinated, and consisted of an airborne magical component as well as a force of more mundane attackers on the ground. Somewhere over the young man's head there came a beating of great unseen wings, sounding far larger than those of any flying creature Valdemar had ever seen or heard before; simultaneously he heard a prosaic thunder of approaching hoofbeats on the ground.

Letting out a hoarse cry Valdemar whirled about, brandishing his Sword, unable for the first moment of the attack to see anything out of the ordinary at all. Then suddenly the sentry found himself confronted by a live man standing where a moment earlier there had been no one at all. The figure was that of a warrior, sword upraised, garbed in the same Blue Temple colors worn by half of yesterday's fallen.

For just a moment Valdemar was frozen by his own imagination, by the terrible image of all those bodies he had helped to rob of food and shoes and weapons, of those dead risen now to claim some kind of vengeance . . .

For a moment only. Then a second swordsman and a third materialized behind the first out of darkness and the desert, and the young man understood that his attackers were only too full of mundane life. He let out a hoarse shout of alarm, realizing even as he did so that his warning must now be too late.

But his companions were reacting very quickly. Around him, friends and foes were scrambling in the darkness.

The first attacker recoiled from the camp's sentry, out of respect for the Sword that Valdemar was holding, if not for his gigantic figure. But now others were coming at him from the sides—and now a gossamer net, more magic than material, came dropping softly toward him from a great blurred form in the softly moonlit sky.

Barely in time he twisted out from under the net, sensing its enchantment. Drawn steel, Valdemar had heard, was the most effective countermeasure an ordinary man could take against a wizard's onslaught, and perhaps the Sword in his right hand, the battle-hatchet now drawn in his left, exerted some measure of protection.

The Lady Yambu, who had been the closest of the other three to Valdemar when the enemy appeared, now rose up at his side, hands spread in a magician's gesture, joining him in his hopeless though spirited defense of the camp.

Part of his mind noted that the Lady did not have Woundhealer—of course, that Sword had been with Zoltan.

"Fight!" she snapped at Valdemar. "We must not let ourselves be taken alive! Not by these—"

Valdemar, with no time to think, only grunted something in return. Brandishing the battle-hatchet in one hand and Wayfinder in the other, and confident in his own strength though mindful of his lack of skill, he faced the enemy soldiers as what looked like a crowd of them came at him.

The young giant wielded both hatchet and Sword with ferocious energy, and by sheer strength he succeeded in chopping down at least one of his attackers.

To his surprise, the others fell back momentarily. The Silver Queen had become a shadow gliding at Valdemar's side, and afforded him some unexpected but very welcome magical assistance.

Still, the odds in favor of the enemy were overwhelming, and they were returning to the attack.

* * *

Zoltan had come wide awake, alerted by some subliminal perception, two or three heartbeats before the attack actually fell on the camp. He was fully conscious and active in an instant, and aware of Ben beside him also springing to his feet. Both were veterans, who needed only a momentary glimpse of the assailants surrounding Yambu and Valdemar, the latter fighting with the Sword of Wisdom, to convince them that the odds were hopeless. But so far Zoltan and Ben were not surrounded; rather, they were at one side of the struggle, and escape appeared to be still possible.

Getting the Sword of Mercy back to Tasavalta came ahead of everything else. Zoltan, with Woundhealer already in his hands, unsheathed the Blade and without hesitation plunged it deep into his own body, holding himself transfixed with a hand on the black hilt. With his other hand he pulled his own short sword from its scabbard, and used it to run through the first enemy trooper to come at him in the dimness of the fading night. The trooper's dying counterstroke cut down on Zoltan's left shoulder, and might have nearly taken off his arm, had not Woundhealer's overwhelmingly benign force prevailed. The enemy's sword fell free, Zoltan's wound closing behind it so quickly that he lost no blood.

Ben, who had been unarmed except for a short knife and Wayfinder, grabbed up the fallen weapon, and killed two men with it in the next few moments of confusion.

Zoltan was running now, with Ben beside him, away from the beleaguered Yambu and her young ally. Zoltan struck down another attacker, receiving another harmless sword-slash in the process and Ben smashed another foe aside. Both of them kept on running, their backs to the noise and turmoil surrounding Valdemar and the Silver Queen.

A flying reptile came lowering out of the sky at Zoltan, talons biting harmlessly, almost painlessly, into his head and face, which were still protected by the magic of the gods. One claw bit through his eye and did no harm, his vision clearing once more with a blink. He could hear, below the harsh gasping of his own lungs, the softly breathing sound made by the Sword of Mercy, mending this new damage to his body as quickly as it happened.

Even as his eyesight cleared, Zoltan's killing sword bit into the airborne reptile's guts. He heard the beast scream, and then fall heavily to earth behind him as he ran on.

Ben kept pounding along beside him, so far managing to keep up. But now a net of magic fell about them both, a gossamer interference with thought and movement that would have stretched them both out on the ground, had not Zoltan been protected from all injury. His senses and his thought remained clear, and he felt the evil magic only as he might have felt a cobweb tear across his face.

Beside him, Ben staggered and stumbled in his run, and would have fallen headlong had not Zoltan managed to sheath his own killing blade and catch the huge man under one arm, pulling and hauling him through torn cobwebs. Grunting with the effort, Zoltan kept Ben on his feet until the last shreds of the magic net had been left behind them.

Still the young man had trouble believing that the two of them were really going to get away; glancing back when they had run another fifty meters, he decided that he and Ben were being greatly helped in their escape by the fact that the attackers were concentrating so thoroughly on getting the Sword of Wisdom into their hands.

Valdemar kept hearing someone in command of the Blue Temple forces shouting orders to take that man alive. He knew the order referred to him. There was nothing to do but fight on, Yambu's warning fresh in his mind, and the Sword in his hands making it substantially harder for the enemy to do what they wanted. If only, Valdemar prayed fervently, this Sword were Shieldbreaker . . .

A rough ring of enemies kept forming around him and Yambu. But he kept muttering rapidly at Wayfinder, asking the Sword of Wisdom to show him the best way to escape. Then, keeping up as best he could with the Sword's rapidly changing instructions, he charged bravely at one Blue Temple weak point after another. The trouble was that soon there were no weak points in the rapidly closing ring.

Yambu meanwhile stayed on her feet, moving with agility to remain at Valdemar's back. She kept doing magical things, things he could not comprehend, but that must be serving to keep the attackers at least temporarily off balance.

But the odds were too great, their resistance could not last. The enemy magic was stronger than the Silver Queen's if not than Wayfinder's. At last Valdemar, the Sword in his hands notwithstanding, felt himself overwhelmed by swirling powers, by rampaging physical forms. Gold and blue faintly visible in moonlight, were everywhere around him. Whether the force that finally overcame him was material or occult he could not have said, and anyway it seemed to make no difference.

Dimly aware that the Lady Yambu was still nearby and shared his fate, he was knocked down, disarmed, made prisoner. Then, with her limp and evidently unconscious body being dragged beside Valdemar, both of them were removed a short distance from their place of capture, to a place where a strange bright light was shone on their faces, and their captors puzzled in mumbling voices over their identity.

That question having been answered to the winners' satisfaction—or else determined to be not quickly answerable, Valdemar could not tell which—the pair were moved another short distance. There they were left on the ground, seemingly temporarily abandoned.

Quickly Valdemar discovered that his arms and legs had been efficiently paralyzed by magic. But within moments after those who threw him down had turned away, he managed to shake free of some kind of cover, evidently a material one, which had been thrown over his head.

His first use of this limited power of movement was to look for Zoltan and Ben, wondering if they were still alive, and what had happened to Woundhealer. Three or four meters away lay the dim, inert form of the Silver Queen. The young man spoke to the lady quietly, but received no answer.

The attack, as Valdemar saw when he once more began to obtain a clear view of his surroundings, had been carried out by a small but powerful force of Blue Temple troops, magicians, and inhuman creatures. A few reptiles had already come down out of the clouded, slowly brightening sky. Larger forms were looming there.

Even as he watched, a pair of the giant wings he had earlier sensed overhead came closer. A creature landed. Valdemar, harking back to stories heard in childhood, realized that it must be a griffin. He could only gaze in wonder.

This was a large creature, much bigger than a riding-beast, with eagle's head and beak and wings, and legs and talons of a gigantic lion. Across its back was strapped a kind of saddle, flanked on each side by a kind of hanging woven basket, a sidecar or howdah. One or two men—Valdemar could not get a clear look at first—were riding on the beast. There would have been room for three, with a driver in the central saddle.

On the ground, the four-legged monster knelt, then crouched. The first of the passengers to disembark was a well-dressed man, short, redfaced and bald, who made an awkward dismount from one of the sidecars.

Moments later, a second elderly Blue Temple official came into Valdemar's field of vision. He was older and less ruddy of countenance than the first. Valdemar could not be sure whether this man had disembarked from the same mount, or from a slightly smaller griffin which had landed close behind the first.

It was soon evident that the attacking force was commanded by the rather short, red-faced man. Valdemar now heard this individual addressed as Chairman Hyrcanus. The elder, obviously second in importance, was called the Director.

Valdemar, with some difficulty raising his head a little farther against the bonds of magic that still held him down, was able to watch and listen as the Chairman expressed his satisfaction at having the solid ground under his feet again.

Now from among the mixed group of Blue Temple military and irregulars who had gathered there emerged a face, and a voice, that Valdemar to his surprise could recognize. Chairman Hyrcanus was greeted by Sergeant Brod, who came pushing forward from amidst the latest detachment of cavalry to reach the scene.

At least the Sarge, having somehow attached himself to the attackers, made an attempt to offer the Chairman such a greeting.

But the official, scowling at this interloper, would not listen. "Who're you?" Hyrcanus demanded; and then, before the man could possibly have answered, turned irritably to his cavalry officer. "Who's this?"

The officer seemed to shrink under his leader's glare. "The man is a local guide we have signed on, Your Opulence. He's been useful—"

"Another expense, I suppose." The Chairman turned away with an impatient gesture. "Get my pavilion up."

Thus brusquely rebuffed, Brod looked about. Catching sight of Valdemar and Lady Yambu, he came to stand over them, an expression of satisfaction gradually replacing the scowl on his ugly face.

"Reckon I've met you folks before. Good mornin' to ye."

"Good morning," said Valdemar, thinking he had nothing to lose thereby. Yambu did not answer; the Lady's eyes were closed, her face relaxed as if in sleep.

While Brod hovered nearby, evidently wondering what to do next, Valdemar saw and heard the officer in command of the small Blue Temple cavalry force, standing at attention before Hyrcanus, respectfully ask the Chairman if there were any further orders? If not, his men had been riding all night and were in need of rest.

Hyrcanus, abstractedly seeing to the careful unloading of a trunk from one of the griffins' cargo baskets, gave the troops permission to rest, once camp was properly established and a guard posted.

Then Hyrcanus, stretching and twisting his body as if he might be cramped from a long ride, exchanged some words with his Director of Security. Both men complained about the weariness and nervous strain brought on by this regrettably necessary means of travel.

The Chairman also congratulated his Director of Security on the fact that that gentleman's wits, such as they were, seemed to have been fully restored.

The Director chuckled, dutifully and drily, at the little joke—if such it was.

Then both of the Blue Temple executives, the Chairman in the lead, came to gaze sourly at their prisoners.

Staring at the supine youth, Hyrcanus demanded: "Who are you, fellow?"

"My name is Valdemar."

"That means nothing to me."

"You—are Chairman of the whole Blue Temple?"

Valdemar didn't know much about how such great organizations were managed, or, really, what he would have expected their managers to be like—but certainly he would have anticipated someone more impressive than this dumpy, commonplace figure.

Brod, evidently still determined to gain points with the greatest celebrity he had probably ever encountered, had edged his way forward, and now took the opportunity to kick Valdemar energetically in the ribs.

"Show some respect to Chairman Hyrcanus!" the Sarge barked.

Someone else, in the middle distance, called: "We have the property ready for your inspection, sir."

Hyrcanus, readily allowing both kicker and victim to drop below the horizon of his attention, turned away. Valdemar got the impression that this man cared little for anyone's respect; the property, whatever that might be, was of much greater interest.

Valdemar supposed that the interesting property ready for inspection was the Sword of Wisdom. He stretched his neck, but couldn't quite make out the object on the ground that Hyrcanus and the others gathered round to look at.

Whatever it was, after a short conference, Hyrcanus was back, looming over Valdemar.

"Fellow, they tell me that you were standing watch, sentry duty, at the time of our arrival." The Chairman had the look of a man who was perpetually suspicious.

"Yes, I was." Valdemar's bitterness at having failed in that duty came through. "What of it?"

Brod, having moved into the background again, was not in sight at the moment. It was an ordinary soldier who kicked Valdemar this time, though Valdemar really hadn't been trying to be insolent. These people, he thought, were really difficult to deal with.

Hyrcanus asked him impatiently: "And you were holding the Sword called Wayfinder as you stood guard?"

The youth saw no reason not to admit that fact.

The red-faced man nodded. "No doubt it looked an excellent weapon—and it is. But perhaps you did not understand its real value?"

"Perhaps I did not."

To Valdemar it seemed no more than a reasonable answer, but there must have been something wrong with his tone of voice, for he was awarded another kick. Soon his ribs were going to get sore.

"Perhaps you were not using the Sword properly? Not engaging its full powers?"

"Perhaps I was not."

Chairman and Director turned away and walked a little distance, to put their heads together for some more mumbling. Then the latter emerged from the huddle to announce: "We'll question him more thoroughly later. What about the woman?"

Soon both officials were bending over Yambu. Magical assistance was called for, and provided. Soon the Director admitted: "She seems to have put herself into some kind of trance. We'll soon have her out of it when we're ready to talk."

Hyrcanus, squinting and frowning, taking a closer look at the woman, ordered someone to bring him a better light. When a magically-enhanced torch, so bright it almost hurt to look at it, was held over the sleeping face, Hyrcanus said in a low voice that she reminded him of the Silver Queen, but that seemed improbable, and in any case this woman appeared too young.

Another subordinate approached the Chairman deferentially, to inquire of him exactly where he wanted his pavilion put up; some soldiers and a minor magician were ready to get to work on that task now.

Hyrcanus considered, and told him. Then he and his

Director continued their discussions, with Valdemar still able to hear most of what was said. One of the soldiers had pointed out that curiously three or four of his comrades had been killed at some little distance from the spot where the two prisoners were taken.

"Killed by whom?"

"That's it, sir. We don't know."

The Director of Security demanded: "Are we sure there were four of these people on the scene before we attacked?"

"Yes sir."

"Then it is obvious that two have somehow managed to get away. You should not have allowed that!"

The military officer's only defense was that orders had been to make sure the Sword was captured, no matter what else happened.

The two high officials moved a little farther off. From what Valdemar could overhear, they were remarking how strange it seemed that the Sword of Wisdom had not only failed to save the camp, but failed to guide its wielder to some means of avoiding death or capture.

The Chairman was coming back. "I wonder if this could be in fact the Lady Yambu."

Sergeant Brod, presented at last with a chance to be useful, did not allow it to go to waste. "Sir! Master Chairman. It is in fact the lady herself that we are looking at. I have seen her before, and I can swear to it!"

"You? Again?" Hyrcanus, frowning, looked around at his subordinates, appealing silently for someone to take this fellow away.

A small squad of soldiers moved to do the job; Valdemar, hearing only a mutter and a scuffle, thought philosophically that he would not be surprised to see Brod back again.

"If she is Yambu," Hyrcanus was brooding to himself, gazing once more upon that silent face, "if she *is* . . . then she at least would have realized the value of the Sword with which her little group was traveling."

"That is certainly the case, Your Opulence," agreed the Director.

Then he raised his eyes to meet Valdemar's. "Well, fellow? Who do you say she is?"

NINE

UNTIL Zoltan was sure that he and Ben had left the enemy behind, he continued running with Woundhealer transfixing his own body, his left hand gripping the hilt to hold the Sword in place. So far he and Ben were managing to stay together, though this required Zoltan to slow down. The young man calculated that Ben's presence would be a mighty advantage toward their goal of getting Woundhealer home.

The continued presence of the Sword of Healing inside his rib cage engendered in Zoltan a very strange sensation, neither pleasure nor pain, but rather a sense that some tremendous experience, whether good or bad, must be about to overwhelm him. The feeling was mentally though not physically uncomfortable.

Both men ran on, without speaking, under the gradually brightening sky of early morning. As soon as Zoltan could be reasonably sure that no enemies were in close pursuit, or ahead of them, he paused and released Woundhealer's hilt; there was no need to pull in order to extract the Blade. Instead it slid itself smoothly and gently out of his heart and lungs, away from his torso. Once more a sighing sound came from the Sword; then it was once more inert.

Zoltan felt physically fine. Taking a quick inventory of

his body, he could discover no residual harm or damage at all from the several deadly blows he had recently sustained.

His giant comrade, swaying and groaning at his side, was in considerably worse shape, and in need of Woundhealer's immediate help.

Ben, completely out of breath, indicated with a silent gesture that he wanted Zoltan to hand over the Sword to him. The younger man complied.

A quick application of Woundhealer abolished Ben's injuries as if they had never been. Now the voice of the older man was clear and strong. "Ah, that's better. Much better."

With Ben retaining the Sword of Mercy, the men moved on together, at the best pace the older man could manage. Their running flight had already put several low rolling, almost barren hills between them and the site where the Blue Temple attack had fallen.

Zoltan, beginning to chafe and fret with the need to accommodate his slower partner, now suggested: "I might take it and run on ahead."

"No." The answer was definite, though made brief to conserve breath.

Making himself be patient, Zoltan allowed his more experienced companion to set their course. The sky continued brightening, but only gradually and sullenly; more spring rain appeared to be on the way. Ben was not heading directly toward Sarykam, but somewhat to the west, where a few trees grew along a ravine that held a trickle of muddy water at its bottom.

Trudging toward the ravine, Ben and Zoltan made plans as best they could.

Both were eagerly anticipating the help promised from Mark, but neither could see any way to guess when such assistance might be expected to arrive.

"No hope for the lady back there, or the young man

either," said Ben, pausing momentarily to look over his shoulder toward the place where their camp had been. All was silent in that direction, but Zoltan thought he could see, beyond a series of intervening hills, the glow of bright, unnatural lights, contending against the slowly brightening sky of morning.

"No. It seems a miracle that we got away." Zoltan shook his head. "They looked like Blue Temple."

Ben grunted. "So they did. That means it's probably not a miracle. Whatever a job may be, if it's nothing to do with counting money, they're as like as not to botch it up."

"I take it we're pushing straight on to Tasavalta."

"More or less straight. I mean to get there," Ben said grimly. "With Woundhealer."

Daylight was coming on in earnest now. The sky continued overcast, now and then dropping a spatter of rain, or lowering patches of drifting fog. The fugitives welcomed this weather, certain to render more difficult the task of any airborne searchers.

"We have to assume there'll be more reptiles."

"Of course. And maybe worse than that."

The few trees along the ravine offered only scanty cover. On a sunny day the Tasavaltans might have been forced to look for somewhere to remain hidden during the day. Clouds, rain, and fog offered some hope, but weather was subject to change.

Continuing their conversation as they hiked, Zoltan and Ben discussed the question of whether or not the Blue Temple attackers would know that they had got away. It seemed almost certain that they would.

"We hacked down a few people as we left."

Zoltan nodded. "And if they know we've got this Sword—they'll certainly be after us."

"Unless they're so distracted by having Wayfinder—

and Yambu and Valdemar, perhaps alive—that they're not interested in us."

"Depends what they do with Wayfinder. If they're going to use the Sword of Wisdom to hunt us down, or hunt this Sword we're carrying, we've got no chance."

Ben grunted stoically. "All we can do is move ahead. Keep trying."

But the day wore on, and still no pursuit appeared, in the air or overland. Pleasantly surprised at their luck, Zoltan and Ben could only pray that it would hold.

"They must have discovered some better use for Wayfinder than tracking us."

"Better than hunting down another Sword?—it sounds strange, but the truth must be that they don't realize that we have Woundhealer. Possibly they don't even know that it was in our camp."

The day passed in hiking, scanning the skies, which fortunately remained clouded, and foraging for berries. When dusk came on, Ben changed course, now leading the way generally north and east, in the direction from which they could expect the approach of Prince Mark and his people.

Half an hour after the Blue Temple attack, morning was brightening slowly and sullenly as Chairman Hyrcanus was establishing himself in an organized field office.

In intervals between his other tasks, Hyrcanus kept coming back to look at the supine figure of the captive woman. Each time he looked, and shook his head, and went away again. He said: "If this is indeed the Silver Queen, it would seem that she has somehow grown young again."

"Magic," offered the Director succinctly.

Another Blue Temple wizard, evidently some kind of specialist brought in for a consultation, sighed uncertainly. "No mere ordinary youth-spell, I can vouch for that." He glanced toward Valdemar, still lying under magical paralysis. "What does her companion say?"

"He says that she might be anyone, for all he knows. We'll conduct some serious questioning presently."

But Hyrcanus and his aides were giving the Silver Queen and Valdemar only a small part of their attention. Much more of their time was spent in gloating over their captured Sword, and getting the field office organized.

A swarm of hustling soldiers heaving poles and fabric, aided by some minor magic, had needed only a few minutes to complete the task of erecting the Chairman's pavilion.

This large tent was put up very near the place where Valdemar still lay, with a light rain falling on his face. From the moment when the pavilion started to take form, he had a good view in through its open doorway. New lights, even stranger than the magically augmented torch, were somehow kindled inside it, to augment the morning's feeble daylight.

Valdemar kept looking toward Yambu. He could see her face rather more clearly now, still unconscious, or submerged in some kind of self-inflicted trance.

A bustle of blue and gold activity continued around the pavilion and inside it. Gradually the movements became more orderly. As soon as the work was finished, the Director ordered that the two captives be brought into the big tent, with a view to beginning their formal questioning.

Valdemar was hauled roughly to his feet, and words muttered over him, giving him movement in his legs, and some degree of control. Then he was marched in through the fabric doorway. Chairman Hyrcanus himself, red-faced and puffing as if the labor of erecting the tent had fallen to him personally, still garbed in heavy winter garments despite the relative warmth of spring, was seated behind a folding table near the center of the pavilion, still grumbling in an almost despairing tone about the sacrifices he had had to make to venture personally into the field on this operation so vital for the Blue Temple's future.

The Director, seated at the Chairman's side, tried to soothe him with expressions of sympathy.

Standing before the central table, Valdemar heard once more, somewhere behind him, the voice of Sergeant Brod. Turning his head, he saw that the Sarge had reappeared, evidently still trying to make himself useful to the Chairman and his people. But Brod had been forced to remain outside the tent.

Hyrcanus himself was wasting no time, but not hurrying particularly either, shuffling papers about in front of him, methodically getting ready to undertake, in his own good time, whatever business might be required.

Behind the Chairman, piled inconspicuously in the shadows toward the rear of the tent, Valdemar could see what appeared to be certain metal tools, looking too complicated to be simple weapons. Vaguely he wondered what they were.

The Chairman cleared his throat. He made an announcement, something to the effect that this session was going to be only preliminary.

Looking sternly at his clerks, seated at another table along one wall, he added: "The fact that we must conduct, in the field, operations more properly performed at headquarters, is no excuse for inefficiency. Everything must be done in a businesslike fashion."

Yambu, having somehow been restored to at least partial consciousness, was now being brought into the pavilion too, and made to stand beside Valdemar. They exchanged looks; neither said anything. Valdemar thought that probably there were no useful words to be said at the moment.

* * *

Rain and wind surged against the blue and gold tent, as if in a fruitless endeavor to get at the papers inside.

Several folding chairs, enough—as Valdemar thought he heard someone remark—for the absolute necessary minimum of meetings, were disposed about within the tent. Two or three of the strange Old World lights had been placed on the tables, and another mounted on a folding metal stand. Valdemar got the impression that there was some kind of heating device as well, Old World or magical, giving off a gentle invisible glow of warmth around the Chairman's feet.

Hyrcanus, mumbling almost inaudibly to himself, was busily extracting more sheaves of paperwork from a dispatch case of dull leather, and laying the stuff out upon his table under the bright, efficient light. Valdemar, watching, assumed that this array of written records must be intended to serve some magical purpose. He could not picture any mundane necessity for it.

At a nod from the Chairman, one of his subordinates gave the order for the prisoners to be moved, one at a time, somewhat closer to the central table.

Before getting down to serious questioning, the Chairman, acting in the tradition of his organization, saw to it that his captives' names and descriptions were noted down, and that they were methodically robbed. Hands went dipping into Valdemar's pockets, and his clothing was patted and probed, by means both physical and magical.

Valdemar realized to his surprise that these people were more concerned with him than with the Silver Queen. The only reason he could imagine for this was that he had happened to be holding the Sword when they arrived.

An exact inventory was taken of all valuables confiscated from the two prisoners. Actually these were very few, and of disappointingly little value.

Valdemar noted that the high officials of the Temple took very seriously this business of accounting for items of trivial financial value.

"Money?"

"Practically none, sir." But the clerk, under the Chairman's cold stare, went on to itemize the few small coins which had been taken from Valdemar and Yambu. This painstaking listing, accomplished in the meticulous Blue Temple fashion, occupied what seemed to Valdemar an inordinate amount of time.

Though Valdemar had never before had any direct dealings with the Blue Temple, he like everyone else had heard a thousand stories exemplifying its legendary greed and stinginess. While the young man had no liking for the picture painted by those stories, the tales inspired in him not terror so much as contempt and wariness. He was now waiting impatiently for a chance to argue that he should be considered a non-combatant here and allowed to go on about his business.

But the Chairman was in no hurry, nor were his clerks, who evidently understood exactly the attitude toward work that was required of them. While Hyrcanus sat shuffling and rearranging his papers at one folding table they were busy writing and calculating at another. Among their other tasks, Valdemar gathered as he listened to their clerkly murmurs, was that of keeping a precise expense account—how much was this mission costing the corporation?

In the background, two or three meters behind and above the droning clerks, a small window high in the rear wall of the pavilion afforded Valdemar an occasional sight of one of the griffins, or perhaps two—he could not be sure whether it was really the same huge, nightmarish head and neck that now and then loomed up in the morning's gloom, as if the beast were curious about what was happening inside the tent. The griffin, or griffins, had evidently been tethered close behind the pavilion.

The griffin or griffins, Valdemar realized at a second look, were eating something out there. Lion-jaws dripped with a dark liquid in the uncertain, cloudy light. Suddenly he had the horrible feeling that the creatures were tearing some animal—or human—body to pieces for a snack.

The Chairman coughed drily. But then, just when Valdemar thought Hyrcanus might at last be ready to get down to business, the Chairman delayed again, turning to his Director of Security to lament the cost to the Temple in time and money of this journey. He had spent some days in getting here, traveling from the unnamed city of his headquarters, and he considered the expense of shipping his necessary equipment to have been almost ruinous.

Talking to his Director of Headquarters Security, upon whose bald head the Old World light gleamed brightly—and who, here in the bright light, looked even older than he had outside—now and then looking up to glare at his new prisoner or prisoners as if he considered them to blame—the Chairman deigned to give them all several reasons why he had felt it necessary to take charge personally of this expedition:

"One, because I feared that Master Wood, on once getting the Sword of Wisdom into his hands, would never relinquish it." Hyrcanus paused thoughtfully. "Of course I suppose Woundhealer is one Sword Wood might be induced to give up—for a price."

The Director, to no one's surprise, expressed agreement.

Now a long strongbox was carried into the tent by a couple of soldiers in blue and gold, who handled the prize warily. After depositing the strongbox at the Chairman's feet, they opened it, lifted out the Sword of Wisdom, and placed it carefully in front of Hyrcanus upon the table, after a blue satin cloth had been meticulously folded and positioned for a cushion.

One of the clerks, moving fussily and nervously, slightly adjusted the Old World lights to provide Hyrcanus with the best illumination.

Only at this point was Valdemar struck by the conspicuous absence of the Sword of Mercy. Since he had been taken prisoner, no one in his hearing had even mentioned Woundhealer—that could only mean, he thought, that either Ben or Zoltan had managed to get away with the Sword of Healing.

At this thought, Valdemar shot the Lady Yambu a sharp glance. And she, as if she somehow knew just what idea had just occurred to him, responded with a glance urging caution.

Yes, Valdemar thought, it must be true. Hyrcanus and his people gave no indication of realizing how close they had come to capturing the Sword of Healing. Had they been aware of how narrowly that prize had just escaped them, they would already have launched an intensive search for it, and not be dawdling through this leisurely preparation for an interrogation.

Of course Wayfinder by itself was treasure indeed. Treasure enough, as Valdemar was beginning to realize, to dazzle at least slightly even the Chairman of the Blue Temple himself. When the soldiers put the Sword of Wisdom down in front of Hyrcanus, his eyes came alight. He touched the black hilt with a tentative forefinger, then stroked it greedily.

Confronted with the reality of Wayfinder, Chairman and Director both appeared to speedily lose interest in their prisoners. Evidently any serious questioning would be allowed to wait.

The Director of Security rubbed his bald head nervously as he stared at the Sword. He said: "Sir, we must get this property to a place of safety as soon as possible."

"Of course." Hyrcanus leaned forward on the table. "But surely we would be at fault, derelict in our duty to the Temple Stockholders, if we did not find one other duty even more pressing, and perform that one first?"

"Sir?"

"We must delay carrying this treasure away to safety, just long enough to make our first use of it."

The Director hesitated. "May I ask what use Your Opulence has in mind?"

"You may ask. Though I suppose it should be obvious." The Chairman, his face displaying a look of satisfaction, paused as if for emphasis. "I intend to require this Sword to indicate to us the location of the greatest treasure in the world."

For a moment there was silence in the pavilion.

Valdemar was suddenly struck by what he considered an ominous indication. Neither Chairman nor Director was displaying the least concern about the fact that their prisoners were listening to this discussion. It was, the young man thought, as if the Blue Temple officials considered their captives already dead.

At last Hyrcanus, standing up, moving carefully, drew Wayfinder from its sheath. The blade caught bright gleams from the Old World lights as the Chairman gripped the hilt in his two soft hands, making the Sword's powers for the moment his own.

"Now, how shall I phrase this request exactly?" This preliminary question seemed to be addressed more to himself than to anyone else, or to the Sword itself.

The worried Director answered with a murmured suggestion that the first care be for safety.

But Hyrcanus stubbornly shook his head. "We have," he said, "had direct assurances regarding our present security from our cavalry commander, and also from your powers, magician. True?"

"True, Your Opulence, but—"

"Tell me, do you believe that our encampment here is now secure, or is it not?"

"At the moment, sir, it is secure enough," the other murmured unhappily.

"Then there you are. Would breaking camp right now make the Sword any safer? Besides, our men and beasts are tired. They are all in need of rest before we undertake another march."

"True enough, Your Opulence."

"While they rest, we at the executive level can best make use of our time by pursuing our further duties to the stockholders."

Now for the first time Hyrcanus addressed the Sword directly. In his dry voice he phrased a simple demand: "Where is the greatest treasure in the world?"

Valdemar, watching with a dozen others, thought that the Sword did not react; or it reacted only slightly, and in an uncertain way.

"What in the world now?" the Chairman demanded, suddenly querulous. Obviously he had been expecting a more dramatic response of some kind. Letting the Blade rest on the table, he rubbed his left hand, the one free of the Sword's hilt, over his bald head.

After a little silence, the Director cleared his throat. "Do you think, Chairman, there might possibly have been some ambiguity in your phrasing of the question?"

"Ambiguity? You mean, some uncertainty as to which of the world's treasures is actually the greatest? Ah, the question of determining the best measure of determined value. Authorities do disagree on that, it's true." Hyrcanus cleared his throat again. "Perhaps I should rephrase my inquiry."

Valdemar hoped that if Hyrcanus did receive from the

Sword a plain unequivocal answer to any of his urgent questions regarding treasure, the Chairman would not feel it necessary to break camp at once, tired men and beasts or not, and follow the direction indicated.

Because what might he do with his prisoners then?

Hyrcanus was now interrupting himself to raise another point: "I wonder whether we ought not to approach Prince Mark—or any successful monarch might do, I suppose—with the idea of making some kind of trade for this lovely piece of magic, or offering it for sale—*after,* of course, we have used it to the best advantage for the Temple."

"Prince Mark," mused the Director, in a non-committal tone.

"I am assuming Mark can raise sufficient treasure to make such a purchase—indeed such a powerful Prince ought to be able to do so."

A brief debate on this point followed, between Hyrcanus and his Director of Security. Finally the latter brought the discussion back to considerations of safety.

Valdemar, listening attentively, gathered that neither the Chairman nor the Director believed Mark had been able to retain any appreciable amount of booty from the fabulous, infamous Great Raid. Both officials seemed to be saying that comparatively little Blue Temple wealth had actually been lost on that occasion.

But neither of the Blue Temple leaders seemed able to believe that Mark had not spent his years in power in Tasavalta amassing more wealth for himself.

Eventually they came back to the business at hand—getting the best possible quick advantage from Wayfinder.

"The more I think about it, Director, the more it seems to me that you are right. To assure that we obtain an unequivocal, useful answer, we must be clear in our own minds about the nature of the specific treasure we are seeking." Hyrcanus toyed meditatively with the Sword.

The Director said: "I should think, Your Opulence, that the most likely site for a truly unsurpassable treasure might well be in one of the Blue Temple's own vaults."

"What do you say?"

"I wonder, sir, if we will know whether this Sword is pointing at our own gold. Do you, personally, know the locations, and certified values, of each and every one of our own hoards? Their bearings from this spot?"

Hyrcanus hesitated fractionally before insisting: "Of course I do! Don't you?"

"Of course—sir."

Valdemar, listening, marveled at the indications suggesting that neither of these men was really sure of the matter.

The young man could see the fires of cupidity beginning to burn out of control in the eyes of the new masters of the Sword of Wisdom, as they huddled close over their prize. It looked as if the Director was beginning to be won over from his concerns of safety by his master's all-powerful greed. They were both staring at Wayfinder obsessively now. Perhaps, Valdemar thought, they were coming to terms with the condition all users of this weapon had to face—that the so-called Sword of Wisdom would never tell anyone Why, or What, or How, or When—or Whether—regarding any thing—but only, with seeming infallibility, exactly Where.

Hyrcanus murmured: "You are right. If our own treasure be not the greatest—then whose?"

Hyrcanus's chief aide said to him: "Possibly some Old World trove that for all our searching we have never been able to discover?"

"Possibly." The Chairman sank back into his chair. "Or possibly it is some property of the Emperor's, to which access is restricted by some tremendous enchantment?"

The Director, who had risen when his leader did, was not really listening. Instead he now waved his arms in the excitement of an inspiration of his own. "Wait! I have it! The Sword's answer to your original question was hard to interpret, ambiguous, for a very good reason—because it was self-referential!"

"Aha!"

"Yes, Your Opulence, the Swords themselves are the world's greatest treasure. And this Sword in particular must be valued above all the others—*Wayfinder itself may be—no, must be—the greatest treasure in the world!* And why? *Because it is the key to all the rest!*"

"Ahh." Hyrcanus, his eyes suddenly gone wide, let out a breath of satisfaction.

He had no need to ponder the Director's claim for very long before giving it his approval. "This very weapon before us, my good Director. Yes, what could be more valuable? I will see to it that you receive a bonus of shares. Perhaps even—a seat on the Board."

Valdemar was thinking that it made sense. Very possibly they were right—from their point of view the Sword of Wisdom had a transcendent value, because it was capable of leading them to all the other Swords, or to any other treasure that they cared to specify.

"Having made that identification," the Director remarked, "are we any further in deciding how best to use our greatest treasure?"

"I think," said the Chairman, "that we must be somewhat more specific, and somewhat more modest, in our next inquiry."

"Indeed. Yes."

"Very well then." He addressed Wayfinder again. "Sword, I adjure you to show us . . . to show me . . . the way to the Emperor's most magnificent treasure." Hyrcanus hesitated, then gave a little nod of satisfaction and plunged on. "I mean, to that thing, or collection of things, that *I* would consider most magnificent were I to see them all."

Valdemar, and Yambu standing beside him, watched and listened, the young man at least hardly daring to breathe. But he was somewhat puzzled. The Emperor? The name evoked only the vague image of a hapless clown, of a legendary figure out of childhood fables, who, even if he really lived, would be far less real and less important than any of the now-vanished gods.

Wayfinder twitched visibly in the Chairman's hands, but that was all. Evidently it was still giving only an ambiguous indication at best.

Hyrcanus evidently found this behavior unacceptable. "Surely you can respond more definitely, Sword. If I said I wanted to find the Emperor, how would you answer me?"

This question was so obviously hypothetical that Hyrcanus scarcely paused before recasting it, with firm Blue Temple legalism.

"Sword, I bid you guide me to meet the Emperor."

But again the Sword only demonstrated uncertainty.

The Chairman set his treasure gently down upon the table, and drummed his fingers next to it. "Well, Director, how are we to interpret this? That we are only to wait here, to meet the Emperor? That does not seem to make much sense—unless he is coming to call upon us." He added drily: "An unprecedented event, surely."

"I agree, Your Opulence."

In the following silence, Yambu's voice sounded quite unexpectedly, so that everyone turned to look at her. "Perhaps the Emperor *is* on his way here, to meet you." Her face wore what Valdemar thought an odd expression, even considering her situation.

Her statement was received with mixed reactions by

the men in power. These were knowledgeable, worldly leaders. They were constitutionally wary of the unknown in all its aspects, and whatever knowledge they possessed about the Great Clown, beyond what ordinary people knew, they did not particularly fear him.

Hyrcanus looked with interest at Yambu. "You know him, then?"

"I am indeed the Silver Queen. I suppose I know him if anyone does. I have borne his child."

"If he is coming here now," said the elderly Director after a time, "do you suppose he will be bringing his greatest treasure with him?"

The Silver Queen said, "I do not know."

Hyrcanus, letting Wayfinder lie on the table but rubbing the hilt as if for luck, stood up, pushing back his chair as if he wished to stretch.

He raised his eyes to find his male prisoner watching him intently. "Well, fellow? Had you any experience similar to this when Wayfinder was yours?"

Valdemar nodded slowly. "I admit it puzzled me a time or two. If that is what you mean."

No one asked him to elaborate, and he did not try.

Standing awkwardly beside him, Yambu was gradually growing more perturbed, as if she found the prospect of an Imperial visit somehow unsettling.

Time passed, very slowly in Valdemar's perception. Outside the pavilion, the Blue Temple's military people were stolidly going about their routine business of guard duty and camp making. Nothing of consequence seemed to be happening.

Not that the two high officials were going to be content simply to wait for the Emperor. No, people kept coming to the door of their tent with practical questions, matters that required answers. The commander of the cavalry, still awake himself though (as Valdemar thought) most of his troops—who had evidently ridden all night—were probably asleep, came in respectfully asking to be informed: Would they be breaking camp first thing the next morning? Would they spend the remainder of the day and night interrogating their fresh-caught prisoners?

Hyrcanus had excused himself, Valdemar supposed probably for a latrine break, and the question was left to his second-in-command to answer.

"Oh, I doubt that." The Director, stretching, allowed himself a smothered yawn. "You might as well haul that stuff away and pack it up again." He gestured toward the rear of the tent; and only now did Valdemar realize what the piled instruments of torture were, as a pair of soldiers packed them up again, and bore them out.

When the Chairman returned, a few minutes later, rubbing his hands together, the Director questioned him about the prisoners too: Was there really any point in dragging the wretches all the way back to headquarters?

"Perhaps, perhaps not. How can we know at this stage? Let us see if my question brings any result within the next few hours."

The morning hours dragged on. Hyrcanus and his Director were, as they thought, being their usual practical, businesslike selves when the clouded sky outside the tent seemed to split in half, and the gold and blue pavilion was torn away from above their heads.

Valdemar closed his eyes and yelled, momentarily certain that the last instant of his life had come.

TEN

IT was still morning, on that cloudy, rainy day, when the young woman commonly known as Tigris, accompanied by ferocious (though not very numerous) supporting forces—including one demon of more than ordinary power—and riding her own griffin, came crashing in with a murderous assault upon the newly established Blue Temple camp.

The Blue Temple griffins, being the cowardly creatures that they were, rose into the air, breaking their tethers, and took flight immediately. At the moment of the attack, Hyrcanus's people were doing their best to be alert, but they were simply overmatched, and the attack was a complete success.

Valdemar had never seen Tigris before, nor had he any means of identifying any of Wood's other people or creatures. The result was that while the fighting raged around him the young man had not the faintest idea of the true nature of this fresh batch of invaders.

On finding himself unhurt after the first few moments of the attack, Valdemar began to hope that he might after all be able to survive. By this time a heartening explanation had suggested itself, namely that these conquerors were the friendly Tasavaltans of whom he had heard so much from his traveling companions; Valdemar's spirits rose sharply with the prospect.

Had the youth been aware that a demon was among the attacking force, this would have dashed his risen hopes. But although the proximity of the foul thing soon began to make him physically ill, the young man was unable to either see or identify the source of his symptoms.

Valdemar's companion in captivity, the Silver Queen, was considerably more experienced and knowledgeable. Quickly recognizing the nature of the latest onslaught, Yambu felt her heart sink. Almost instantly she was able to recognize Tigris, and the presence of a demon as well.

The Silver Queen would have made some effort to enlighten her fellow prisoner, but she could neither talk to him effectively nor help him at the moment.

As had been the case in the previous assault, the struggle in magical and physical terms was intense but brief. Too late, one after another, the pair of high Blue Temple officials tried to grab up the Sword of Wisdom. But the neat tables full of paperwork had already been knocked over, and the top of the pavilion ripped away before either of the Executives could get his hands on Wayfinder. The Sword fell to the ground, and was covered in folds of collapsing fabric. The clerks ran in panic, or writhed in pain as enemy weapons struck them down.

At this point the magical bonds constricting Valdemar's movements began to slacken, and the youth enjoyed a few moments' hope that he would be able to escape. As he looked, Hyrcanus himself was slain. Valdemar, watching, could not have named the cause of death; one moment the Chairman was grimacing in alarm, and the next he was slumping inertly to the earth.

A moment later Valdemar himself was buried under the folds of collapsed fabric. Struggling ineffectually, the youth could tell by the sounds reaching his ears that more swordfighting was taking place. He could see nothing of the conflict.

With some strength and feeling coming back into his tingling limbs, Valdemar struggled against the enveloping folds that were keeping him a prisoner. He could only hope that Yambu, luckier or more skillful in the arts of magic, or perhaps both, might be able to get free in the confusion.

During the few moments in which the Director and the Blue Temple troops continued to make a fight of it, all local Blue Temple spells were shattered; and Yambu, given such an opportunity, did what she could to make the best of it.

Valdemar at last managed to crawl partially out from under the folds of the collapsed pavilion.

Before him the latest attackers, as they came slicing their way in, led by a woman, concentrated their efforts on getting control of the Sword of Wisdom.

And these attackers, in blue and silver livery, were ruthlessly successful.

In a few minutes at the most, the female leader and the her forces had stunned, scattered, or killed all Blue Temple opposition. The warrior woman had fairly got Wayfinder into her pretty white little hands.

At the last moment, the Director of Security, emerging from some obscure hiding place, attempted to escape. Valdemar saw him first, scuttling on all fours, then slowly trying to crawl away, and finally trying to play dead—but he was discovered and pounced on, captured alive.

And what of the Silver Queen? Valdemar, looking in all directions, realized with a faint dawning of hope that he could no longer see Yambu anywhere.

The young woman who had led the attack took a moment to examine the Chairman's body.

She then complained to some of her subordinates; evidently she was dismayed to find this eminent person dead.

Her anger flared at those who had killed him, and Valdemar thought she would have been angrier had she not been distracted by the discovery of Wayfinder.

Someone asked her whether the body of such a leader could be put to any use magically. No, she said that it was worthless—perhaps she did not want to divert her time and effort from a greater opportunity. "Might as well feed him to my griffin."

And now Tigris, annoyed at having been forced to waste even a few moments on other problems, was picking up Wayfinder, claiming the great Sword for herself.

She looked at the Sword of Wisdom with great satisfaction, and, thought Valdemar, considerable surprise. It seemed to him as if this lady warrior had not been expecting this Sword at all. Again he wondered about Zoltan and Ben, and prayed to Ardneh that one of them at least might be able to keep Woundhealer safely away.

The Director, somewhat dazed, was being brought before his conqueror. He managed a slight bow. "Lady Tigris," was all he said.

She was still absorbed in the contemplation of her new treasure. The prisoner being held before her would have fallen had not the grips on his arms held him up. Now he looked about him as if uncertain of where he was.

At last giving him some attention, Tigris remarked: "You're not looking well, my friend."

The Director only stared at her wanly.

She added, speculatively: "You know, sometimes people never completely get over the kind of treatment that you received from my Master in your Temple."

The elderly man smiled, as if that idea pleased him.

The smile, in the circumstances, made him look like the village idiot.

But now Valdemar's opportunity of leisurely observation was coming to a sudden end. A soldier had discovered him, and in moments he had been disentangled from the wreckage of the pavilion. Soldiers in mixed dress, looking like a gang of peasants, were dragging him before the Lady Tigris.

Gesturing for the Director to be taken away, she frowned at Valdemar. Her free hand moved in a subtle gesture, and her blue eyes narrowed as she stared at the gigantic young man.

"You are not Blue Temple," Tigris said. It was not a question.

"No ma'am. I was their prisoner."

Tigris adjusted the swordbelt she had so recently fastened around her slender waist. Meanwhile her gaze at Valdemar did not waver in its intensity.

"I more or less expected to take a few prisoners," she murmured to herself. "One can always find good use for prisoners. But . . . "

She raised the Sword she was still holding in her right hand, so that for a moment Valdemar thought she was going to kill him right away with Wayfinder.

Then, to his immeasurable relief, he realized that she was only going to ask the Sword a question.

"Sword," she whispered again, "where am I to turn to win—that which I most desire?"

Valdemar at the moment was physically closer to the enchantress than any other person. No one else, perhaps, except the stolid soldiers who were holding his arms, was near enough to have heard the question. No one else, perhaps, observed the look of sheer surprise in her eyes when Wayfinder, in response, swung up in the enchantress's grip to point directly at Valdemar.

He was at least as astonished as the young woman holding the Sword of Wisdom.

"This one?" she muttered, in slightly louder tones. "And what am I supposed to do with him—sacrifice him?"

But that kind of question, as the questioner herself appeared to understand full well, was not the kind to which Wayfinder could be expected to reply.

Meanwhile other matters began intruding, frustrating her evident wish to concentrate on the Sword. The blue and gold pavilion had been thoroughly wrecked in the skirmishing, and one of the young woman's aides was wondering what to do about it. She commanded him to see that the wreckage was got out of the way and searched for whatever of value it might contain.

"And are we to camp here, Lady Tigris?" the soldier asked.

The lady, seemingly indifferent to the rain which darkened and plastered her blond hair, muttered some kind of an answer that Valdemar did not really hear.

In Valdemar's eyes the young woman's face was so hard and ruthless that he felt morally certain she could not really be as young as she appeared.

Now she came a few steps closer, pointing Wayfinder deliberately at his midsection, so that momentarily he once more felt in danger of being skewered. From the steady way she held the heavy Sword, it was apparent that her slender wrists must be stronger than they looked.

Fiercely she demanded of Valdemar: "You . . . very well, what is important about you? There must be something. What are you good for, what use am I to make of you?"

The only response that came to the lips of the dazed youth was: "Well, you are certainly not the Emperor."

One of the lady's eyebrows rose. "I should hope not."

It was a wary, calculating answer. "Were you expecting him?"

She sounded as if she thought the Emperor's arrival not a totally ridiculous idea. Why, Valdemar wondered, were all these knowledgeable people apparently taking the Great Clown so seriously?

To his captor he replied: "Someone just moments ago—I mean the Chairman—was asking that Sword about the location of the Emperor's treasure."

"I see." Again what he said was being taken seriously.

Meanwhile, Tigris was evaluating her young captive as impressively arrogant. At first glance he was only a peasant, but of course there had to be something special about him, for the Sword of Wisdom to pick him out as her ticket to freedom.

He was continuing to stare at her in what she considered to be a very insolent way—allowing for the fact that men did tend to stare at her. The look had some fear in it, as might be expected of anyone but a madman in his situation. But it contained a measure of haughty defiance too.

Just as Tigris was about to speak again, a small bird, unperturbed by drizzling rain and sullen cloud, began singing somewhere nearby. Her reaction, the way she turned to get a look at the bird, made Valdemar turn his head too. Yes, there was the little feathered thing, looking quite ordinary, perched in the branches of a tree not far from the destroyed pavilion.

The diminutive songster, seemingly indifferent to the affairs of humans and the weapons of the gods, produced a few more notes, then flew away, as if suddenly frightened by something beyond the range of Valdemar's senses.

Tigris turned her attention to her prisoner again.

Valdemar felt a sudden return of the physical sickness. Still he was unable to assign a cause.

The lovely young woman regarded him in silence a little longer. Then she said: "I am still trying to fathom why the Sword of Wisdom should have pointed you out to me. Have you any idea why?"

Before Valdemar could attempt a reply, one of the lady's human subordinates came up to request orders, interrupting her train of thought. Turning aside, she commanded this man to dispatch a message to Master Wood. "Inform the Master that we have had great success."

"Shall I tell him, my lady, that the Sword we have taken here is not the one we were expecting to find?"

"No, fool! The Master will know of that already. Use just the words I have just spoken: 'great success.' Nothing more and nothing less."

"Yes, my lady." The soldier bowed himself away.

Tigris returned her full attention to Valdemar.

"Where is the Sword of Healing?" she demanded abruptly.

"I don't know."

Tigris stared at him. If she was really determined to find Woundhealer, he thought, all she had to do was put to work the Sword she had just captured. But he was sure that she had had some other goal in mind when she put her first question to Wayfinder. And she had been quite as surprised as he was at Wayfinder's answer.

In another moment Tigris, still with the Sword of Wisdom in hand, was giving orders that the camp be guarded well. She herself, she proclaimed to her subordinates, was about to go apart from them, because she needed solitude to work a certain special spell.

With that accomplished, a new word and a gesture from the sorceress sufficed to grant Valdemar another degree of freedom from the magical restrictions on his movement. Suddenly he felt he could walk normally; he wondered what would happen should he attempt to run.

Brusquely ordering him to follow, her eyes on Wayfinder, which she held in front of her, Tigris led the way out of what had been the Blue Temple camp.

Stiffly Valdemar followed. His legs still moved only slowly, his powerful arms hung almost useless at his sides. Maybe, he thought, he could use both arms and legs effectively if he really tried. But probably that thought was delusion. The confident small woman who had just turned her back on him did not seem to be worried about anything that he might do.

She continued to carry the Sword extended horizontally ahead of her, and he thought she was muttering to it again, though he could not make out her words. As if she might be asking Wayfinder for the best place to take Valdemar—for what purpose? He supposed that he was going to find out soon.

As they paced on across the sandy wasteland, Lady Tigris still in the lead, the rain continued, a sullen dripping from a lowering, overcast sky. The birds were silent now, or absent, having taken flight from the ominous presence of the demon.

This stalwart, healthy-looking youth, as far as Tigris could tell, was a damned unlikely candidate to be of any magical or political prowess or importance whatsoever.

Physically, of course, he was impressive. It occurred to her to wonder whether he might have been someone's personal bodyguard. Not Hyrcanus's or the Director's, because he was not Blue Temple. But then who . . . ?

"Who are you, fellow?" she demanded, turning to stare at him again, but almost as if asking the question of herself.

He shook his shaggy head, perhaps to rid his eyes of rain. Looking down at her from his great height, he answered simply: "My name is Valdemar, lady."

"That tells me almost nothing."

"I am a grower of vines and grapes."

For a moment Tigris regarded this reply as brave mockery indeed, and was on the brink of administering punishment. Then, reconsidering the tone of the answer, she came to the belief that it had been sincere.

She shook her own wet blond curls, impatient but wary, pondering, ready to kill or to bless, as might be required. "I can smell some kind of magic about you, I believe . . . though not, I think, any impressive power of your own. What have you to do with the Swords?"

Again the towering youth shook his head. "Nothing at all. Except that the one you now hold, lady, was once given to me."

That surprised her. "Given to you? Why?"

The young giant sighed. "I wish someone could tell me why."

"Who gave it?"

"I don't know that either."

Tigris made a disgusted sound. "I fear that getting at the truth about you is going to take time, and my time just now is in extremely short supply. If I thought you were being wilfully stubborn . . . but of course that may not be the case at all. You may in fact know nothing, and still be vitally important—somehow."

When Valdemar's feet slowed, and his shoulders moved as if he wanted to wave his arms and argue, Tigris with a gesture of her own increased the paralytic restriction on the movement of his arms. "Keep moving, and be quiet!"

Then she once more consulted the Sword, murmuring: "Guide us to the safest place within a hundred meters."

Following Wayfinder's indication, she continued to march her prisoner quickly along until after another forty meters or so they reached a place where the Sword indicated that they should stop.

Here Valdemar thought at first that the two of them

were now entirely alone. But when he looked and listened carefully, calling into play such sense of magic as he did possess, he became aware of a faint disturbance in the air, just at the limit of his perception. They were in fact being attended by certain immaterial powers, of which his human captor evidently was well aware.

And in another moment these magical attendants were gone, dismissed by a wave of a small white hand.

Their mistress looked steadily at Valdemar. "When Hyrcanus had this Sword," she asked, "what question or questions did he put to it?"

"As I have already mentioned, lady, he spoke chiefly of the Emperor, and the Emperor's treasure. Why the Chairman of the Blue Temple should do that I do not know—I have always thought that the Emperor, if he really existed, was no more than a clown."

The lady was not interested in Valdemar's opinions. "And what exactly did Hyrcanus ask of this Sword?"

"I don't remember the exact words. He wanted to be shown the way to the Emperor's greatest treasure."

"And what answer was he given?"

"Nothing very definite. The Chairman discussed this with his colleague—the man you were just talking to back there—and they thought the ambiguity might mean the Emperor was actually approaching. But . . . you arrived instead."

The red lips smiled faintly. "Perhaps the real answer was that the Great Clown has no treasure." The smile vanished. "But you and I, grape-grower, we have no time to worry about that now."

"What are we to worry about instead?"

Tigris did not reply.

Her one overriding worry was Wood, escape from whose domination was the single thing in the world which she most desired. Now she caught herself instinctively looking over her shoulder. A useless gesture, of course, and she was irritated to catch herself doing it more than once.

Valdemar took note of this quirk of behavior, and of the expression on the young woman's face when she looked back toward the encampment where her troops were busy with the tasks she had assigned them. He wondered silently who or what it was that this mighty sorceress feared so much.

He asked: "You are very powerful in magic. Also you have just won a victory, and captured one of the gods' own weapons, which you now hold in your hands. What are you afraid of?"

She raised the Sword a little, as if she wanted to pretend that she would strike him with it. "Yes, this is indeed one of the gods' own weapons—but remember that the gods are dead. Or did you know that, grape-grower?"

"I think the gods are not all dead, my lady. I still pray to Ardneh. Ardneh of the White Temple, who never allowed himself to be caught up with the other deities in their games—"

"Ah yes—well, grape-grower, it may surprise you, but I could wish sometimes that Ardneh still lived, and still ruled the world—not that I believe he ever really did."

"Why should such a wish surprise me? I could share it. I was once," continued Valdemar, not really knowing why he chose this moment for his revelation, "a novice monk in a White Temple."

"So? And did those fat Brothers in their Temple warn you, when you abandoned safety for the great world, that you should choose to stay instead?"

Without waiting for an answer, Tigris once more raised the Sword of Wisdom.

Careless of the fact that Valdemar watched and listened, she couched her next question in clear terms: "Hear me, Sword! Show me the way to gain freedom from the one I fear above all others! I do not mean my own death; that road to freedom I could find without your help. I want a long life, in safety from any harm that he may try to do to me."

And again Wayfinder pointed, immediately and steadily, straight at Valdemar.

"Just who," he asked the enchantress, "is this one you fear above all others?"

She ignored him. She gave the impression of a woman fighting back panic, trying to remain patient. There was a faint tremor in her voice. "Very well, Sword. I now have firmly under my control this great clod of farmyard mud that you keep pointing at. You are able to perceive that, I suppose? Well, what do you expect me to do with him next? Sacrifice him, eat him alive, lie with him? You will have to give me some further sign."

The Sword, of course, was not to be commanded thus, and it said nothing in reply. It still pointed where it had been pointing—straight at Valdemar—and that was all.

Valdemar cleared his throat. "I have noticed, that this Sword's way of conveying meaning can sometimes be rather hard to interpret." Though his voice was calm enough, he could feel how his ears had reddened, oh so foolishly, with the echoing in them of those three words: *Lie with him.* Odd, that now, with his very life at stake, he should be so affected by that suggestion.

Tigris did not notice Valdemar's reaction. She cared nothing for her captive's ears, or for his whole head, come to that. Her trained senses, contemplating the Sword whose hilt she gripped so hard in both her hands, could perceive the intricate knots of magic interpenetrating the hard steel, strands invisible to ordinary vision, stretching forth and fading away in all directions, becoming lost in bewildering complexities of power. . . . Even she, long accustomed to the tremendous capabilities of

Wood, was awfully impressed by this, forced to an attitude that had in it much of reverence.

And this enigmatic Sword, each time she questioned it, only kept reinforcing the importance of her captive, this otherwise inconsequential youth who called himself Valdemar.

Letting Wayfinder's point sag to the ground, looking keenly at the bold and ignorant fellow, Tigris was totally convinced that there must be something more to him than he admitted. Whether he himself realized what his peculiarity was or not.

Haughtily she insisted: "Who *are* you, fellow? What are you holding back? I must somehow determine your importance to me."

The giant shrugged. "I have told you my name, and who I am. Tell me who you are. Perhaps a meaningful connection can be established. Maybe I have heard of you."

"You have a kind of serene insolence about you, unusual in a peasant. Very well. My name is Tigris."

That much he had already heard. He blinked rain from his eyes. "The name means nothing to me. I don't suppose you are from Tasavalta?"

"I am not—are you?"

"No, I have never been near the place."

"And have you," Tigris asked her captive, "any connection with Prince Mark of that land?"

Valdemar answered as usual with the truth: no, he had never seen Prince Mark, and knew very little about him. He volunteered no information about having made contact recently with Prince Mark's friends.

Tigris next asked him if he knew anything of a magician called Wood. "He has other names as well."

"I have heard," said Valdemar, "that that one is a powerful and evil man."

Tigris muttered under her breath: "This is getting me

nowhere." She tried another tack in her interrogation. "When I arrived, you were a prisoner of the Blue Temple."

"Yes ma'am, I certainly did spend an uncomfortable hour or two in that condition. It seemed like days. I thank you for putting an end to that. I believe they would have killed me."

"How polite he is. That's good. Yes, certainly the late Hyrcanus and his associates would have killed you, if they thought there was any profit to be made that way—making your hide into parchment perhaps—but they did not. What did they actually want of you?"

"Actually it was only the Sword Wayfinder they wanted. And when they got it, they were so busy worrying about what to do with it that they never got around to wanting anything much from me . . . except to ask me where I had got Wayfinder, and from whom."

"And what did you tell them?"

"Lady—Lady Tigris—I could give them only the same poor answers I have given you."

With every heartbeat of time that fled, she could feel her brief allotment of opportunity rapidly running out. Every moment Tigris spent asking questions, puzzling over the answers, and yearning to rend this poor fool to bloody ribbons with her nails, the inevitable end was drawing steadily nearer. Her end would come when Wood learned that she had taken the Sword of Wisdom, and was keeping the discovery from him. At that moment her gamble for freedom would turn out to have been a catastrophic blunder.

Valdemar, in the moments when her attention faltered, had begun to tell her the story of his life. The existence of a grape-grower sounded extremely dull.

Still she forced herself to listen patiently, hoping to gain the clue she needed, even though the timekeeper in her head was running, as regularly as her speeding pulse.

Now the first real suspicion has been born in his mind. Now he is considering sending out a demon to check up on me . . .

"Cease babbling about grapes!" she shrieked at her captive. "Why are you here? Why were you in the camp of Hyrcanus?"

Valdemar, with an effort maintaining his own calm, revealed to his questioner his purpose in setting out on the journey which had brought him first in contact with the Silver Queen, and then afoul of the Blue Temple.

He did not say anything to Tigris about the Sword of Healing, and she did not raise the subject.

All this seemed to Tigris to be bringing her no closer to understanding what she ought to do next. It was maddening to think that the Sword on which she had abruptly decided to risk her life was giving her the answer she had to have, but she was unable to interpret it. Her anger flared at this babbling fool of a peasant, at the Sword, at the whole world and her life in it. And then her rage began to settle, to congeal into a deadly calm that tasted bitterly of despair.

She said: "All very fine . . . for a grower of grapes. But I don't see how any of that helps me." She raised the Sword of Wisdom again, glaring at it. "All right! Powers of the Sword, I have accepted that for some reason you want me to make this grower of grapes my own. Whatever happens, I intend to keep him, until you deign to show me what his usefulness may be. And when are you going to get around to that?"

Valdemar shook his head. He offered mildly: "Wayfinder will never answer a question of that type. But it occurs to me that, being a sorceress yourself—no offense intended—you may be making too much of the idea of sacrifice and magic."

"What do you mean?"

"I mean the Sword might simply be indicating that you are to take me with you somewhere."

Her blue eyes widened. "Is that it, Sword? Am I now to travel to another place, taking this peasant along?"

At once, to the young woman's immense relief, the Sword responded strongly. The tip moved away from Valdemar, and now pointed almost straight west.

"You do know something, fellow, after all." Her spirits rising abruptly, Tigris half-jokingly remarked: "Perhaps your function is going to be that of counselor, interpreter of Swords for me."

Valdemar shrugged his enormous shoulders. "It is only that I have had that Sword, and tried to use it, longer than you have. And you appear somewhat distracted at the moment. As if something were preventing you from thinking clearly."

But his companion was no longer listening. Once more addressing Wayfinder, Tigris demanded: "And where are we to go? How far? But no, never mind, of course you cannot tell me that. I have been given a direction. The real question is, should we walk, or run, or will we need a griffin?"

Again Valdemar shrugged. Of course the Sword was not going to tell them how far away the goal, whatever it was, might be.

The young man saw little future in trying to do anything but cooperate with this woman for the time being. She was evidently a practitioner of evil magic, but she had also rescued him from death and perhaps worse.

Once shown a clear course of action, Tigris was decisive. Already she was giving a magical command, together with a shrill whistle, calling her own griffin from the camp a hundred meters distant.

In another moment it was Valdemar's turn to be distracted. He was awed, and frightened, watching the griffin approach and land beside them.

Getting aboard the hideous winged beast required some courage of Valdemar. It was not, of course, that he really had any choice. His huge frame was cramped in the small space available in the left side pannier, but the extra weight seemed to make little difference to the griffin. The young man had heard that these creatures' powers of flight depended far more on magic than on any physical strength of wing.

His captor was already aboard, straddling the central saddle, glaring down at Valdemar in his lower seat with imperious impatience. In a moment they were breathtakingly airborne. Tigris steered the beast, sometimes by kicks, sometimes by silken reins, or murmured words, or all of these means in combination—steered so that the Sword always pointed straight past the creature's leonine and frightful head.

They were heading approximately west.

Tigris soon resumed her conversation with Valdemar, demanding help from him, impatiently listening to his replies, revealing more than she intended about her desperate situation. She was trying every approach she could think of, in an attempt to fathom this youth's mysterious importance, perhaps absolute necessity, to the success of her effort to escape Wood's dominance.

Suddenly she demanded: "What do you know about me, grape-grower?"

"Not much, lady. Only the very little you have just told me. And . . . one thing more."

"What?"

"It's plain enough, isn't it? When I had the chance to hold Wayfinder in my own hands, and demand guidance from it—that very Sword that you are now depending on—it guided me to you."

"What?"

Patiently Valdemar explained what his question had been, and concluded, "The Sword must have directed me to you. I asked my question of Wayfinder, and followed its directions consistently—and here you are."

The enchantress almost laughed—but not quite. Though inexperienced with Wayfinder, her theoretical knowledge of the Swords was substantial. She realized that this one's devious indications, like the powers of any Sword, had to be taken very seriously indeed.

She said: "You mean you think I am somehow going to help you find your bride-to-be?"

"I hardly think that you are meant to be my bride, so I suppose it must be that." Valdemar added after a pause: "First I was led to another woman, who was not the one I wanted to marry, but I suppose somehow brought me closer to her. And now I have been brought to you."

Tigris allowed a sneering comment to die unsaid. She supposed that in a way the Swords were all quite democratic; to Wayfinder, the status of its wielder, or the gravity of the quest, would not matter in the least. Vine-grower or duke, king or swineherd, princess of magic or homeless beggar, all would be on an equal footing to the gods' weapons. And so would the goals they sought.

Wayfinder still pointed straight ahead; the griffin still bore on untiringly. A good thing, Tigris congratulated herself, that she had not decided to try walking.

"It could be worse, grape-grower. Had this mount not been available, we might be riding Dactylartha's back." Even as Tigris spoke, she looked round warily once more.

"Is that the name of another griffin?"

"No creature so mild and friendly as that."

The youth looked back too, seeing nothing but the clouded sky. Was this mysterious Dactylartha the being that she feared? He inquired: "This creature, as you call it, follows us?"

"It does, right closely—but at my own orders."

Then your fear, the young man thought, must be for someone or something else.

Valdemar gritted his teeth and continued to endure the journey. At moments when, because of weather or an unexplained lurching of the beast beneath him, things got particularly bad, he tried closing his eyes. But being deprived of sight only made things worse.

Once or twice he asked: "Where do you expect the Sword to guide us?"

"To a place where I can find what I need."

From time to time Tigris spoke again to Wayfinder, questioned it, in a language Valdemar did not know. He inquired: "Is it too much to ask—I couldn't hear you clearly—exactly what query you have just put to our guide?"

Tigris ignored the question. Her face was grim.

The great wings beat on, marking out slices of time and space. With every fleeting moment Tigris felt an incremental growth of fear. An increase of the driving, nagging, growing terror that she would not be able to reach her goal before her Ancient Master caught wind of her treacherous intention. The goal to which the Sword was guiding her, for all she knew, might still be halfway around the world.

She had not asked the Sword of Wisdom for safety.

And Wayfinder, upon which her life now depended, was forcing her to bring this peasant clod along. And still she had no inkling why.

ELEVEN

ON having Wayfinder fall so unexpectedly into her hands, Tigris had needed only a moment to make her great decision. She would strike for freedom, gambling impulsively on the Sword of Wisdom's tremendous power. After all, there was no telling when, if ever, an equal opportunity would arise. She had expected quick meaningful answers from this weapon of the gods, affording her a fighting chance of success in her revolt against her Swordless Master.

But so far, to her growing terror and rage, things were not working out as she had hoped.

In her anger, she lashed out at the grape-growing peasant Valdemar. He was the handiest target; and besides, there was something intrinsically irritating in the very nature of this young man with whose presence the Sword had saddled her for some indeterminate time to come.

Bridling her impatience and fury, concentrating her attention, straining to be logical, she resumed her questioning as they flew. She dared not harm this oaf seriously until she could determine just what his purpose in her life might be.

The peasant answered her questions with an irritating lack of fear—as if he were confident in being indispensible to her.

But she had practically no success in extracting useful information from him.

In something like despair she demanded: "So, what am I to do with you when I reach the end of this flight?"

"You will let me go my way, I hope. Perhaps my bride will be there."

Tigris told him what he could do with his bride. Then, as the griffin bore them over a lifeless wilderness of splintered rock, an idea struck her, with the force of inspiration.

"I wonder if I have now carried you far enough," she mused aloud. "Perhaps the Sword will be satisfied if I leave you in safekeeping here, while I go on, unencumbered, to solve the next step of the puzzle, whatever it may be."

Safekeeping? Valdemar, not knowing what she had in mind, or whether to be pleased or worried, clung to his seat in silence. Decisively the young enchantress reined her griffin around in a horizontal loop, and caused the beast to land on a rocky pinnacle perhaps twenty or thirty meters high. The small flat space that formed this spire's top was totally inaccessible from the ground.

"Now get off," she commanded.

"Ma'am?"

"You heard me, insolent fool! Get out, get off. If this mode of transportation bothers you, you may be free of it for a time at least. I will be back for you, I suppose, when I have performed the next step required by the Sword."

Silently, somewhat awkwardly, Valdemar climbed out of his basket, planting one foot after the other carefully on the one square meter or so of flat rock not occupied by the crouching body of the griffin itself. He stood there carefully, not saying anything. He was thinking that the Sword had brought him to this pass, and there must be some benefit in it for him. At least in potential.

Tigris settled herself in the central saddle and flicked the reins. Her mount sprang back into the air.

But then, when she would have urged on her steed again, she found the damned Sword in her right hand pointing inexorably straight back to the abandoned man.

Muttering abuse and imprecations, she steered the animal back to land on the spire again, a process that made Valdemar crouch and cling in fear, ducking under one of the great wings to keep from being knocked into a deadly fall.

"Get on!" his persecutor commanded.

The youth needed no second invitation. In a moment they were airborne again, the satisfied Sword once more pointing almost due west. Valdemar, settling himself more comfortably in his basket, remarked against the rush of air: "So, it seems that Wayfinder insists that our fates are somehow bound together."

Tigris did not answer.

"Do you know where we are going?" he asked patiently.

Eyes of blue fire burned at him. "Plague me with one more question and I'll slice out your tongue!"

"No, you won't."

The griffin, urged on by its mistress, was swiftly gaining speed, far beyond anything attained in the first leg of their flight; the terrible wind of their accelerating passage whipped Valdemar's words away and tore them to shreds. Now Tigris made a magical adjustment to screen the wind somewhat, and managed to hear what her captive had said when he bravely repeated it. But she said nothing in reply.

Valdemar, fighting to keep calm, continued: "As I see it, you can't afford to do me any serious harm. Because the Sword insists that you need me for something, but you don't know what it is. I'd like to know the answer too, and it might help me figure it out if I knew exactly what you are trying to get the Sword to do for you."

Tigris, resisting the urge to commit magical violence upon this fool, stubbornly remained silent.

Still she had no more idea than did her reluctant passenger of where they were going, and under her controlled calm the terror of her own ignorance, her fear of Wood, was threatening to overwhelm her. Her imagination could readily supply a hundred destinations, objectives to which Wayfinder could be sending her. But she had no real reason to credit any of them.

Hours passed, tempting Tigris to despair, while their great steed still hurtled toward the west, now angling somewhat to the south, at mind-numbing velocity. Valdemar was stunned to see how the sun's normal westward passage slowed, then stopped for them, then began to reverse itself. The griffin's wings had long ago become an almost invisible blur. Great masses of cloud, above, below, and near them churned past.

Tigris, almost lost in her own thoughts, became chillingly certain that Wood had by now had more than enough opportunity in which to suspect, if not actually prove, her treachery. And it was not the Ancient One's habit to delay punishment until he was presented with airtight proof.

And then, just when the enchantress had begun to wonder if her Master's magic had already found her and begun to destroy her life, and the terrible flight was going to endure forever, the Sword of Wisdom suddenly swung its sharp point downwards.

Tigris hastily moved to instruct her magic steed, directing it carefully toward the indicated goal.

Obediently the griffin descended, through layers of cloud and slanting sunlight to the waiting earth.

They emerged from the clouds at no more than mountain-top altitude. Valdemar, reviving from a kind of trance brought on by cold and monotony, observed in a dull voice that the object of their journey appeared to be nothing but an extensive desert. He had no idea how far they were from the wasteland where their flight had started.

Tigris, moved by some impulse toward human feeling to engage in conversation, agreed. Thinking aloud, she speculated that Wayfinder might have brought them here in search of the Sword of Vengeance.

"Farslayer? How would that help you?"

"A dullwitted question. A bright young man like you must know the virtue of that Sword."

Within a minute or two the griffin brought its riders safely to a gentle landing on the earth.

Muttering words of control into the nearest ear of the huge leonine head before her, Tigris climbed lithely from her saddle with drawn Sword, to stand confronting a harsh, lifeless-looking landscape under a midday sun. Valdemar promptly joined her, without waiting to be commanded. All was quiet, except for a faint whine of wind moving a drizzle of sand around their feet.

The Sword in the young woman's hand was pointing now in the direction of a barren hillock nearby.

Together Valdemar and Tigris began to walk that way.

As they drew near the hillock, he raised a hand to point toward its top. Up there, the cruciform outline of a black hilt showed against the distant sky, as if the point of a Sword were embedded in the ground, or in something that lay on the earth.

Silently, keeping their discovery in view, the pair trudged toward the modest summit. What at a distance had appeared to be a Sword was one indeed. At close range the weapon was identifiable as Farslayer. The Sword of Vengeance was stuck through the ribcage of a half-armored skeleton, nearly buried in the sand.

"So," Tigris breathed, "I was right. It is to be his death. That is my only chance to escape from him. So be it, then."

Valdemar noted that the garments adorning the anonymous skeleton had once been rich, and gold rings still adorned some of the bony fingers.

Tigris, murmuring some words of her art in an exultant tone, stretched out her hand to take hold of the black hilt. But scarcely had she possessed Farslayer, when there sounded a deep, dry whispering out of the low clouds above. Valdemar, looking up sharply, could see them stirring in turmoil.

"What is it?" the young man asked in a hushed voice. At the same time he unconsciously took a step nearer his companion, as if some instinct told him that he needed her protection.

Before Tigris could reply, there emerged from the lowering cover of clouds a churning gray vortex, a looming threat the size of a griffin, but barely visible to Valdemar. He found the silent onrush of this phenomenon all the more frightening because his eyes were almost willing to believe that nothing at all was there.

"It is Dactylartha," Tigris said in a low, calm voice. "Just stand where you are."

Valdemar nodded. Meanwhile, though his eyes had little to report, wind shrieked and roared about his ears, and those of the woman standing beside him on the hill.

That was only the beginning. The wind soon quieted, but Valdemar's stomach was literally sickened by the presence of the creature that now appeared; now he realized that this entity in the air above him, or something like it, must be what had sickened him before.

But Tigris was speaking to the thing, then boldly challenging it, with the businesslike air of a woman long inured to facing things this bad, and even worse.

Valdemar stood swaying slightly, averting his eyes

from what was almost impossible to see anyway. He did not need his companion to tell him that, for the first time in his life, he was having a direct encounter with a demon.

Tigris, facing the thing boldly, appeared to be perfectly comfortable and in control. She spoke to the demon sharply, calling it by the name of Dactylartha.

Valdemar, retching helplessly despite his empty stomach, his knees shaky, had all he could do to keep from collapsing to the ground. Instead he forced himself to stand almost upright.

To his relief the great demon was paying him no heed. Dimly Valdemar could hear the voice of Dactylartha, a sound that reminded him of dry bones breaking. The demon was speaking only to Tigris, saying something to the effect that it would join her in rebellion, or at least refrain from reporting her to the Master, provided she immediately loaned it the Sword of Wisdom.

"Never."

"Then will the gracious lady consent to ask the oracle of the gods one question on my behalf?"

Tigris sounded as if she might have the wit and nerve to be able to win an argument with the creature. "Why do you want that?"

"I wish to locate my own life, great lady," muttered the ghastly voice of Dactylartha. "Where it has been hidden I do not know. But only by finding it again shall I be able to free myself of the power that the Ancient One now has over me."

Valdemar, trying to remain sane, and to understand, remembered with a shudder what little he had ever heard of the man who was sometimes called the Ancient One. Valdemar could also recall hearing somewhere that the only way to truly punish or control a demon—or to kill one—was to get at its life, which was almost invariably hidden, sometimes a long way from where the creature appeared and acted.

Whether Dactylartha was telling her the truth or not, Tigris did not, would not, believe him. She was thinking that she dared not trust any of his kind—this one, perhaps, least of all.

Valdemar watched her as she balanced the Sword of Vengeance in her hands. Such was Farslayer's power, he knew, that Tigris—or anyone else—armed with it would be able to cut down Wood himself, or any other foe, at any distance. Only one other Sword, only Shieldbreaker itself, could provide a defense. What, then, was holding her back? Only the ominous presence of Dactylartha, it would seem.

"Will you ask the question I want asked of the Sword of Wisdom?" the dry bones snapped.

"After I have won my own struggle. Support me in my fight first!"

They were shrieking at each other now, the woman and her demonic antagonist. Valdemar reeled and shuddered.

He put his hands over his eyes, then brought them down and stared. To his horror the demon had now assumed the form of a giant manlike shape in black armor, standing frighteningly close.

"Will you fight for *him,* then?" Tigris, her voice become unrecognizable, demanded of the thing. "You had better revolt, with me!"

"It may not be, great sorceress, it may not be! When *his* life ends, so does mine." The aerial blur of Dactylartha's presence seemed to intensify. A crushing weight seemed to be descending upon the stomach, and the soul, of Valdemar.

The woman was ready for combat. She had sheathed Farslayer, and her hands, one holding Wayfinder, rose in the subtle gesture of a great magician. "If I must slay you first, I will!"

The struggle was closed between Tigris and Dactylartha.

To Valdemar's limited perception, the outcome appeared horribly uncertain.

Made more desperately ill than ever by the increased activity of the monstrous demon, the young man thought he might be dying. But suddenly he found himself completely free of illness, for the moment, as the magical powers of the two contestants strained and nullified each other.

Terror of the demon overrode all other fears. Valdemar lunged desperately for the Sword still sheathed at the slender waist of Tigris. In a moment he had seized the black hilt of Farslayer, pulled it from its scabbard, and was hurling it with all his strength at Dactylartha's overwhelming presence—it was a crude effort, such as any unskilled fighter might make in desperation, throwing any sharp object at a foe.

The Sword of Vengeance, relentlessly indifferent to its user's skill or lack thereof, shot straight through the demon's flickering, half-substantial image, and in a moment had vanished over the distant horizon.

Valdemar had forgotten for the moment that the demon's life must be hidden elsewhere.

Dactylartha, frozen in position, stared for a long moment at his two human foes, glaring with eyes that were no longer eyes, out of a face no longer even a passable imitation of humanity. And in the next moment the demon died, shrieking a great shriek, his image exploding in spectacular fashion, and yet so quickly that he was able to do no harm to Tigris or Valdemar—nor carry any reports back to the Ancient One.

His guts hollow with fear, but his eyes and mind once

more clear, Valdemar discovered Tigris down on one knee, struggling with the after-effects of the contest.

Stumbling closer, he seized her by the arm. "It's gone. I think it must be dead."

"Dead and gone," Tigris confirmed, in a dull voice. Moving slowly, also stumbling at first, she regained her feet. Then some energy returned. Shaking herself free of Valdemar's grip, she cursed him for a peasant coward: "I could have managed that demon without wasting Farslayer on it! But nothing else will give me a chance to kill my Master, or to break free! I will be helpless without it . . . Damn you! Damn you, grower of poisoned grapes! I might have coped with the fiend by my own strength! You have cost me my chance for freedom, and damned me to hell!"

The youth recoiled, shaken. "We might get it back—"

"There will be no time."

Valdemar asked humbly: "What do we do now?"

For a moment Tigris brandished Wayfinder, as if she meant to cut him down with it. Then, in a voice bleak with depression, close to despair, she admitted: "Still I dare not hurt you."

Valdemar could find nothing helpful to say.

The woman cried out: "Sword, what am I to do? How am I to survive?"

Wayfinder, displaying the infinite patience of the gods, silently indicated Valdemar.

Tigris glared speculatively at her silent counselor. Then a gleam of hope appeared in her eyes. "Is it possible that the Sword of Wisdom has allowed for your idiocy in wasting Farslayer? In that case, peasant, it appears there may still be hope."

"I suppose we are to travel again?"

"Is that it, Sword? Yes, I'll drag him with me again, wherever you command. But which way?"

Promptly Wayfinder directed her to the griffin, which

had been cowering like a beaten puppy in the demon's presence. Now, with Dactylartha gone, Tigris was quickly able to reinstill in the lesser creature something like a sense of duty.

As soon as she and Valdemar were airborne, Wayfinder aimed them back eastward, in approximately the same direction from which they had come. Tigris accepted the command without comment.

Once more they went hurtling above the clouds. Their speed soon filled Valdemar with awe by bringing on a premature sunset behind them. Both of the griffin's passengers drew the obvious conclusion from their direction: that Wayfinder was guiding them back to somewhere near—perhaps very near—their original point of departure, at the overrun Blue Temple camp.

Tigris said little as they flew. Her thoughts were dominated by the notion that the pair were getting closer to Wood with every passing moment.

Once her companion was able to hear her questioning herself, or fate: "Am I to go to him, try to lie to him, defend my actions? That cannot be! As well plead with him for mercy."

The young man, despite his own desperate situation, felt a stirring of something like sympathy.

The enchantress muttered several somewhat amended forms of her wish for survival and for freedom, asking the Sword for some means of protection against the Ancient One, rather than the ability to destroy him.

"Sword, save me from him! Save me, somehow!"

From the very beginning of her contemplated escape, Tigris had been aware of the extreme danger involved in defying a wizard as powerful as the Ancient One. And Tigris knew, far better than most people, how powerful he was.

Even so, she now feared that she had almost certainly underestimated the truth.

"What am I to do?" she breathed. She was looking at Valdemar as she spoke, though perhaps not really seeing him.

He glared at her sourly. "Do you now want my willing cooperation?"

The sorceress snarled back, "From the first moment I saw you, I have suspected that you could not be as innocent as you appeared. Very well, if you have any revelations that you have been holding in reserve, let's have them now.

"Or else," she continued a moment later, speaking now as if Valdemar were not there, as if she were talking to her griffin, "some other power may be cleverly using this peasant as a catspaw." Suddenly she faced her prisoner again. "What say you to that, grape-grower?"

He shook his head, as calmly as he could. "Why is it necessary for me to be something other than what I am?"

The eyes of Tigris, filled with pain and fear, seemed to be boring into him. "When one has lived with Master Wood for any length of time, as I have, nothing can any longer be considered simply what it is. It is necessary to approach every question in those terms."

"Why did you choose to serve him, then?"

This, it appeared, was an unanswerable question. Tigris faced forward again, and the griffin flew on, magically tireless. Valdemar wondered if it would ever have to stop and rest, or feed.

When Tigris's attack had fallen on the Blue Temple encampment, Sergeant Brod had been close enough to observe the results, and to be shaken by the experience. But by good fortune he had also been distant enough to survive, unnoticed by the attackers.

In Brod's estimation, the new conqueror, even if she

did appear to be hardly more than a girl, was obviously powerful enough to be a worthy patron. He wanted to attach himself to her somehow, if that were possible without taking too much risk.

Torn between fear and ambition, the Sarge considered approaching the camp, and representing himself to its new masters as a victim of the Blue Temple. But soon caution prevailed; there were events in progress here that he could not begin to understand. Later, perhaps, when he had learned more. For the time being he decided to sneak away instead.

Ben, hiking industriously toward home, warily scanning the skies ahead, was just saying that, in his opinion, they might be going to get away with Woundhealer after all. At that instant he heard Zoltan scream behind him.

Spinning round, Ben was almost knocked off his feet by a swooping griffin. The thing must have come down at them from behind, and was now rapidly gaining altitude again with both Zoltan and the Sword of Mercy in its claws. While Ben stared, open-mouthed and helpless, the great beast swung round in the air, and rapidly departed in the direction of the Blue Temple camp.

On the ground Ben ran hopelessly, shouting curses, after the rapidly receding griffin. "Drop the Sword!" he screamed at his hapless comrade. "Drop—"

But Zoltan either could not hear him, or was powerless to obey.

Meanwhile, the Ancient One's most malignant suspicions of Tigris were in the process of being inflamed by a whispered report from a certain lesser, junior demon. This creature had just arrived at Wood's headquarters with the report that Dactylartha had been slain.

And even that was not the worst news: To the surprise of the attackers, the Sword of Wisdom had been in the

Blue Temple camp—and Tigris had seized that mighty weapon for herself, and taken it away with her.

Wood, seated now on a plain chair in a small room near his laboratory, did not move a muscle. He said quietly: "She sent me no report of any such discovery."

The bearer of bad news offered no comment on that fact.

"Her official report," the great magician continued, "was very vague. Something about 'great success'—and that was all. I suppose there is no doubt of any of these disquieting things you tell me?"

The creature made no attempt to conceal its unholy glee. "Absolutely none, my Master! And—no doubt of this fact either, great lord!—Dactylartha was slain by Tigris herself!"

"So."

"With the Sword of Vengeance!"

Wood sat listening carefully to the few additional details that he was told. His eyes were closed, his face a mask. He tended to believe the allegations against Tigris. Yet he could not be *absolutely* sure that his most favored aide has in fact turned traitor—this report might be a mistake or a lie, the result of some in-house intrigue.

But with at least one, and perhaps more, of the ten surviving Swords at stake, he was certainly not about to take any chances.

One thing that the Ancient One did secretly fear intensely, without trying to deceive himself about the fact, was Farslayer. Though he betrayed no sign of this externally, in his imagination he could feel the great cold of that steel as it slid between his ribs, or split his breastbone.

But the Sword of Vengeance had evidently gone to finish Dactylartha.

Wood actually did not know where that demon's life had been hidden, except that he thought it had been at a reassuringly great distance. Well, there was nothing to be done about that problem just now.

But Tigris. . . . If she was indeed now armed with the Sword of Wisdom, she would be very dangerous. He could not afford to put off action for a moment.

As night fell, and the stars came out above her speeding griffin, Tigris, still mounted in the saddle with her prisoner Valdemar huddled beside her in his basket, felt increasingly certain that her treachery must now be known to Wood. She knew a foretaste of the terrible punishment that it would no longer be possible to avoid.

Her worst fears were coming true. In an abyss of terror, feeling her mental defenses crumbling, Tigris realized that nothing could keep her Master from trying to wreak terrible vengeance upon her.

Valdemar stared at his companion helplessly. He could see by Tigris's behavior that she thought something terrible was happening or about to happen to her, and he was afraid of what this would mean to him.

At this point Tigris in her panic redoubled the urgency of her demands on Wayfinder. She stormed and pleaded with the Sword, that it must show her a way to escape.

"Help me! Save me!"

The Sword still pointed straight ahead, along the griffin's rippling neck.

Then, staring hollow-eyed at the Sword, the blond sorceress almost despaired. "Or is it," she whispered, "that even the gods' weapons cannot help me? That you can only guide me straight back to him—that *he* is too strong—even for you?"

A moment later, with her passenger watching and listening in frozen horror, the terrified young woman was retracting that statement, fearful that she had offended the mighty powers ruling Wayfinder.

Valdemar, hesitant to speak, gaped at his companion.

In this raging, cursing, pleading woman there remained no visible trace of a figure he thought he had once glimpsed, a wistful girl who had once paused to listen to a robin sing.

Suddenly some part of her terrible rage was directed at Valdemar. She glared at him and snarled.

Turning in the central saddle, she raised the Sword of Wisdom in both hands, to strike.

This madwoman was on the brink of killing him! There was no way to dodge the stroke. He was trying to straighten his cramped legs in the basket for a hopeless effort to seize the deadly Sword—when a sudden and violent change transformed the finely modeled face above him.

Suddenly and unexpectedly, the last curse died in the throat of Tigris.

Her body lurched in the saddle. Her eyelids closed. Wayfinder, which she had been brandishing for a death-stroke at Valdemar, slipped from her hands and fell.

TWELVE

ZOLTAN was gone, and Woundhealer with him, and there was nothing Ben could do about either loss. Doggedly the huge man had resumed his trudge into the north. From that direction, as the bird-messengers had told him, the Prince of Tasavalta and his force were now advancing; and if all went well he ought to meet Mark soon.

But Ben was unable to make much headway. Time and again flying reptiles appeared in the sky, forcing him to lie low, waiting in such shelter as he could find until the searchers were out of sight again.

At night, great owls, dispatched by Mark as forerunners of the advancing Tasavaltan power, came to bring Ben words of counsel and encouragement. They kept him moving in the right direction, and helped him to remain hidden successfully through the hours of darkness. Freighted with tokens of Karel's shielding power, the owls drifted and perched protectively near Ben while some of Wood's lesser demons prowled through the clouded skies above.

Yambu lay in another self-imposed trance, placed by her captors in a newly erected tent in what had once been the Blue Temple camp. The Silver Queen's condition was the subject of cautious probing by minor wizards who had been part of Tigris's attacking force. These folk were prudently waiting for orders, from their vanished mistress or from Wood himself, before they took any more direct action regarding this important prisoner.

Only partially, intermittently aware of the world around her, Yambu lay drifting mentally. Her dreams were often pleasant, rarely horrible, on occasion only puzzling. Most of the dreams in the latter category concerned the Emperor.

As often as not, Yambu's recent near-rejuvenation now seemed to her only part of the same continuing dream.

At the moment when Wood's vengeance fell upon Tigris, a thunderbolt no less startling for having been expected, her last coherent thought was that the Sword of Wisdom had somehow failed her.

The crushing spell aimed at her mind permitted her a final moment of mental clarity in which she gasped out some curse against the Sword. After that she was aware of crying out in desperation for her mother. And then a great darkness briefly overcame her.

Tigris—or she who had been Tigris—was still in the griffin's saddle when an altered awareness returned, and her eyes cleared; but when her lids opened they gazed upon a world that she no longer knew.

When Valdemar saw the hands of stricken Tigris relax their grip upon Wayfinder's hilt, he lunged upward and forward from his basket. He was making a desperate, almost unthinking effort to catch the Sword of Wisdom as it fell.

The hilt eluded his frantic grab; the blade did not. Cold metal struck and stung his hands. His try at capturing the

Sword succeeded, but the keen edges gashed two of his fingers before he could control its weight.

For a long moment he was in danger of falling out of the swaying basket. At last he recovered his balance, now gripping the Sword's hilt firmly, in hands slippery with his own blood. Valdemar glared at the dazed woman whose face hovered a little above his own. In a tone somewhere near the top of his voice he demanded: "What happened? What's wrong with you?"

The young woman was slumped down in the saddle, the reins sagging in her grip. She swayed so that he grabbed her arm in fear that she might fall; but still she appeared to be fully conscious. Her only reply to Valdemar's question was a wide-eyed smile and a girlish giggle.

Meanwhile the griffin, evidently sensing that something well out of the ordinary had occurred, was twisting round its leonine head on its grotesque long neck, trying to see what was happening on its own back.

Tigris giggled again.

"Fly!" Valdemar yelled at the curious beast. "Fly on, straight ahead for now!"

The hybrid monster, presented with these commands by an unaccustomed voice, kept its head turned back for a long disturbing moment, fixing the youth with a calculating and evil gaze, as if to estimate this new master's strengths and weaknesses. After that long moment, to Valdemar's considerable relief, it faced forward again and went on flying. The reins lay along the creature's neck, where Tigris had let them drop.

The evening sky was rapidly darkening around them. Demon-like masses of shadow and cloud went swirling by with the great speed of their flight.

The young woman raised her head and spoke in a tiny, childish voice.

"What did you say?" he asked.

She blinked at Valdemar. "I just wondered—where are we going?"

Her smile as she asked the question was sweet and tentative. She looked somewhat dazed, but not particularly frightened. She seemed really, innocently, uncertain of where she was.

The dropped Sword, the cut fingers, the sudden change, were briefly all too much for Valdemar. He felt and gave voice to an outburst of anger. He threw down the Sword—making sure it landed safely in his basket—and raved, giving voice to anger at his situation and at the people, all of them by his standards crazy, most of them bloodthirsty, among whom the precious Sword had plunged him.

Meanwhile, the strange young woman who was mounted just above him recoiled slightly, leaning away from Valdemar, her blue eyes rounded and blinking, red mouth open.

What was wrong with this crazy woman now? But even that question had to wait. The first imperative was to establish some real control over the griffin. Now the beast's unfriendly eyes looked back again. The course of their flight was turning into a great slow spiral.

The first step in dealing with this difficulty, obviously, was to use the Sword. Valdemar did so. While Tigris looked on wide-eyed but without comment, the young man asked to be guided to a safe place to land. Wayfinder promptly obliged.

The indication was toward an area not directly below. Therefore Valdemar was required to head the griffin there. Strong language and loud tones accomplished the job, though only with some difficulty. When he thought the creature slow to turn, he even cuffed it on the back of the neck. As a farmer's son, he had had some practice in driving stubborn loadbeasts, and saw no reason why the same techniques might not work in this situation—at least for a little while.

Presently they were over a good-sized lake, with a single island of substantial size visible near the middle, a dark blob in a great reflection of the last of the sunset. Soon Valdemar managed to guide the creature to a successful landing on the island.

Tigris, her face, arms, and lower legs pale blurs in the deep dusk, remained in her saddle until her companion told her to dismount.

At the same moment Valdemar began to climb out of his own basket, then hesitated, worried lest the griffin fly away once they both got off. But he could not very well remain permanently on board. Tigris had already leapt from her saddle to the ground, and in a moment he followed.

The griffin turned its head and snarled; the young man spoke harshly and gripped his Sword, wondering if the great beast might be going to attack them.

Well, that was simply another danger they would have to accept for the time being. Still carrying Wayfinder, and keeping an eye on the griffin, the youth went over to where Tigris was standing uncertainly. Angrily he began to question the woman who, an incredibly short time ago, had taken him prisoner.

Truly, the change had been drastic, whatever its cause. Valdemar was now confronted by a stricken girl who looked back at him anxiously.

Feeling angry all over again, he demanded: "What is this, some kind of joke? Some kind of pretense?"

Recoiling from him, the young woman abruptly burst into sobs. There was a convincingness about this sudden relapse into childishness that caused Valdemar to feel the hair rise on the back of his neck, an unpleasant sensation that even the demon had not managed to produce. This was no game or trick, but something completely out of her control.

She mumbled something through her tears.

"What's that you said?"

"I'm—afraid," she choked out. Tears were making some kind of cosmetic run on her eyelids, blotching her cheeks. Another moment, and she was clinging innocently to Valdemar as if for protection.

Automatically he put his arms around her, comforting. Paradoxically, Valdemar found himself even angrier than before at Tigris. Angry at her and at his general situation.

Not only angry at her, but still afraid of her in a way. What if she were to recover from this fit, or whatever it was, as abruptly as she had fallen into it? He didn't know whether he wanted her to recover or not.

Whatever magic might still have been binding Valdemar at the moment the sorceress had been stricken—obviously there had not been enough to keep him from lunging for the Sword—was now undone. He had felt the last remnants of that enchantment passing, falling from him, like spiders' webs dissolving in morning sunlight.

"Where are we?" she was asking him again, now in what sounded like tearful trust. She wiped at her eyes. "Who are you?" she added, with more curiosity than fright.

"Who am I. A good question. I ask that of myself, sometimes. Here, sit down, rest, and let me think." Seating his oddly transformed companion upon a mossy lump of earth—she obeyed directions like a willing child—Valdemar paced about, wondering what question he ought now to ask the Sword.

His cut fingers, still slowly dripping blood, kept him from concentrating, and he used the peerless edge of Wayfinder to cut a strip from the edge of his own shirt, thinking to make a bandage. The crouching griffin kept turning its head watchfully from time to time, as if estimating its chances of successful escape or rebellion. Valdemar thought that the beast's eyes glowed faintly with their own fire in the deepening night.

Tigris, sitting obediently where he had put her, had ceased to weep and was slowly recovering something like equanimity. Now, when he got close enough in the gloom to see her face, he could tell that she was smiling at him. It was a vastly transformed smile, displaying simple joy and anxious friendliness. A child, waiting to be told what was going to happen next.

As Valdemar stared at the metamorphosed Tigris, a new suspicion really hit him for the first time: the suspicion that this impossible, dangerous young woman could be, in fact, his Sword-intended bride to be.

Going to her, he unbuckled the empty swordbelt from her slender waist, and, while she watched trustingly, fastened it around his own. Then he sheathed Wayfinder. Waving the little bloodstained rag of cloth which he had been trying to tie up his hand, he asked: "I don't suppose you could help me with this?"

"What?"

"It's just that trying to bandage my own fingers, working with one hand, is rather awkward."

And when he held out the cloth to Tigris, she made a tentative effort to help him. But the sight, or touch, of blood at close range evidently upset her, and the bandaging was only marginally successful.

Gripping the black hilt of the Sword of Wisdom in his now precariously bandaged hand, Valdemar drew it and asked: "Safety for myself—and for my intended bride—*whoever* she may be!"

The Sword promptly gave him a direction. Generally south again. He decided that, since this island had been certified safe for the time being, further travel would have to wait till morning.

The next question, of course, was whether the griffin was going to get restless and fly away before sunrise. Or grow hungry, perhaps, and decide to eat its erstwhile passengers.

Valdemar sighed, and decided they would take their chances here for the night.

The remaining hours of darkness were spent uncomfortably, with each passenger sleeping, or trying to sleep, in one of the side-baskets, which were still fastened to the griffin's flanks. Some cargo in the right basket—the most interesting items were food and blankets—was unloaded to make room for Tigris. Valdemar thought it would be hard for the magical beast to attack them while they were on its back; and if the thing felt moved to fly during the night, it could hardly leave its passengers behind. As matters worked out, the griffin remained so still during most of the night that Valdemar wondered from time to time whether the beast had died. But he definitely felt more secure staying in the basket.

As if his current crop of problems were not quite enough, Valdemar continued to be nagged by worries about his untended vines back home, and about his lack of a wife. The images rose before him of several of the women with whom he had had temporary arrangements; all of them, for various reasons, had proven unsatisfactory.

At last he slept, but fitfully.

In the morning, when it seemed that no more sleep was going to be possible, Valdemar stretched and took stock of the situation. Tigris, as he could see by peering across the empty saddle, was still sleeping like a babe. She actually had one finger in her mouth.

The griffin, on feeling its heavier passenger stir, looked

round lazily; but at least it had done nothing—yet—in the way of a serious rebellion.

Valdemar had the Sword of Wisdom still gripped in his right hand. Raising it again, he bluntly demanded: "Where is the woman I should marry?"

His wrist was twisted by an overwhelming force. Remorselessly the weapon continued to point out Tigris.

Dismounting with a grunt, straightening stiffened limbs, Valdemar walked around to the animal's right flank and awakened his companion, who rewarded him with a cheerful, vacant smile.

Then, chewing on some of the food they had removed from that cargo basket, he attempted to nail down the Sword's meaning beyond any doubt. Addressing Wayfinder, he demanded: "Are you trying to tell me that this, this one with me now, is the very woman? That this creature is not simply meant to be a help of some kind to finding my rightful bride?"

The Sword, without a tremor, still indicated Tigris.

"Oh, by all the gods!" the young man roared. Such was his disgust that he felt a serious impulse to throw this Sword away.

He did in fact make an abortive gesture toward that end, but such was his practical nature that the Sword went no farther than necessary to stick the sharp point in a nearby tree. A moment later and Valdemar had hastened to retrieve the weapon of the gods. Wayfinder might produce some unpleasant surprises, but still it seemed to be the only hope he had.

A few minutes later they were preparing to fly again. This time Valdemar occupied the saddle, and Tigris went indifferently into the left basket, where he had ridden as her prisoner.

Time for the orders of the day. Valdemar put some thought into his request. "Sword . . . I want to go home, to my own hut and my own vineyard. I want to reach the place safely, and I want the world to leave me in peace once I am there. Also I want to have there with me—someday, somehow—the woman who should be my wife. Whoever she may be."

Pausing, Valdemar eyed Tigris. Sitting obediently in the basket where he had put her, she returned his gaze with an eager, trustful look that he at the moment found absolutely sickening.

He returned his concentration to the sharp Blade in his hands. "With all those goals in mind, great Sword, give me a direction." The response was quick and firm. "Very well! Thank you! Griffin, fly!"

He gave the last command with as much confidence as possible. If the griffin only turned its head and looked at him, he was going to be forced into some act of desperation.

Fortunately, things had not yet come to that. Gathering its mighty limbs beneath it, the creature sprang into the air.

This morning's flight lasted for about an hour, and during its entire course, controlling the griffin continued to be something of a problem. Tigris, giggling and babbling what Valdemar considered irrelevancies, distracted him and made his job no easier.

Wayfinder at least was predictably reliable. In response to Val's continuing requests for safety for both passengers, the Sword guided them through several aerial zigzags that had no purpose Valdemar could see. And then, point tugging sharply downward, it indicated a place to land.

At that same hour, a great many kilometers away, the Ancient One found himself able to spare a little time and thought to contemplate the treachery of Tigris, and to decide upon the most satisfactory method of revenge.

Another of Wood's inhuman secret agents had just

brought confirmation that he, Wood, had been able, from a distance, to inflict a severe loss of memory upon his most faithless subordinate.

"And not only that, Master, but a complete regression to near-childhood. The foul bitch is deliciously, perfectly, helpless!"

"It is a rather powerful spell." Wood nodded, somewhat complacently. "I am not surprised at its success. If the Director of Security for the Blue Temple could not resist it, our dear Tigris had no chance . . . of course in her case, this treatment is meant as no more than a preliminary penalty. One might say it is not really a punishment at all, only a form of restraint. I want to neutralize the little wretch until I can spare the time and thought to deal with her—as she truly deserves." He frowned at his informant. "Now who is this companion you say she has? No one, I trust, who is likely to kill her outright?"

"Only a man, Master. Don't know why she brought him along. Not much magic to his credit. Youthful, physically large. A lusty fellow, by the look of him, so I don't think he'll want to kill her very soon. He has of course taken over the Sword Wayfinder now."

"And I suppose he has been making use of it—but to what end, I wonder?"

"No doubt I can find out, great lord. Indeed, you have only to give the word, and I will step in and take the Sword away from him. I, of course, unlike the faithless Tigris, would bring the prize directly to you, without—"

"You will not touch that Sword, or any other!" Wood commanded firmly. "From now on that privilege is mine alone!"

"Of course, Master." The demon bowed, a swirling movement of a half-material image.

"I," the Ancient One continued, "am presently going to take the field myself."

There yet remained in the old magician's mind some nagging doubt that his lovely young assistant had really turned against him—his ego really found it difficult to accept that.

Perhaps it would be possible to learn the truth from her before she died.

At first she had been somewhat frightened, coming awake out of that awful dream—or sleep, or whatever it had been—to find herself straddling the back of a flying griffin. A griffin was an unfamiliar creature—certainly there had been nothing like it on the farm, home of her childhood, scene of most of her remaining clear memories—but it was not completely strange. She remembered—from somewhere—certain things about the species. Thus it proved to be with many other components of this strange new world.

By now, the young woman who had been Tigris had just about decided that this world in which she found herself—the world that had in it such an interesting young man as her companion—was, taken all in all, a sweet, wonderful place.

She who had been Tigris, her sophistication obliterated and her knowledge very drastically reduced by the magical removal of most of the memories of the later half of her life, continued to be very confused about her situation. But in her restored innocence the young woman was mainly unafraid.

From her place in the passenger's basket she gazed thoughtfully at Valdemar, looked at him for the thousandth time since—since the world had changed. Since—whatever it was, exactly, that had happened.

Since, perhaps, she had awakened from a long sleep of troubled dreams—and oh, it was good to be awake again!

She found herself still gazing at the strong young man. And she found him pleasant indeed to look upon.

It was something of a shock—it was almost frightening—to realize abruptly that she did not know his name.

In a loud clear voice she asked him: "Who are you?"

Turning a startled face, the youth in the saddle stared at her. "It is now something like a full day, my lady, since we met. I have told you almost as much as I can tell about myself. Have you no memory?"

She who had been Tigris did her best to consider. "No. Or, I have *some* memory, I suppose, but—I don't remember who *you* are. Tell me again."

The young man continued to stare at her. For the moment he said nothing, only shaking his head slightly.

Gently she persisted. "But who *are* you? Where are we?"

When Valdemar did not answer, she began to be a little afraid of him. She saw him as a very formidable person—even apart from his obviously gigantic physical strength. He had an air of confidence and reliability.

After a while she told him as much, in simple words.

He gazed at her with returning suspicion. "So, I am to believe that you are only a child now, and easily impressed? Is that it?"

She laughed girlishly. She could not really remain afraid of this young man for long. He was too . . . too . . .

"Ah, Lady Tigris, if only I could be sure . . . but how can I determine what you are really—but you have let me have the Sword, haven't you? Oh, truly you are changed!"

The lady was frowning. "What did you call me?"

"Tigris. Lady Tigris."

"But why do you call me that? Are you playing some game?"

"No game, no game at all. Not for me, certainly. By what name should I call you, then?"

"Why, by my own."

"And that is—?"

"How can a friend of mine not know my name?" She paused, thinking, her red lips parted. "But then I didn't know yours, did I? . . . my name is Delia. And now I remember that you did tell me your name before—Valdemar. That has a strange sound, but I like it."

He looked at her for what felt like a long time. "What else do you remember about me?"

"Why, that you are my friend. You have been helping me to—do something." Gradually, with an effort, Delia was able to remember a few other things that he had told her about himself, before—before the world had changed.

Valdemar asked: "And what do you remember about the Sword of Wisdom?"

She blinked at him. "What is that?"

He stared at her, the wind of flight whipping his long dark hair. "We'll talk about it later," he said at last.

The longer the flight went on, the longer she looked at him, the more definitely she who had been Tigris began to flirt with Valdemar, innocently and sensuously at the same time.

Valdemar at first took no real notice of her smiles and subtle eyelid-flutters, and occasional voluptuous stretches. He was watching the griffin grimly, and from time to time he repeated his latest question to Wayfinder: "Point me—point both of us—the way to safety."

Under his inexpert piloting, the great winged creature, continuing to change course on demand at frequent, irregular intervals, carried the couple back to some place that was half familiar-looking; Val, who as a rule had a fairly good sense of direction, had the feeling they were not far from the armed camp from which Tigris had marched him—it seemed like a terribly long time ago.

Obviously Wayfinder was not guiding them directly toward his vineyard. Well, having once decided to trust his life to the Sword's guidance, he supposed he had better trust it all the way. And anyway, he wouldn't want to arrive home with a griffin.

They landed in the middle of a small patch of forest.

Wood, once having made his decision to take the field in person, had not delayed. Within a few minutes he was airborne, flying on his own griffin.

On his arrival at the camp which had been taken by Tigris, he took charge at once, and ruthlessly. By dint of seriously terrorizing her former subordinates, he was soon able to confirm—if any confirmation was still needed—that Tigris had indeed captured the Sword Wayfinder, and had deliberately failed to notify him.

All of Tigris's people who remained in or about the camp automatically fell under grave suspicion in the eyes of the Ancient One. Those who Wood thought should have prevented her defection were placed in the hands of interrogation experts.

Wood had been in personal command of the camp for less than an hour when an alarm was sounded. But this time the news was good: another griffin, bringing in the Sword Woundhealer, along with a prisoner.

After gloating briefly over the Sword—no hands but his own took it from the semi-intelligent beast—Wood turned his attention to the prisoner. At the moment the wretch looked more dead than alive.

Thinking he recognized the fellow as Prince Mark's nephew, the Ancient One employed the Sword of Mercy to heal his injuries—quite likely he would be worth something in the way of ransom.

In a moment, as soon as Zoltan's eyes were clearly open, Wood asked him gently: "Where is she now? Tigris?"

On recognizing where he was, and who was speaking to him, the youth looked gratifyingly sick with terror. "I don't know," he whispered hopelessly.

"No? Well, I suppose there's really no reason why you should. But I'm sure there are interesting things you *do* know, young man. Things that I shall be pleased to hear—you and I must have a long chat."

That was postponed. More news arrived: yet another new prisoner had just been picked up in the vicinity of the camp, upon which he appeared to have been spying.

Wood turned his attention to this man.

Brod, dragged in and supported by several guards, tremblingly assured the wizard he had only been watching the camp because he had long wanted to devote himself to the service of the mighty magician Wood as a patron. He had been trying to find the best means of approach when he was taken.

The Ancient One stared at him. Nothing pleased him so much as a proper attitude of respect in those he spoke to. Brod, who thought he could feel that gaze probing his bone marrow, clutched at the only hopeful thought which he could find: at least he had not been trying to tell a lie.

"Tell me, Brod . . . "

"Yes, sire?"

"What would you ask, if you were given the chance, from the Sword called Wayfinder? I take it you know what I am talking about."

"Oh yes sir, yes sir. I know that Sword." The Sarge swallowed with a great gulp. "Well sir. I'd ask a way, a direction, that would let me fill my ambition of getting into your service, Lord Wood sir, and continuing in your service, successfully, for a long, long time . . . "

The Sarge stopped there, because the great wizard called Wood was laughing; it was a silent and horrible display.

THIRTEEN

PRINCE Mark was heading south. He rode astride a great black cantering riding-beast, with the bulky form of the old wizard Karel similarly mounted at his side. They were long out of sight of home. Days ago the Prince had ridden forth from the great gate of Sarykam at the head of a hundred cavalry, supported by magicians, beastkeepers, a couple of supply wagons, and semi-intelligent winged scouts and messengers. Ever since their departure the Prince and his expeditionary force had been riding hard to reach the region where his friends and enemies were still contending for a pair of priceless Swords.

The Prince was wearing two swordbelts, each supporting one sheathed Sword, so that a black hilt showed on each side of his waist. During most of the day Mark had little to say. His gaze was usually fixed straight ahead, and his countenance grim. He was ready for a fight, armed to the teeth, coming to the struggle with both Sightblinder and Shieldbreaker in his possession. The Swords Stonecutter and Dragonslicer, considered unlikely to be of much use in the current situation, had been left in the armory in Sarykam.

The swift-moving Tasavaltan column kept moving generally south, in the direction of the region from which

Ben had last reported his position. Scouts, both winged and human, ranged ahead continually.

Mark as he rode was nagged by the feeling that he ought to have brought Stephen with him. But he knew it was better that he had not; he felt comforted by the idea that the boy would be with his mother and perhaps afford her some relief from her endless gloom.

At sunset, the Prince and his troops reached the fringe of the barren country lying to the southwest of the Tasavaltan border. Mark ordered a halt. This would be a dry camp; tomorrow would be time enough to look for water.

Several times during the past few hours, winged scouts had returned from the southwest to meet the column on the march. Now yet another of these great birds, speeding from the same direction across the twilight sky, arrived at the encampment.

This scout reported the ominous presence of griffins in the area.

The Prince cursed at the indications that the enemy was now in the field too, in force. Mark ordered the beastmaster to dispatch more birds to investigate.

"Day-flyers, sir, or night?"

Mark ordered some of each sent into the air.

In the light of a lowering sun, Mark glanced at the three or four specially trained loadbeasts accompanying the column, which appeared to be bearing hooded human riders. Actually the figures on the loadbeasts' backs were the swathed forms of giant owls, whose heads and shoulders became visible as the hoods were removed. These birds would presently be launched to scout and harass the enemy under cover of darkness.

When Mark chose the campsite, Karel and his magical assistants busied themselves weaving protective spells around the area. The Prince personally oversaw the posting of sentries, ate lightly, then entered his small tent. Grimly impatient for morning, he wrapped himself in a blanket, stretched out on the ground, two swordbelts beneath him, his body in contact with both of his sheathed Swords, and tried to get some sleep.

The Prince sometimes tried to calculate whether he had spent more of his life in the field, in one way or another, than he had under a roof. Certainly he sometimes felt that way. The familiar sounds of a military camp—low voices, a fire crackling, someone sharpening a blade—were soothing rather than disturbing. Yet sleep eluded Mark. His mind could not cease struggling with plans and calculations.

The ominous signs of Blue Temple presence, and worse, in the land ahead suggested that one of his chief enemies might well now be in possession not only of Woundhealer, but of Wayfinder as well. But the Prince could take comfort in the fact that against the Sword of Force, even the Sword of Wisdom would be no more useful than a broken dagger. Wayfinder, Mark felt confident, could never tell its owner how to locate Shieldbreaker or Shieldbreaker's holder, or how to avoid any danger posed by him.

The Prince shifted position on his blanket, feeling as wide awake as ever. What would he do if he were Wood?

Of course, Wayfinder would be able to tell its owner the whereabouts of the magician Karel, say—or the location of the Sword Sightblinder—and from that information an enemy might well be able to deduce that Mark was somewhere near. No Sword or combination of Swords could solve all problems.

Sleep eventually came to Mark, in the form of a troubled doze. And with sleep came disturbing dreams that shattered into unrecognizable fragments as soon as he awoke, leaving a feeling of anxiety.

And one thing more. He had awakened with a new plan.

The Prince conferred with the wizard Karel just before dawn, and Karel agreed that Mark should ride on, alone but carrying both his Swords, ahead of the main body of his troops.

The old wizard had some forebodings about what seemed a chancy scheme, and at first had argued against it. But Mark was impatient, and stubborn enough to adopt the idea even against Karel's opposition.

At sunrise, as the Prince swallowed hot tea and chewed on a hard biscuit, preparatory to riding out alone, Karel warned him that carrying Shieldbreaker and Sightblinder at the same time, even with both Swords sheathed, could cause him problems.

"I must warn you, Prince, that holding both of these Swords drawn at the same time may well produce some powerful psychic effect even on you, who in some ways seemed to possess a curious partial immunity to the Swords' power."

"I have done as much before."

"Perhaps. But I warn you that your immunity is far from complete."

"I understand that, Uncle."

"Have you, since leaving home, tried either of the Swords you carry?"

"Not yet."

"Then do so."

Now, in the relative privacy of his uncle's tent, Prince Mark drew from its sheath the god-forged blade that rode on his right hip.

Sightblinder, as always, produced some spectacular effects when it was drawn. Mark was aware of no change in himself. But he knew that in the eyes of his uncle he was somehow transformed into a figure evoking either terror or adoration. Even the great magician Karel, here in his own tent, surrounded and supported by all his powers, and knowing intellectually that the figure he saw was only a phantasm of magic, was powerless to see the truth behind the image.

"What do you see, Uncle?"

The old man passed a hand across his eyes. "The details of the deception do not matter. I no longer see you in your true nature, of course, but an alien image which frightens me, even though I know . . . " The old man, averting his eyes from Mark, made a gesture of dismissal.

Prince Mark sheathed Sightblinder, which he had held in his left hand, and saw Karel relax somewhat. Next the Prince drew Shieldbreaker. The Sword of Force was silent, and inert, because no immediate danger threatened. Mark gripping the black hilt was aware of the vast power waiting there, but he felt no more than that.

Then, still gripping Shieldbreaker, the Prince pulled the Sword of Stealth from its sheath once more, and stood holding both Swords at the same time.

He saw by the change in his uncle's face that his own appearance had once more altered, perhaps even more terribly than before. The nerves in Mark's arms and shoulders tingled; the effect was strange, but well within his range of tolerance.

Carefully Mark sheathed both Swords again, Sightblinder first.

He tried to reassure Karel, but the old man remained cautious, and perturbed. He warned the Prince, unnecessarily, not to be caught in combat with an unarmed foe whilst holding Shieldbreaker.

"I know that," Mark patiently reminded his counselor.

Karel still looked worried.

The Prince, putting a hand on the old wizard's shoulder, reminded him that he, Mark, was no stranger to the Swords. And he assured the old man—though not without a certain mental reservation—that the effect of holding the two Swords at once had not been strong enough to cause him any real concern.

At the same dawn hour when Mark set out alone from his camp, Ben was urged out of a light sleep, into instant alertness, by the tug of a rapier-pointed claw upon his garment.

Crouching over him where he sat with his back against a tree was a winged messenger from Mark. This helpful, friendly bird, having been instructed by Karel, brought Ben the welcome news that Tasavaltan troops were not very many kilometers away, and the Prince himself was even closer.

The birds' sense of horizontal distance was notoriously inaccurate, so Ben did not derive as much comfort from this news as he otherwise might have.

As the hours passed, Valdemar continued to observe the destruction of the personality, even the physical identity, of the sorceress who such a short time ago had come riding at the head of a force of demons and human thugs to slaughter her enemies and kidnap him.

Not that Delia appeared to care in the least—she kept humming little snatches of simple, cheerful songs—but her clothing was now sodden with rain and getting dirty. Evidently it was now deprived of what Valdemar supposed must have been the magical protection afforded the garments worn by Tigris. Even the woman's face was notably changed from that of the conqueror who had devastated the Blue Temple camp. Valdemar wondered if he could have recognized this as the same individual, had he not seen with his own eyes the several stages of the change. Rain and circumstances seemed to have washed and scoured away an aura of bad magic, and perhaps some subtle though mundane makeup as well, from her countenance.

Only the physical parts of the transformation had taken any time at all. Never, since the thunderbolt fell, had Valdemar caught any hint that any part of her older, wasted and vicious personality might have survived.

Valdemar had no doubt that the metamorphosis had resulted from a blow struck at Tigris by the great and mysterious magician she had feared so terribly, and from whom she had been so desperately trying to escape. One of the oddest things about the whole situation, as Valdemar saw it, was that the blow, the sudden transformation, had not really done her any harm. As far as he could tell, quite the opposite.

And here was another turnaround to consider: He, who had been the prisoner of Tigris, was now Delia's captor. Or more properly her keeper. Now he, the simple farmer, had become the worldly, experienced mentor. It was not a role he relished, but there was no one else to take responsibility for her, and the idea of simply abandoning her was unacceptable. Though in her previous persona she had treated him unjustly, still her new helplessness was disarming. And her new childlike personality was charming in its innocence.

Delia was more talkative than Tigris had been. Almost every time Valdemar looked at her, he found her gazing back at him as if she sought his guidance. And she kept asking naive questions.

Earlier, under relentless questioning from this young woman, Valdemar had tried to explain how he had been guided to her by the Sword of Wisdom. He thought that Tigris had never quite believed that story; she had been chronically suspicious, and perhaps incapable of understanding a simple truth. Now, when he told Delia the same tale, she somehow had no trouble at all believing if not comprehending what he had done.

"This Sword has brought us together, you and I," Valdemar, patting the black hilt, assured his new companion.

"That's good." Her tone suggested complacent acceptance, if nothing like full understanding.

"It is a magic Sword."

"Magic. Ah." And Delia nodded solemnly, with an appearance of wisdom.

"Are you acquainted with magic, then?"

"No," she said vaguely. "No, I don't think so. Except—"

"Yes?"

"Except sometimes, when I still lived on the farm, I think . . . there were things that I could do."

"What kind of things?"

"When plants were sick, sometimes I could make them well."

"Really? Then I will have to tell you about my vines."

A shadow, as swift as it was insubstantial, abruptly fell over the two young people.

Simultaneously Valdemar was once more stricken with the helpless sickness in his guts; this time he recognized the cause, and now his fear was greater than before.

The presence this time was smaller and more nearly bearable than Dactylartha's had been. But the young man had no doubt that this sudden intruder was a demon too.

He clutched for dear life at the Sword of Wisdom, and cried to it for help. He did his best to lift it, as if to strike a blow.

The demon only chuckled, a truly hideous sound. The

ghastly wraith-shape of it drifted in the air in front of Valdemar.

"What do you mean to do, young man? Strike me with your Sword?"

"I . . . " At the moment, brave words seemed impossible to come by.

"Wayfinder will not protect you . . . nothing will . . . if I simply reach out to you . . . like this . . . "

Fear and nausea gripped him, then dragged their slimy presences away. Val wondered why the demon did not simply seize Wayfinder out of his almost paralyzed hands. But the shadow drifted on, and the Sword of Wisdom was still his.

It was, it had to be, only playing with them, like a cat with a pair of mice.

Delia, utterly miserable, pathetically ignorant, clung to him, wanting to be comforted.

Val's fears were confirmed. The vile creature had only pretended to depart, for now it came drifting back. Its vague shape gathered over Delia, and it whispered something frightful into the young woman's ear.

Shocked, uncomprehending, Delia screamed and wept.

Valdemar tried to summon up his nerve, his will, to rise to her defense, but physical and mental cramps assailed him, and he fell back groaning.

Delia shrieked again. Horrible memories had stirred in her when she heard the demon speak Wood's name.

Then, as unexpectedly as it had come, the demon was gone.

Delia expressed her fear that the Ancient One was coming to get her. "Val, that's what it meant. That—*thing* which spoke to me just now—whatever it was. It told me things that made me start to remember—Val, hold me!"

And Valdemar, still sick and trembling from the recent

presence of a demon, found himself doing his best to comfort Delia.

He held her while she wept, and promised to protect her—and in his ignorance he could even believe for a time that he might be able to afford her such protection.

As for the Ancient One himself, with every passing hour, each incoming report, he was becoming more firmly convinced of his former assistant's treachery. Though by this time, as Wood assured himself grimly, the objective truth concerning her guilt or innocence really no longer mattered. He had decided to consider her guilty, and that was that.

Whatever she had really done or not done, after this he would never again be able to trust her even minimally. Too bad; at one time she had shown great promise . . .

Wood now welcomed back—as warmly as he ever welcomed any being—the demonic scout who had just tormented Tigris.

Listening attentively, the Ancient One received from this creature a new report. The news, related with much demonic merriment, was that Tigris had certainly been reduced to childish helplessness. And now—this was the crowning effect—seemed to be on her way to a new existence as a farmer's wife.

The Ancient One reacted to this announcement with a great deal of amusement and satisfaction.

He went so far as to reward the messenger—at least, he promised a substantial, though unspecified, reward, to be delivered in the future.

The demon praised its master's generosity—its gratitude sounded as sincere as the virtue that it praised. And it slavishly rejoiced at having brought good news.

"Yes. Well, well." The human nodded. "All things considered, such a fate will do quite well as the first phase of our settlement of accounts with her."

"And the next phase of her punishment, Master?" The servile creature almost gibbered with delight. "When may we expect to enjoy that?"

Tersely, in a voice tinged with regret, the Ancient One explained that for the next few hours or perhaps days he was going to be too busy dealing with his chief opponents to pay this traitress much attention.

He concluded: "But do keep me informed."

"Most gladly, Master!"

Valdemar still asked the Sword for safety, and the Sword still required him and Delia to fly. The flights thus commanded were random jaunts, as far as Val could see, getting them nowhere in particular, but rather keeping them in the same area of almost uninhabited country, uncomfortably close to the camp from which Tigris had kidnapped him—how very long ago that seemed!

And Val was growing increasingly worried about the griffin. He supposed that the creature had grown tired, lacking its proper magical nourishment, or reinforcement. Or perhaps, thought Valdemar, the beast was simply becoming increasingly restive in the control and company of these two milksops.

When he asked Delia if she remembered anything about the animal's diet, she only shuddered and insisted that she knew nothing whatever on the subject. Valdemar couldn't decide whether she was telling the truth or not.

When he asked the Sword for help in feeding their chief means of transportation, Wayfinder obliged. Evidently there was some kind of food the griffin favored, and when Valdemar turned to the Sword for help, Wayfinder directed them to a landing place where the creature browsed contentedly for a time, burrowing its head into the dense foliage of a grove of peculiar trees. Valdemar was unable to tell at first glance whether the beast was eating leaves, fruit, or perhaps something more meaty that dwelled in the high branches; he made no effort to find out.

"Is it a very big magic, then?" The young blond woman was staring gravely, wide-eyed, alternately at Valdemar, and at the Sword he was consulting with regard to their next move.

He was disconcerted by the way she put a thumb or knuckle in her mouth, her pink lips sucking at it.

Also he wanted to tell her that her garments needed some adjustment. He was more certain than ever that in her previous persona her clothing must have been protected by some magical means. Now this enhancement was no more, and seams and fabric, not made to withstand rough usage without help, here and there starting to give way. Her blouse, or tunic, or whatever the right name was for the upper garment she was wearing, was tending to come open in front. Matters were tending toward the immodest. How could he think of her as a potential bride?

Valdemar told himself that he was not really accustomed to dealing with children.

He said: "Of course this Sword is magic, magic of tremendous power. Haven't I just been telling you?"

The griffin was showing signs of reasonable contentment as it continued feeding. Valdemar assumed that he and Delia would soon be riding on the monster's back again. He wondered if some curse was on him too, that circumstances kept arising to delay his return home.

Of course, once he had reached that goal, another problem would arise: What ought he to do then with the Sword? Any such treasure would inevitably draw trouble, as Valdemar saw the situation. He would have to hide it, get rid of it, trade it off somehow as soon as an opportunity arose.

But that could wait until he was safely home. Once Wayfinder had seen him that far, Valdemar was sure he wanted nothing more to do with any magic of the gods.

As for his wife . . . whoever she might be . . .

He sat looking long and soberly at Delia.

"What am I to do with you, girl, when we've got that far? I don't know. Will you at least be safe from demons when we've reached that point?"

She could no more answer that question than an infant. She looked back at her caretaker with mild concern, waiting for him to find some reassuring answer.

"At least," Valdemar growled, "I'll know where *I* am then, and I'll be able to do something . . . "

He picked up the Sword and once more asked it to show him the way home.

FOURTEEN

THE Sword of Wisdom failed to respond at all to this important question, or to the others Valdemar asked. Valdemar took this to mean that he too should adopt a course of inactivity. That would be all right if it didn't last too long; he could use the rest. Anyway, the griffin had not yet finished its protracted feeding.

Also Val was still being bothered by his cut fingers. The skin around the little wounds was red and sore and even felt warmer than the adjacent flesh, as if he were getting a local fever. Healing was slow, not helped by the fact that he had to keep using his hand.

Delia, despite her claim to have spent her childhood on a farm, protested that it bothered her to have to deal with blood and injury. But when Valdemar coaxed her, she agreed to do what she could to help him.

First, wearing an absentminded look, she searched among the nearby bushes and eventually came up with what she said were useful herbs, varieties to help the small wounds heal.

While engaged in this search, she took time out to complain, she had not been able to find the kind of berries she would really like to eat. "There should be little red berries, in the spring . . . "

"I suppose your farm was a long way off from here."

"I suppose it was," the young woman answered vaguely. Then she lifted her head sharply. "Listen!"

"What?" Valdemar turned uneasily, hand groping for his Sword.

"The birds. Hear them? Except they're not the same kind that used to sing on the farm."

Eventually, with Delia's assistance, Val succeeded in getting an effective bandage on his hand. The poultice of leaves that she bound on stung a little at first, but then felt vaguely comforting.

As Delia finished tying the last knot in the little bandage, he continued to stare at her thoughtfully. Long ago Valdemar had abandoned the last suspicion that this shocking innocence was some kind of a trick, a pose on her part. And she showed no signs of snapping out of it. No, it seemed that she was his responsibility now.

So far the pair of them had had enough to eat; fortunately the griffin had been carrying some field rations, mostly hard bread and cheese, in one of its panniers. But those supplies were quickly running out, and Valdemar realized that to keep himself and his supposed bride going he was going to have to somehow scrounge more nourishment from other sources.

He would have to think seriously about that problem soon. At the moment he was very tired.

The Sword of Wisdom would of course lead them to good things to eat, as soon as he wanted to make that his priority. But Valdemar had the feeling that they were under pursuit, if not direct attack, and he had learned that the Sword could only handle one question—or one main goal—at a time. He would not risk his life and Delia's for food until actual starvation threatened.

Sitting against a tree, he was pulled back from the brink of sleep by his companion leaning over him.

"Is it a very big magic?" Delia now repeated, innocently. She was gazing thoughtfully at the Sword, which lay in Valdemar's lap, his hand on the black hilt.

Earlier, Valdemar remembered with a sense of irony, this woman—or rather this woman's other self—had been the one to accuse him of feigning an innocence too great for the real world.

"It is indeed," Valdemar replied at last, with the slow patience of near exhaustion. "It is a gigantic, tremendous magic. And also very sharp—be careful!" He had thought for a moment, from the eager way his charge was leaning forward, that she had been about to run a testing finger right along the edge of Wayfinder's Blade.

She who had once been Tigris had never objected to Valdemar's having complete charge of the Sword of Wisdom. But from the way she was gazing at the weapon now, it was obvious that something—whether it was the bright beauty, the supernal keenness, or the intricate under-the-surface pattern of the steel—held a strong fascination.

He slid Wayfinder back into the sheath still fastened at his waist.

And then he leaned back against the tree. His eyelids were getting very heavy, and he would rest for just a moment.

Delia, feeling a mixture of mischief and curiosity, reached for the Sword again as soon as Val, losing his battle to exhaustion, dozed off.

And at that moment the griffin, as if sensing that something of importance was about to happen, silently turned its head, watching Delia keenly as she reached for Wayfinder.

She could not test the sharpness of the edge while the Sword remained sheathed. Softly she put her hand on the black hilt and drew the weapon forth, so quietly that Valdemar slept on.

Holding the Sword with a double grip on the sturdy hilt, made Delia feel strange. Her arms and hands were going tingly in a way that she knew—somehow—had something to do with magic. The sensation made her forget about testing the physical edge. She held up the Sword to smile at it in innocent admiration.

Val had told her that the Sword answered questions, and helped people. "What should I ask?" she whispered aloud. The question seemed addressed more to herself than to the instrument of the gods.

The griffin, at the moment chewing its mysterious nourishment, chewing with the jaw-motions of a cow, and the fangs of a gigantic lion, had no answer for her.

Warily Delia turned her head, looking carefully at Valdemar to make sure that he was still asleep.

Then inspiration came. Small hands white-knuckled with the strain of gripping the black hilt, she raised the heavy Sword of Wisdom and whispered to it again.

"Show me the way to make him want to keep me with him," she whispered devoutly. And smiled a moment later—because sure enough, Wayfinder had just twisted slightly in her hands—pointing at what?

At nothing in particular, that she could see. Just at some bushes.

Moving eagerly and quietly, holding the heavy Blade extended carefully in front of her, Delia investigated. The Sword led her through a screen of brush, and on a few meters more, to a point where she heard the sounds of murmuring water just ahead.

Still following the Sword's guidance, she soon arrived at a small stream, partially dammed by a fallen tree and lodged debris. Above the dam a pleasant little pond had formed, partially shaded by standing trees. The day was warm and sunny for a change, and the pool invited her to test it with her fingers. Not prohibitively cold. Certainly it looked deep and clear enough to provide a bath.

Sniffing fastidiously at her armpits, she grimaced, and could not remember ever before being this dirty.

What had awakened Valdemar he did not know, but full consciousness suddenly returned. Sitting up straight, with a reflexive wrench of all his muscles, he felt a cold hand at his heart when he saw that the Sword of Wisdom was no longer in its sheath, which was still belted securely at his waist.

Delia was missing too. Maybe she had only stepped into the bushes to relieve herself. Jumping to his feet, Val called her name, first softly and then at considerable volume. To his vast relief, an answer came drifting from somewhere in the middle distance. A moment later, he thought he could hear prolonged splashing.

Quickly the young man pushed his way through the bushes to investigate.

He stopped abruptly as soon as the pond came into view. The Sword at least was safe, stuck casually into the moist earth at the water's edge.

Delia's clothing, including an undergarment or two which Valdemar had never seen before, lay beside the upright Blade. The young woman herself, completely unclothed above the waist, covered by water below that, waved at Valdemar from midstream, no more than an easy leap away. She called cheerfully for him to join her in her bath.

"Val, come in, come in!"

"I'm coming!" he heard himself reply. His voice was a mere croak. Already he was striding forward, as if hypnotized. Somehow it was as if he were watching his own behavior from outside. He was aware of stripping off his own garments, and stepping down into the current . . .

Half an hour later, Delia, still unclothed, lying at ease amid the spring grass and early flowers a little inland from the water's edge, was frowning prettily. She had hold of the huge hand of Valdemar, who, as naked as she was, lay almost inert beside her, and was turning it this way and that, as if interested in the articulation of the wrist.

"And now your bandage has come off again," she was complaining. "What are we to do for your poor fingers?"

"Never mind my fingers." Valdemar's voice had a newly calm and thoughtful quality.

Something crackled in the brush nearby, galvanizing him into action, first lunging, then crawling awkwardly, to reach the Sword. With his bandaged hand on the black hilt he turned—to find himself facing nothing worse than the griffin, driven by curiosity to see what its two masters were about.

Delia, who had crawled after him, started tickling him playfully.

Another half hour had passed before Delia asked Valdemar whether the magic Sword could heal his fingers.

"No, there is another Sword, called Woundhealer, that would be needed to do that."

"Woundhealer? Where is it?"

"I don't know. It was with me for a while, before I met you—or rather I was with some people who were carrying that Sword. But where it is now . . . just help me put on a bandage again. My fingers will be all right, and we face bigger problems than a couple of little wounds."

The bandaging went more easily this time, perhaps because Delia was less afraid of hurting him.

As she tied the last knot, Val said regretfully: "Better get dressed. We must be moving on."

The griffin appeared to be through feeding, for the time being anyway. But Val's renewed questioning of the

Sword, with safety as his goal, this time elicited no clear indication from Wayfinder.

Valdemar, strolling about with his arm around Delia, bending now and then to kiss her, kept trying to picture her as his wife, working beside him in the vineyard. Yesterday such a vision would have seemed impossible. Now it was much clearer.

He began to talk to her about his vines and grapes, and about the good wine that could be made from them in a year or two when the plants were fully matured.

Delia, listening to Val's description of his work, and his plans for the future, saw nothing frightening or unpleasant in the prospect. In fact she found herself quite pleased.

His description of the vineyard stumbled to a halt. "Does this suit you, then?" he asked.

"Yes," she told him simply. "All I want now, Val, is to stay with you."

"Oh. Oh, my dear. Delia."

When the pair of them were busy gathering what food they could, foraging to augment the supplies still remaining from the griffin's fast-diminishing store, she demonstrated a definite magical affinity for growing things—making thorny vines bend to and fro, to yield her their juicy berries without pricking her reaching hands and arms.

"I foresee a great future for you in the country, little woman."

"I keep telling you, I have always lived on a farm."

"And do your parents live there still?"

"I'm not sure." A shadow crossed the young woman's face. "I don't want to think about them."

"Then don't."

* * *

Once more Delia, at a moment when her companion was inattentive, got her small hands—hands no longer as pale and soft as they had been—on the weapon of the gods. In simple words she whispered a new question to the Sword of Wisdom, asking it to guide them to the Sword called Woundhealer, so that her lover's cut fingers could be healed.

Yet again they mounted the griffin. Valdemar, thinking that his own most recent query was the one to which the Sword was now actively responding, gave the beast commands. Quickly they were airborne.

They had not flown far before the young man noticed that a flying reptile was following them. He could not be sure whether it was actually trying to catch up with them or not, but the griffin was flying so slowly that that seemed a possibility.

Grimly Valdemar urged their mount to greater speed. The nightmare head turned on the long neck. The eyes, seeming to glow with their own fire, looked straight at him. But the griffin ignored the command.

"Faster, I said!" Val waved the Sword, as if threatening the beast with it.

The threat was a bluff, and it proved a serious mistake.

With a move that appeared deliberate for all its speed, the beast reached up, with an impossible-looking extension of one of its almost leonine hind legs. The blow from the great claws caught Wayfinder cunningly, knocking the Sword of Wisdom neatly out of Valdemar's hand.

Val uttered a hoarse cry of surprise and dismay. There was no use trying to grab for the Sword, it was already gone. In the next moment he saw the pursuing reptile catch the falling treasure in mid-flight, and with the gleaming blade between serrated teeth, go wheeling away on swift wings, carrying the prize.

At the moment of the Sword's fall, as if a successful

and unpunished act of rebellion had given it courage, the griffin became totally unmanageable.

Skimming low over forest and wasteland, it launched into a series of aerobatic moves, as if determined to dislodge at once its two uncongenial masters from its back. Val and Delia hung on all but helpless, shouting at the creature and at each other. Sky, wasteland, and patches of forest spun round them as the griffin looped. The couple clung desperately to saddle and basket.

Suddenly a blue-white wall of water loomed, a pond or miniature lake. Hardly had the body of water come into sight, when the crazed animal plunged straight into it, diving and swimming like a loon.

The water's liquid resistance finally dislodged the humans. Valdemar, choking, almost drowning, felt a piece of basket rim break off in his hand. Swimming in water over his head, he fought his way to the surface, just in time to see his escaped means of transportation floundering ashore. From the wooded shoreline the griffin leapt into the air again, displaying magical celerity.

Where was Delia?

Treading water, turning this way and that, Val hoarsely called her name.

A long moment passed before he saw her—floating face down.

Desperately he stroked to reach her, got the muddy bottom of the pond under his boots, and carried her ashore. By that time, to his great relief, she was coughing and moaning feebly. She spat out a mouthful of muddy water.

When he would have helped Delia to sit up on the bank, she cried out in pain. Her back had been somehow injured in the watery rough landing. She protested that she could not walk, could hardly move.

Standing now on the shoreline, with a chance to look around, Valdemar thought that this territory looked vaguely familiar. As far as he could tell, they had returned to a point at no very great distance from the place where a young woman named Tigris had kidnapped him, and their adventures with the griffin had begun.

The scouting reptiles informed the Ancient One that Tigris was not very many kilometers away.

A beastmaster relayed the information. "She is in worse shape than ever, Lord! The peasant who is traveling as her companion strips off her clothing, and uses her at will."

Wood chuckled. For the moment he continued to be satisfied with the progress of his punishment.

"And we have taken their Sword from them!" the reporting human gloated.

The Ancient One's demeanor changed. "I hope that none among you has dared to touch it?"

Hastily the subordinate explained. No one had disobeyed orders. One of the more simple-minded flying reptiles had caught the falling Sword Wayfinder in midair, and was bringing it in, flying slowly under the unaccustomed load.

Wood was not really surprised by the news regarding the Sword. He had been working for some time, and on several levels, to get Wayfinder away from Tigris and Valdemar, and into his own hands.

It had been part of his plan to obtain the Sword without letting any of his associates possessed of human intelligence, or greater, get it into their own hands even for an instant.

The task had been further complicated by the fact that Wayfinder itself had doubtless been employed to protect its possessors from him. But as matters had turned out, his plan succeeded anyway. Perhaps, he was tempted to believe, the Swords' magic was not invariably supreme.

Soon the Sword itself was brought in. But, almost

immediately after getting Wayfinder into his hands, Wood was distracted again from thoughts of pleasant vengeance by reports from both demons and reptiles, confirming that a force of about a hundred Tasavaltan riders was on its way south, heading almost directly toward his camp.

On hearing this, one of the Ancient One's currently most favored human subordinates immediately suggested evoking a large force of demons, and dispatching them all against the hundred cavalry and their support people and creatures.

The proposed tactic would undoubtedly serve well to determine whether Mark was accompanying this main Tasavaltan force or not. But if Mark was indeed there, the discovery might cost the discoverer, Wood, a whole force of demons.

He decided prudently to begin by sending only one or two of the vile creatures.

As for attacking Mark personally, he had other ideas about that.

Having been aware for some years of the presence of Shieldbreaker in the Tasavaltan arsenal, Wood assumed that the Prince would be coming against him armed with the Sword of Force. Shieldbreaker was undoubtedly the mightiest piece of armament in the world, capable of nullifying the power of any other weapon, even another Sword, that might be deployed against it.

With these facts in mind the Ancient One, pleased as he was to be finally holding Wayfinder, took it for granted from the start that any attempt to locate Mark directly by using the Sword of Wisdom was bound to fail.

So Wood, on first obtaining the Sword of Wisdom, made only a perfunctory attempt to locate Mark. When that was unsuccessful, he acted rather to locate the wizard Karel, or the Sword Sightblinder, on the assumption that Mark would be found very near that person or object.

When the Ancient One's small squad of demonic skirmishers attempted to strike at the force from Tasavalta, they would encounter, in fat old Karel, a magician of sufficient stature to beat the attackers off—though not as quickly and effectively as Mark would have been able to repel them.

In Karel's archives, as he was soon explaining to an anxious pair of military officers in his tent, were listed the locations of many demons' lives. And the old magician gave assurance that he knew how to find out more such locations very quickly, if and when the need arose.

Besides, Karel had the power to make things unpleasant for a lot of demons whose lives he lacked the knowledge to terminate—so unpleasant that they would even prefer to incur Wood's displeasure, rather than persist in this attack.

Wood, observing the fate of his demon skirmishers as closely as he could while still remaining at what he considered the best distance to exercise command, felt reasonably confident that Mark was no longer accompanying his cavalry and his chief magician.

Then where was the Prince of Tasavalta? Mark's arch-enemy chewed a fingernail, heretofore well-kept, and pondered.

Wherever the Prince might be, Wood felt sure that he would be armed not only with the Sword of Force, but also with the Sword of Stealth. Such a combination would make a formidable antagonist out of the veriest weakling; in the hands of a warrior like Mark, the effect was bound to be overwhelming, against all but the strongest and most crafty defense.

Well, Wood considered that he was ready.

In less than a minute, before Wood's demons could begin their serious attack, even before most of the Tasavaltan force had been made aware of the impending threat, Karel's magic had slain or dispersed the handful of magical skirmishers.

But the confrontation, once begun, continued between Mark's uncle and the Ancient One. The two commenced sparring at long range.

Wood had long wanted to test directly the occult strength of Kristin's overweight uncle. Now, having at last made immediate contact, the Ancient One had grudgingly to admit that, although he felt confident of being able to wear this veteran adversary down in time, the struggle was bound to be a long and draining one. Wood did not choose to spare the time and effort to fight it to a conclusion now. He was going to need all his powers to deal with Mark, armed as the Prince must now be.

Not that Wood thought Mark was going to represent the ultimate test. The Ancient One had received certain magical indications that his own final success or failure, in his bid to dominate the world, was going to depend upon another confrontation, now still relatively remote.

Against the Dark King, and the horde of demons that one could call up? Wood considered it unlikely that his rival Vilkata had really been permanently removed from the scene. But no, not even the Dark King would represent the ultimate challenge.

Sooner or later, the Ancient One was thinking now, it would be necessary to concentrate his efforts with the Sword of Wisdom on locating the Emperor, in anticipation of a final combat with that man.

The Lady Yambu, lying on an ebon couch, covered with a white sheet, her head now pillowed on rich fabrics, was being more or less forcibly maintained by her newest captor in a state of responsive consciousness. Finding it necessary to converse with him whether she wanted to or not, she expressed to Wood her surprise that his first questions to the Sword of Wisdom did not seem to have been concerned with establishing his own safety.

She asked him the reasons for this lack of caution.

He assured the Silver Queen that he scorned to be so timid.

"You will understand that, I am sure, my lady. You yourself have never been accused of excessive caution."

"No doubt that is intended as a compliment."

"Of course. I have always regarded you with the greatest respect." Wood paused, before adding in a low, convincing voice: "I would never have deserted you in your time of need."

"Meaning that the Emperor, who was my husband, did?"

"You are the best judge of his behavior in that instance." Without hesitating, the Ancient One continued: "Support me now, and I will give you real youth. Eternal youth and beauty, a far more lasting change than even Woundhealer will ever be able to provide."

Her head turned on the brocaded pillow. "And Tigris? Did she have the same promise from you?"

"What has happened, is happening, to that woman is no secret. But dear lady, I made her no promises. I never found that woman half as interesting as I find you."

"I have no interest in what is happening to her. Now will you let me rest?"

"Of course, dear lady. For a time."

Walking alone, a few moments later, Wood developed a shrewd suspicion: this lady was really trying to find, to rejoin, her former husband. Though he thought it doubtful that the Silver Queen herself was fully aware of her own motivation.

Perhaps he, Wood, ought to announce his readiness to help her in this quest.

Because he really wanted to find the Emperor too.

On an impulse drawing Wayfinder, Wood took time out from his immediate struggle to command that Sword to guide him to the Great Clown.

The Sword's reaction was simply to point straight down to the spot of earth on which Wood was standing. He could readily find one interpretation of this answer: If he remained where he was, the Emperor would come to him.

Of course there were other possibilities.

"Am I to dig into the earth? I hope not. Or do you simply mean that I must wait? Faugh! The secrets of the gods are welded into this bar of metal, and all I can do is ask questions like any other supplicant, and hope, and wait!"

Faced with this behavior by the Sword of Wisdom, the Ancient One began to wonder if his calculations regarding Mark's behavior could have been wrong.

He wondered also whether it might be the Emperor, instead of Mark, who was now armed with Shieldbreaker.

When Wood tried to locate Mark directly, Wayfinder became as inert as any farmer's knife.

Wood, who had also taken possession of Woundhealer on entering the camp, was considering that he might eventually want to trade that treasure for a Sword he wanted more—though he would dislike having to give up the Sword of Healing, having certain uses for it in mind.

He thought that the next time he talked with Yambu, he would elicit some comment from her on the subject of trading Woundhealer.

FIFTEEN

MARK in a grim mood kept riding forward. The country through which he traveled was largely desert, and for a time remained almost flat. The land got rougher as he drew closer to a river's rocky gorge.

He had now been traveling alone, ahead of the advancing column of Tasavaltan cavalry, for more than a full day.

The Prince had had no conscious contact with anyone, friend or foe, since he had separated from his hundred picked troopers, from Karel, the assistant magicians, and the rest of the fast-moving force.

On parting from his friends, Mark had ridden for a short time without drawing either Sightblinder or Shieldbreaker. But rather soon the Prince decided that he had better not advance any farther without having in hand one of his two Swords—or, better, both of them.

Mark wanted to have the Sword of Stealth in hand before he was seen by the enemy's reptile scouts.

And he wanted to draw Shieldbreaker before coming within range of any enemy weapons.

Since leaving Karel behind, the Prince had several times sensed the power of contending magical forces, and he realized that something might be happening to delay his uncle and the cavalry. But even with Sightblinder in hand to enhance his powers of observation, he had been unable to perceive the details of the magical combat between Karel and Wood, or of Karel and Wood's demons.

Mark supposed that, barring such magical hindrance, his Tasavaltan escort ought to be not much more than a couple of hours behind him.

Carrying Sightblinder drawn for protection deprived Mark of information he might otherwise have received from scouting birds and made him unable to send winged couriers to his friends. Confronted by magic powerful enough to deceive humans, the birds, with their limited intelligence, could hardly be expected to disregard the visual image—they would either perceive Mark as some fearful presence, and refuse to approach him, or they would see him as some beloved object—another bird, he supposed, or a favorite handler—not the two-legged master for whom they had been trained to carry messages and fight.

Thus on occasion, when he saw a friendly messenger in the air, Mark risked sheathing Sightblinder again.

Under these conditions, the Prince had received indications that Wood himself was now somewhere in this general area. The most recent of these communications was a note from Ben, explaining that the Blue Temple force had been destroyed, and its camp taken over by an expedition under the command of Tigris.

Mark observed several flying reptiles at irregular intervals of time. Their paths in the sky converged at a place no very great distance ahead of him. This fact warned the Prince that he was almost certainly closely approaching some enemy; from this point on he rode with the two Swords continually drawn.

And now the subtle blending of their two powerful magics, Shieldbreaker in his right hand, Sightblinder in his left, both Swords more fully activated than when he had tried them in Karel's presence, gave Mark strange, exotic feelings of power and glory. Wave after wave of giddiness threatened to unbalance him in his saddle. His uncle's warnings clamored in his memory, but Mark forcibly put them from his mind—just now, both of his Swords were necessary.

Old Karel had more than once cautioned him that these, like other forms of power, could be addictive. Not that Mark had needed the warning; he had long been old enough to understand that for himself.

The Prince retained a firm faith that Shieldbreaker's protection would hold absolutely against any spells or other attacks that Wood might launch personally, or might order to be made by others.

As Mark grew closer to the enemy, the powers slumbering in the Sword of Force awoke and made a tapping sound. He knew that this noise signalled a hostile presence, somewhere close enough to represent an immediate danger.

Now and again, as Mark moved forward, the dull sound arose, only to sink back almost to inaudibility. In the circumstances, knowing the power of this Sword, the Prince found the faint noise more comforting than alarming.

As when the duel commenced between Karel and Wood, Mark's experienced senses provided him with a vague but disturbing warning of evil magic, strange presences, nearby. He could feel these groping in the air around him, and then withdrawing thwarted.

Wood, on taking over the camp established by Tigris, had quickly reorganized its layout and defenses.

The Ancient One now occupied a blue and silver pavilion in the center of an elaborate and heavily safeguarded bivouac.

The powers, human and inhuman, who had come here

with the treacherous young enchantress had all by now been formally charged with incompetence or worse. Every one of them had now been taken away in chains, or the magical equivalent thereof.

Having, as he thought, magical capabilities to spare, and no real concern for problems of logistics, the Ancient One had also set out to make this facility luxurious.

In the few moments he thought he could spare from more immediate concerns, he studied the condition of his prisoner Yambu, and talked with her on several subjects.

The Ancient One, with the help of several subordinates, was also conducting, or preparing to conduct, experiments with some new magical techniques. He nursed at least feeble hopes that these would enable him to get around the defense posed by the Sword of Force.

But it did not take long to confirm his most gloomy auguries regarding the new methods. These were doomed to fail as absolutely as any other inferior magic ever set in opposition to a Sword.

He was angry, but he had really expected no other result.

"It is no use," he admitted, his voice descending to a quiet rasp of rage. "Shieldbreaker's protection remains absolute."

These new techniques had required some human sacrifice, and the Director had been chosen. The Lady Yambu had asked whether she was being considered as a candidate, and Wood had looked pained at the suggestion.

The Ancient One did truly regret that Tigris was not currently available in his camp, so that she could do him a final service as the sacrifice.

It would be hard, he thought, to imagine anything more satisfactory than watching her be fed slowly to a demon—unless of course he should manage to lay his hands on Woundhealer and Tigris together. Then new possibilities would open. He would be able to treat her, after all, to that little vacation in one of his remote strongholds for which she had once so eagerly expressed a wish . . .

Yes, Wood already missed his little comrade, and he was going to miss her more. Oh, if only she had remained loyal to him a little longer! It was unsatisfying to have the decision on when to end a relationship taken out of one's hands, so to speak.

Wood talked with Brod, and in the course of this discussion he formally enlisted the Sarge as one of his followers.

Brod groveled in gratitude.

"You may demonstrate your thankfulness by performing a certain mission for me. Do this job well, and I will give you something more important."

"Anything my Master commands!"

"I want you to seek out a certain woman—you will be given her approximate location, and magical means by which you will be able to certainly identify her—and bring her back here, to me, for my personal attention. You need not be too concerned about her sensibilities while she is in your charge."

"I take your meaning, Master."

"I think I made it plain enough."

Ben, forced to seek shelter almost continually, had been able to make little or no progress to the north. But he kept trying.

On rounding a bend in a path that wound its way through scrubby forest, he suddenly came upon a vision that stopped him in his tracks—he was confronting a young woman, tall and strong, with clear blue eyes and bright red hair, who stood regarding him steadily.

It was Ariane, his long-lost love.

Intellectually, Ben knew better. He realized almost at

once that he had really encountered Mark, carrying the Sword Sightblinder, so that the Prince must appear to his old friend, as to anyone else he met, as some object of overwhelming love or fear.

Knowing well the powers of Sightblinder, and also that Mark would almost certainly have armed himself with the Sword of Stealth, Ben had braced himself mentally for such a moment. Still the shock was almost overwhelming.

Mark, on seeing his friend turn pale, and sit down as if his knees had betrayed him, sheathed Sightblinder, and advanced to offer words of greeting and reassurance.

In a minute Ben had pulled himself together, had given Mark the bad news about the loss of Zoltan and the Sword of Healing, and was ready for whatever had to be done next.

The Prince took a turn at walking, loaning weary Ben his riding-beast for an hour or two. In this manner the pair headed south again. Mark told Ben that he had been for some time reasonably certain that an enemy camp was not far, because he had observed the converging reptile flight-paths.

Ben confirmed that his the lost Sword of Healing had been carried that way too.

At dusk, advancing cautiously, the two men observed sparks of firelight ahead, suggesting the presence of a camp.

Taking counsel together, the two experienced warriors decided that, armed as they were with Swords, they stood an excellent chance of being able to launch a successful raid without waiting for the arrival of the Tasavaltan troop and Karel.

Mark emphasized: "If Wood is indeed in this camp, I

want to get my hands on him before he has a chance to fly off with the Sword I need."

Ben raised a hand to silence him.

Someone was approaching.

Valdemar had been forced to leave the injured Delia in an abandoned hut, which at least offered shelter against the intermittent cold rain, while he sought help.

Even in the gathering dusk, he quickly recognized Ben's hulking figure.

But standing beside Ben . . . in that first moment . . . was an almost-forgotten horror out of Valdemar's own childhood, a faceless figure of which he could be certain only that it was frightful.

And in the next moment, even as he recoiled in horror, the young giant beheld the image of horror replaced by one of his beautiful wife to be . . . and then that form faded too. Beside Ben there was only a tall man, sheathing what appeared to be a Sword.

In a few moments introductions had been made, and explanations begun. From Valdemar Mark soon heard, in a drastically condensed version, the story of how the woman who had been Tigris was now lying in an abandoned hut, reformed and injured, in dire need of help.

Valdemar in the course of this relation reported how Tigris had abducted him from this site, and mentioned the loss of Wayfinder.

Ben expressed his doubts. "You think she's reformed, young one? Maybe her magic's been taken away, but I'll shed no tears for that. It's some kind of trickery she's worked upon you."

"It's not!"

Quickly and firmly the Prince squelched this argument. There was no time for quarreling now. Even if the situation was in fact just as Valdemar described it, he, Mark, could not, would not, go off on a tangent now to help some woman in distress, however deserving she might be.

And then the Prince made a plea of his own. "Help me now, Valdemar. Help Ben to guard me against attackers when we invade this camp, and I swear that I in turn will help you as soon as I can. With all the power of Tasavalta, and of the Swords, that I can bring to bear."

The towering youth let out a sound of frustration, something between a sigh and a snort. "I must accept your offer, Prince. It seems I have no choice."

Mark decided that they would not attack the camp till dawn, giving them all a chance to eat and rest. He shared out the food from his saddlebags. Before bedding down for the night, Mark and Ben discussed tactics with the inexperienced Valdemar. The two veterans made the point that the only enemy tactic they really had to worry about, whatever forces might oppose them here, was that of people deliberately disarming themselves and then hurling themselves on the Prince who carried Shieldbreaker.

Valdemar nodded; the theory of the situation was easy enough to comprehend. As for putting it into practice: "I will do the best I can."

"Can't ask for any more than that."

In the first gray light of dawn, the three men soon came close enough to Wood's encampment to hear the sounds of people stirring, and smell the smoke of campfires.

Evidently the Ancient One, confident in his strength, had made no particular effort to conceal his position.

Mark, made wary by this lack of concealment, wondered whether Wood was more or less expecting him, perhaps even trying to lure him into making a solo attack.

It turned out that Wood's camp was magically protected against casual discovery, but with Shieldbreaker in one hand and Sightblinder in the other the Prince crossed the invisible boundary unharmed and unimpeded. Had it not been for a softly augmented thudding from the Sword of Force, he would not even have realized that he had encountered any defenses.

Matters were different for the two men who formed his escort. Ben, despite his experience and alertness, was unaware of the magical protection until unnatural light flared around him and Valdemar, and immaterial weapons slashed at their minds and bodies.

Shields and snares of magic closed on the three intruders, only to recoil an instant later like snapped bowstrings, broken by the unyielding central presence of the Sword of Force. Shieldbreaker's voice beat loudly, light flared across the early morning dimness, and the claws of magic lashing out at it were instantly blunted and beaten back. Valdemar and Ben were staggered momentarily, but the power that might otherwise have destroyed them was quenched before it could have serious effect.

Hoarse cries in human voices went up from near the center of the camp. Ben thought that perhaps the backlash of the broken spells had taken toll among the minor wizards there. Certainly by now the entire enemy camp was aware of an intrusion. Soldiers in blue and silver, magicians, and others came pouring out of their tents. The trio of invaders stood in plain sight of most of them, and Sightblinder immediately provoked primary confusion among the defenders, human and inhuman.

The first human sentry to get a clear look at Mark, near the edge of camp, ran forward hesitantly, sword half-raised by an arm that jerked uncertainly, as if the man himself did not know whether he meant to salute or strike. Evidently this man perceived the invading Prince as Wood himself, or as some hideous demonic power.

An instant later, a real demon came hurtling down out of the lowering morning sky. Even had Mark been lacking Shieldbreaker, he would have confronted the foul thing with a wary respect, but not with terror. As the Emperor's son, he had always possessed the power, without understanding why or how he had it, to drive away even the most powerful of those evil creatures, simply by commanding them to depart. In the past the Prince had been forced to demonstrate this ability several times, often enough to give him confidence in it now.

And the Sword of Force, he felt sure, added another impenetrable layer of protection against demons. Such beings, as old Karel had once explained to Mark, were creatures of magic and pure malevolence, born of great explosions at the time of the Old World's dying. They could will nothing but evil, and Karel thought that they could take no action of any kind except by means of magic.

Magic employed to inflict injury was by definition a weapon, and Shieldbreaker was proof against all weapons, material or otherwise. A human being abandoning all weapons could win barehanded against the Sword of Force—but a demon could hardly disarm itself without ceasing to exist.

Perhaps, Sightblinder notwithstanding, this morning's demon understood at once just what antagonist it must be facing. Because the thing vanished out of the air again, as quickly as it had appeared, and of its own volition.

And now—inevitably but foolishly—a few material weapons were deployed directly against the holder of the Sword of Force. Mark's body, no longer under full control of his own will, stretched back and forth with magical celerity, darted to right and left, executing parry, cut, and thrust with ruinous violence and precision—but all under cover of Sightblinder's cloak of deception. The visible counterfeit of Mark—some image of terror or love—beheld by each friend or enemy, more often than not appeared weaponless and unmoving, a single enigmatic figure standing immobile in the midst of causeless carnage.

Enemy swords, spears, missiles and shields were hacked and harvested in a spray of fragments. Shieldbreaker chopped up human flesh and body armor with ruthlessly complete indifference. The Sword in Mark's right hand—in those moments when that weapon could be glimpsed—became a silver blur. The hammer-sound blurred also with its speed, and swelled up to a steady thunder-roll.

Valdemar had never seen or dreamed of anything like this before. Few people had. There was, there could be, in the whole world nothing else like this to see. The young man was momentarily stunned into immobility.

One man, Mark, advancing with his weapons, sent the first wave of blue and silver opposition reeling back in confusion.

So far the Prince's double bodyguard had not been required to do anything but stay close to him. If they stayed close enough, they remained within the aegis of protection of the Sword of Force. Shieldbreaker flashed invisibly between their bodies and around them, smashing slung stones and arrows out of the air.

But now, sooner than either Val or Ben had expected, some of the enemy began to come against Mark unarmed.

Val saw the first one, a squat, strong soldier in silver and blue, come charging barehanded between two of his fellows armed with short spears. The Sword of Force put out its flickering tongue of power, and both spearshafts were severed in a blink. The unarmed enemy who would have charged between the spears to grapple with the Prince instead encountered the battle-hatchet swung accurately at the end of Val's long right arm. The vineyardist had never killed before; but he was left with no time now to meditate upon the fact. Another unarmed foe was coming.

Ben and Val, stepping forward one on the Prince's right hand and one on his left, acquitted themselves well in the first fight with the initially disorganized foe.

There came a brief lull. Panting, Mark gave his orders: "We go forward again. I must find Wood! Whatever Swords are here will be with him."

Advancing boldly, pressing their initial advantage, he and his escort penetrated to one of the central tents. Ripping open fabric with a Blade, the Prince cursed on realizing that his chief antagonist was not here either.

But a moment later, to their joy, the three attackers discovered in this tent a pair of important prisoners. Zoltan and Yambu were both stretched out on narrow beds, eyes staring and bodies rigid, obviously under some magical constraint. Any humans who might have been stationed to guard them had already taken to their heels. In only moments the Prince and his flankers were able to set the pair free.

Into the right hand of each prisoner, briefly and in turn, Mark pressed the hilt of the Sword Shieldbreaker. This instantly and permanently broke the grip of the magic Wood had bound them with.

Zoltan, on being released from imprisonment, sat up with a strangled gasp of relief, to see Valdemar and Ben before him, standing one on each side of a black-eyed mermaid. Zoltan understood that he was facing the Sword of Stealth, when a moment later the mermaid's image turned into that of Wood himself, and then into a nameless, shrouded figure of horror, a memory from nightmares of his childhood.

Whatever horror the Lady Yambu might have experienced in her captivity, or on waking to see Mark wielding Sightblinder, she bore the burden well.

* * *

Less than a kilometer away, the young woman who had once been Tigris was still lying injured, half delirious, inside some peasant's half-roofless and long abandoned hut.

Fearing equally for her own survival and for her lover's safety, Delia drifted in and out of feverish sleep. In her lucid moments the young woman hoped and prayed to all the gods that the two of them would be able to get away from this seemingly endless conflict, to the peaceful vineyard Val had so proudly described to her.

Almost Delia felt that she already knew that place, that she and Valdemar had already lived there together. In dreams she saw the little house, the garden, a green and summery vision of delight, a paradise once possessed, now gone again and unattainable.

In her pain and distress she had lost track of how much time had passed since Val had left her here alone. Many hours, certainly. She was afraid it had been days. She feared, in her state of suffering, that the man she loved had suffered some horrible fate. Or, worse, that he had cruelly deserted her.

Zoltan, still suffering somewhat from Wood's maltreatment, could provide little relevant information about Wood, nor could he guess what Swords the Ancient One might hold. But Yambu was able to confirm that Wayfinder had been here, in this camp, and in Wood's hands.

Where the Ancient One was now, or whether he had with him that Sword, or any other, she did not know.

Mark assumed that Wood had carried the Sword of Wisdom away.

Now, in the center of the camp, Mark and his augmented bodyguard faced a development the Prince had not really expected—a carefully prepared series of enemy counterattacks by a surrounding composite force of armed and unarmed men, specially trained to fight against Shieldbreaker.

At the next pause in the action, Mark suspected, and his panting friends agreed, that the Ancient One must be somewhere near at hand, directing these attacks.

The beleagured handful craned their necks, trying to spot their enemy in the clouded sky. The Prince grunted: "He'll be riding on a griffin, or I'm surprised. He'll be too shrewd to mount a demon, when he expects me to be present."

Before anyone could answer him, there sounded from somewhere in the distance what Mark and his compatriots could recognize as a Tasavaltan horn.

"That's Karel, thank all the gods."

"Let us hope some cavalry is with him."

Karel himself, riding forward with a courage matched only by his physical clumsiness, doing his best to keep up with the cavalry, had been able to determine with fair accuracy, despite Wood's attempts at concealment, just where the enemy camp had been established. Some of the Tasavaltan scouting birds had been deceived by enemy magic, and others temporarily outfought by reptiles. But the uncle of the Prince and Princess could also determine, even without much help from feathered friends, that Mark was now in the vicinity.

He signalled to the cavalry commander to sound the charge.

In moments the Tasavaltan mounted troopers, supporting and supported by a truly formidable magician, were heavily engaged with the forces surrounding Prince Mark and his small bodyguard.

Drawing a deep breath, Mark commanded an advance, toward their allies.

There were plenty of fallen weapons about with which the former prisoners could arm themselves.

They advanced.

Meanwhile Wood, still carrying Wayfinder, was airborne. Mounted on his own especially large and vicious griffin, he circled above the fighting, dispatching relays of reptiles with urgent messages to his officers below. He sent other winged couriers with orders to speed the advance of his additional ground forces already marching to the scene.

What had once been an orderly camp was now a ruined, trampled field of mud, fallen bodies and ruined and discarded weapons, and collapsed tents. Time and again, the Prince's personal bodyguard saved his life by beating off unarmed attack. He, and the unmatchable power in his right hand, rescued them in turn. The onslaught of the Tasavaltan cavalry had relieved some of the pressure from surrounding forces, but still Mark and his handful in the center had all that they could handle. So far, thanks to skill and luck and the weapons of the gods, none of them were more than slightly wounded.

Wood, hovering on his chosen griffin, darting away and coming back, now and then swooping low enough to get a good look at the figure he knew must really be Mark, sometimes perceived instead a man he recognized as the Emperor. Again the Ancient One beheld a shadowy figure, insubstantial yet angular, somehow almost mechanical, something out of the Old World. He knew that the Sword of Stealth was tricking him into seeing Ardneh.

Though Shieldbreaker had prevented Wood from using Wayfinder effectively to plan his counterattack on Mark, the Sword of Wisdom continued to be effective against Mark's allies, Karel and the Tasavaltan cavalry. The trouble was, as long as Mark himself was on the scene, Wood could not spare the time to accomplish their destruction.

The next time he dove his mount low enough to get a close look at the fighting around Mark, the Ancient One beheld, to his own freezing horror, the hulking, foul image of the king-demon Orcus—a being now ages dead, along with Ardneh his great antagonist.

Putting aside the initial shock of this perception, Wood summoned up his intelligence and will, gritted his teeth, and stubbornly denied what both his eyes and his best magical perception were assuring him to be true.

That was Mark. And with the two Swords, Mark was winning.

A number of Wood's people, who as a rule were more afraid of their master than of any other conceivable enemy—or at least of Mark—fought like fanatics.

But on encountering the armed Prince of Tasavalta, a majority of these unfortunates perceived Mark as Wood, and they saw confronting them a figure even more terrible in its wrath than the original. And the very terror with which the Ancient One had sought to bind his fighters to him, resulted in their defection.

Yambu had been struck down, and was out of action for the time being.

Those of the Prince's friends who were still fighting beside him could only hope, if they should lose sight of Mark for a moment, that when they again saw a figure they took to be him, it was not really that of Wood or another enemy instead.

For Wood, snarling rage was giving way to a kind of calm. He prepared to risk everything on a single move.

"My plan is failing, because my fools down there lack wit and nerve to execute it properly. Very well, then. I see I must grapple with him myself."

Wood, meaning to hurl himself unarmed on Mark, reined his griffin round to circle in a wide loop, gaining momentum for a final charge. Meaning to hurl himself unarmed on Mark, he began divesting himself of weapons right and left—but stopped when he came to Woundhealer and Wayfinder, sheathed at his side.

"Not yet. Both Swords may have to go, but only at the last moment, when I'll know that he still has Shieldbreaker in hand."

Mark's tiring riding-beast tripped and fell, hurling him violently to the ground. Though protected against all enemy weapons, Mark had been knocked out of the saddle by accident.

The Prince lay temporarily stunned.

Zoltan, being closest to him on his right side, grabbed up Shieldbreaker.

Val, who was in the best position on the other side, took up Sightblinder, which had fallen from Mark's left hand.

Moments later, having seen from a distance how their Prince went down, Karel and some of the Tasavaltan cavalry attacked fiercely, and broke through to surround and defend him.

In the double confusion of a melee and a joyful reunion, Valdemar was easily able, even though he lacked Sightblinder, to step away without being noticed.

The Ancient One, circling away momentarily, failed to see Mark go down.

Coming back, swooping very low to the ground for a final attack, Wood observed only a confused struggle in the place where he expected Mark to be. The Ancient One's hopes rose—perhaps his plan of attack had succeeded after all.

The griffin, great wings blurring with its speed, roared

low above the struggling throng, sustaining what to it were minor wounds from Tasavaltan stones and arrows.

Closing swiftly on the knot of central activity where Mark must be, Wood saw Zoltan standing in the Tasavaltan ranks.

Shieldbreaker would be down on the ground there, somewhere underneath that scramble. The direct attack on Mark would have to wait for his next pass—or if the Prince was already slain, such a desperate tactic would be, after all, unnecessary. But here was another choice target, and this run would not be wasted. Swerving his mount slightly at full speed to meet the altered target, the Ancient One swung Wayfinder with all his strength against Zoltan—and the world seemed to explode with tremendous violence in Wood's face.

The shocked griffin literally somersaulted in midair, and the body of its rider went hurtling from the saddle. Some of the onlookers were quick-witted enough to realize almost immediately that Wood must have swung Wayfinder against Shieldbreaker, and that the Sword of Wisdom had been dazzlingly destroyed.

In every quarter of the field, increasing numbers of enemy soldiers were panicking into flight. No matter how thoroughly their secret training had prepared them for a fight against two overwhelming Swords, the reality was overwhelming, and they found themselves unable to stand against it.

The surviving Tasavaltan troopers, taking heart from the fall of their archenemy, fought all the harder.

The physical combat flared and receded and flared again. The fighting was fierce, the slaughter great, the number of fallen in blue and silver much larger than those in blue and green. Wood had been determined to wear down his foe by numbers, if he could win in no other way.

* * *

Mark, still sprawled on the ground, but now fiercely protected by his friends and his surrounding troops, was starting to regain consciousness.

Part of his trouble was due to the strain of carrying two such Swords into battle at the same time. Karel now was at the Prince's side, mumbling a reminder of his own warnings on the subject; but at the same time the elderly wizard protected Mark and all the Tasavaltan forces against anything that Wood's lesser magicians were able to try against them.

Valdemar, his perceptions enhanced by having Sightblinder in his grip, went running toward the place where he had seen Wood's plummeting body strike the earth. The crashing weight had half-collapsed a large tent in an area of the battlefield now otherwise deserted.

Inside the standing portion of the tent, Valdemar discovered that the falling body, half-armored in bright metal, had torn its way right through the fabric as it came down. The corpse lay on its back, rain falling on the face, the whole head looking hideously altered from the human. The terrible wound of Shieldbreaker's latest riposte showed plainly in the center of the chest, where armor of steel and high magic had been shredded as effortlessly as skin.

The Sword of Mercy still reposed in its sheath at the waist of the dead wizard.

The proof of the identity of this deformed and otherwise nearly unrecognizable corpse was in its right hand: dead fingers still gripping the black hilt of what had been the Sword of Wisdom, the hilt itself still bearing a stump of broken blade, once-magnificent metal dulled and lifeless now.

After the briefest of hesitations, the young man identified the sheathed and intact Sword beyond any doubt: he did this by drawing it forth and using it to treat his own small injuries recently received in battle.

Then Valdemar, working quietly and quickly and unobserved inside this half-collapsed pavilion, wrapped up Woundhealer in tent fabric, having used the blade itself to cut a piece to size. And then he promptly made off with it, trusting to Sightblinder in his right hand to afford him an unimpeded exit from the battlefield.

Valdemar had no trouble justifying this action to himself. The fight seemed to have been won, or at least was in a lull, with every prospect for an eventual Tasavaltan victory.

He told himself that he had done his share, and more than his share, of the necessary fight against the evil folk who would have hounded Delia to her death or worse—their glorious enemy, the Prince of Tasavalta, was still alive, now protectively surrounded by his own fiercely defensive troops, all of them, unlike Valdemar, trained fighters.

Overshadowing all other considerations, of course, was the fact that Delia desperately needed help, the help that he could bring her now—and that he feared might never reach her, if he were to trust the Sword of Mercy to someone else.

With both leaders now fallen, a lull had fallen over the field of combat. The enemy had retreated to regroup, or were perhaps recovering from a rout, or else they were following the Tasavaltans who in turn were trying to retreat with their injured Prince. Val could not immediately see just what was happening, and in fact he did not greatly care. He moved out boldly, armed with the Sword of Stealth.

Making steady progress, not looking back, he separated himself from whatever was left of the battle. He was going to bring help and healing to the woman he loved.

He told himself as he trudged away that after he and Delia were safely out of trouble, the Prince of Tasavalta would be welcome to the Sword—to all the Swords.

The Prince had not seemed a bad man, but Valdemar really put little faith in Mark's promises of help—obviously the Prince was going to be fully engaged in his own problems for some indefinite time to come.

Val could not blame him. In Mark's place, he would have done the same.

Presently the fighting flared up again around the Prince and his close companions, so that their search for the now-missing Valdemar, just tentatively begun, had to be abandoned for a time.

Zoltan and Ben exchanged guesses as to whether Valdemar had been killed. Of course there was nothing to be done about it if he had been.

Men had been dispatched to look for Wood's body, for he might have been carrying a Sword or two. The corpse of the fallen wizard was discovered, and, with the help of Karel, recognized. But no unbroken Swords were with it.

Sightblinder was gone from the field, but Shieldbreaker in Zoltan's hand fought on, with devastating effect. Any minions of Wood whose morale had survived the loss of their leader, and who were still misguided enough to strike directly, with material weapons, at the holder of the Sword of Force, saw their spears and swords and missiles shattered and broken, and they themselves were slaughtered when they came within range of Shieldbreaker's matchless force.

Similarly, any who tried to attack that person with magic saw their spells, too, broken by the Sword of Force. Some minor wizards in Wood's camp expired with startling visual effects.

And again and yet again, cleverly trained and fanatically led, one frantic would-be wrestler after another cast down his weapons and tried to close with the figure assumed to be Mark.

Again and again that man's new bodyguard beat back these attempts with ordinary blades, cudgels, skill and strength.

SIXTEEN

VALDEMAR, struggling against exhaustion after the prolonged fighting, kept moving as fast as he could, trudging on through rain and muck. He snatched brief periods of rest, when quivering knees and faintness told him that he must.

In the first stage of his journey, carrying two Swords, he passed many wounded, numbers of them crying out pitiably. Setting his jaw, he closed his ears to the sounds of pain and carried Woundhealer wrapped and hidden past the victims of the fighting, telling himself that he had already done more than his share for the Tasavaltan cause. At moments when he closed his eyes, every groan of pain seemed to be sounding in Delia's voice. He kept on moving as quickly and steadily as he could, back toward his beloved.

When Valdemar was half a kilometer from the camp, he thought he heard the sounds of battle started up behind him yet again. He did not look back, but kept going, and the noises slowly faded once more.

Resting only when his weariness compelled, Valdemar traveled for about an hour before coming in sight of the abandoned hut where he had left Delia. Running the last few meters, calling her name, he heard a welcome answer, and found her inside waiting for him.

He remembered to put Sightblinder away before he entered.

Delia, lying almost exactly where Val had left her, cried out to him in weak but joyous welcome.

Woundhealer drawn, he rushed forward to his woman's side.

Minutes later, the couple were resting and eating, preparatory to starting their long journey to Valdemar's vineyard, when a dull shadow fell across the doorway, blocking the dim light of the rainy day. Val looked up to glimpse a massive figure clad in Wood's blue and silver livery.

The young man had taken off his belt, and left both Swords imprudently just out of easy reach. In the next instant Val lunged for them, only to be felled by a stunning blow on head and shoulder.

"Good day to you both, young folks," said Sergeant Brod.

Delia hurled herself on the intruder, but Brod, laughing, easily caught her and clamped her wrists behind her back in one of his huge hands.

He said: "Things have gone a little wrong with the Master's magic—but I see the spell he gave me to find you here is still working just fine."

But on taking a good look at the woman he had just caught, who continued to squirm and hiss and scratch, Brod had some difficulty in believing this ordinary-looking female had once been Tigris—even though he had never had a good look at the enchantress. It seemed to the Sarge that Wood's long-range punishment had been devastatingly effective. In fact, if Wood had not thoughtfully provided him with a certain magical means of identification, he would probably have failed to recognize her at all.

Val lay on the floor of the hut groaning, by all indications unable to move.

The Sarge, making sure he had Delia in a safe grip, bent over to get his first good look at the weapons on the earthen floor, the tools Val had just been trying to reach. He was astonished and momentarily distracted by what he saw.

"Swords!—by all the gods!"

Shifting his grip on Delia's arms, he muttered: "Let's jus' see which ones we got . . . " And bent over, meaning to look closely at the black hilts projecting from the swordbelt.

It was now or never. Val, seeing double, his head and neck aflame with pain, a deadly weakness dragging all his limbs, summoned up what strength he could and hurled himself forward, grappling Brod around the knees.

Brod struck viciously at his assailant, stretching the already injured man out helpless on the floor. But he had to let go of Delia in the process.

In the moment when Brod was busy defending himself from Val, Delia managed to pull one of her hands free. Diving to reach the Swords, she was able to pull Sightblinder from its sheath.

With the same movement of her arm, she threw the weapon as far as she could, so it went flying into a far corner of the hut.

When Brod instinctively released her and went plunging after the Sword, she stuck out a leg and tripped him, so that he came down with a slam that drove the breath out of his body. A moment later she had seized Woundhealer and without hesitation thrust its bright blade straight into her lover's chest.

The Sarge, regaining his feet and lunging forward once more after the tantalizingly available Sword of Stealth, had almost got his fingers on its hilt when the great weight of Valdemar's body, once more fully functional, landed on him from behind. Skidding forward with Val's momentum, both men went crashing out through the old hut's flimsy wall.

Wrestling hand to hand, the two went rolling over and over. Brod's effort to knee his opponent failed. Valdemar's huge arms quivered, straining against muscles every bit as powerful as his own.

Suddenly the Sarge stiffened, looking over Valdemar's shoulder at a terrible male figure that towered above them both. The figure's blue eyes glared, its empty hands were extended in the gesture of a wizard about to loose a blasting curse.

Valdemar saw nothing of this apparition. He only felt Brod's body convulse, and heard him scream out: "Master Wood!" before he retched up blood and died.

Turning, Valdemar beheld only Delia. He saw her in her true form, for she had let go the hilt of Sightblinder, whose blade remained embedded deeply in Brod's heart.

Val, struggling to his feet, recalled once urging Ben to use Woundhealer to save this very man. And Val muttered now: "No. No more. You've had enough chances."

Tethered at a little distance from the hut they found Brod's riding-beast, along with a spare mount saddled and ready. The saddle-bags of both animals contained food and other useful items.

"He said something, didn't he, about having been sent to bring me back?" Delia shuddered.

"It wasn't you they really wanted, love. It was that other woman, Tigris."

"I don't want to hear about her, or think about her."

In less than half an hour the pair, wishing with all their souls to put the horrors of their last few days behind them, were hastening away from the scene of their most recent struggle.

* * *

Delia, her spirits risen again with the return and triumph of her lover, began to play with Woundhealer, giggling and marveling at the inability of this sharp Blade to cut her fingers off, or even scratch them.

How different this Sword from the one that had so treacherously hurt Val's fingers earlier!

Watching her perform such tricks gave Val the shivers, and he ordered her to stop. For once in a meek mood, she obeyed without a murmur.

Valdemar noted also, with belated apprehension, that the Sword of Mercy had only partially, if at all, restored Delia's memory. He supposed that Wood's expunging of her evil experiences, both as perpetrator and victim, would not be construed as an injury.

Somehow, out of renewed spirits and talk of a future that suddenly seemed clear, the topic of marriage came under discussion.

The urge for wedlock came with the greatest intensity upon Valdemar. His sense of propriety, an innate conservatism in matters of society and morals, was really stronger than Delia's.

Delia wondered aloud if she was too young for matrimony, and whether she ought to take such a step without consulting her mother.

"Would that be possible?" her companion asked, vaguely surprised.

"No. No, I don't see how. I don't know if she's still alive."

Valdemar was in a mood to insist on a ceremony. "Otherwise it would be shameful to continue to take advantage of you in this way."

"Is that what you call it? 'Take advantage'? Come, take advantage of me again!"

* * *

On the next morning the couple awakened to idyllic sunshine. From the state of the morning sky it seemed likely that, for a change, a whole day might be going to pass without rain.

"Delia?"

"Yes?"

"I think perhaps the most proper thing for us to do is to perform some kind of wedding ceremony ourselves."

Chewing on a grass blade, the young woman thought over this idea. "Yes, we can do that if you like."

Having won his point, the youth still felt it necessary to explain his thoughts and feelings. "Otherwise the difficulty, as I see it, is going to be in finding someone qualified to marry us.

"Even when we get back to my vineyard, there'll really be no one. The nearest village is about a day's walk distant. And I don't know if there's anyone in that village I'd want to perform my wedding ceremony."

"That's too bad." But in fact Delia did not seem very much upset.

Val continued: "A White Temple priest or priestess would be the best, I think. Maybe someday we can get to a White Temple somewhere. I pray to Ardneh sometimes. Actually I pray to Ardneh a great deal. He's not dead like the other gods."

Delia was now listening carefully, wide-eyed and nodding. As far as her companion could tell, she was accepting everything he said as truth. That made him feel the importance of weighing his words carefully.

He added moodily: "I could almost wish that we still had the other Sword. Wayfinder would show us where to find the right priest or official."

"Is it that important to you, finding someone to say words over us? We could pretend we still have the Finding-Sword."

Half in jest, half seriously, Valdemar closed his eyes,

held out his hands gripping an invisible hilt, imagining or pretending that he still had the Sword of Wisdom.

He said: "Sword, if you can do so without keeping me longer from my vineyard, or putting us in danger—show me the way to someone who could marry us."

Of course there was really no weight tugging at his hands, no bright metal to point and give him a direction.

But Delia's fingers were pulling at his sleeve. Opening his eyes, Valdemar discovered that they were no longer alone.

Standing on the other side of the little clearing, regarding them in a friendly way, was a middle-sized, dark-haired, thirtyish man wearing boots and practical trousers of pilgrim gray, his upper body covered by a short white robe which made him look like a White Temple priest on pilgrimage. He appeared to be unarmed.

Valdemar scrambled to his feet. "Greetings to you, sir. I am Valdemar, and this is Delia."

The man nodded his head briskly. His eyes were faintly merry. "And greetings to you, in Ardneh's name. I am . . . the man you see before you."

"Sir?"

"The truth is that I have taken a certain vow. For a time I may not speak my real name."

Delia appeared to find this interesting. "A vow to a god? Which one?"

The other shrugged slightly, a deprecating gesture. "A vow to myself, that's all. You might call me Brother White, if it is easier for you to call me something."

"Brother White—" Valdemar was suddenly anxious. "Are you a priest of the White Temple, as your robe suggests?"

The newcomer nodded in acknowledgement. "I am. Among other things."

"Then . . . Reverend Brother? Would you be willing to perform a certain ceremony for us, sir?"

"That is what you both want?"

Delia and Val looked at each other, then said together: "It is."

"Then it would please me to be your witness, if you will perform the ceremony for yourselves."

Valdemar looked again at Delia, then agreed. He was beginning to have the distinct impression that he had known this man somewhere before, but he could not recall where or when.

And then, abruptly, a hint of insight came to Valdemar. He asked: "Sir, do you know the Lady Yambu?"

"I do."

"Then—sir, are you, possibly, he who is called the Emperor? She spoke to me once of such a man, who was once her husband."

"Indeed I am." The answer was very matter-of-fact, neither a boast nor an apology.

Val didn't know exactly what to say next. At last he announced: "Sir—the Blue Temple covets your treasure."

"I'm sure they do." The Emperor smiled, then looked almost wistful for a moment. "But I doubt they know how to get at it."

Delia's thoughts were elsewhere. "If we are to be married," she murmured thoughtfully, "I wish I had a new dress to wear." There had been nothing of the kind in Bord's saddlebags.

"Let me see," said the Emperor. And he bowed to Delia slightly, as if asking her permission for what he was about to do. Then he took her by one hand and turned her, spun her gently, considerately, as if he were the skilled partner of the world's most graceful dancer. "White? Perhaps white would be best. Why, I see nothing in the least wrong with what you are wearing now." And with the spinning, in the time it took young legs to dance a step, her stained, frayed garments changed, became a dress, a gown, of purest ivory.

Val would have expected a White Temple priest presiding at a wedding to read from some kind of a book, but instead the Emperor—or Brother White—simply took each of the young people by the hand, held their hands clasped together in his own, and asked them questions about their commitment to each other.

The girl became very solemn for a time when this rather ordinary-looking man looked at her, and spoke to her and to Valdemar.

The setting was a pleasant place, and, true to the morning's promise, for once it was not raining.

When the ceremony had been concluded, and Valdemar had kissed his bride, he turned to Brother White and said: "Sir, we are young and healthy. We intend to avoid war in the future—so we have no need of either of these Swords that we are carrying. Or, rather, others have greater need of them than we do. And we have had proof, more proof than we needed, that the possession of such treasure can bring disaster as well as healing. So—I want to give them to you."

Brother White listened carefully, and nodded. "A noble gift, and I thank you. And I am proud to accept. Still, others have greater need than I. So my acceptance must have one condition."

"Yes sir?"

"That you carry these Swords, which are now mine, with you a little longer. Hand them over to the next person you meet who appears to be in need of their powers."

Valdemar and Delia nodded.

The Emperor waved them on their way.

Very well pleased to be formally united as man and wife, Delia and Valdemar continued their progress homeward on Brod's pair of riding-beasts—not hurrying now, but not wasting any time. She had noticed, with no great surprise, that as soon as she and her husband were alone again her wedding dress had turned into clothes very much resembling her own garments, but not worn or grimy.

They pressed on. At times when the way ahead still seemed long and difficult, Valdemar reminded his new bride and himself that he had come on foot, in no very great number of days, from his home to this region; and that they therefore ought to have no great trouble walking home again. Especially not with the Sword of Stealth to guard them on their way.

The land around them had become more hospitable, and there were increasing signs of human habitation, and Valdemar had begun to ride with Sightblinder sheathed instead of drawn. Perhaps he had also begun to lose a little of his alertness. He was halfway across a narrow bridge, spanning a small stream, when he raised his eyes to see Ben of Purkinje, armed and mounted, waiting for him on the west bank.

Val slowed his riding-beast, and put a hand to the black hilt at his side.

He hoped devoutly that Delia would know what to do—to stay in concealment where she was, back on the east bank. They had not yet entirely foresaken caution as they traveled.

The bridge was a single great log, carved flat on its upper surface. The brisk stream splashed and gurgled underneath. Speaking a little more loudly than was strictly necessary, Valdemar called out: "Ben. Surprised to meet you here."

The ugly face smiled faintly. "Can't say I'm that surprised to meet you. Matter of fact, a lot of us have out been looking for you—and for a couple of Swords—and for a certain woman—ever since we won the battle."

"I was sure our side had it won. Else I would not have left." Even as Valdemar spoke the words, he wondered if they were strictly true. Urging his mount slowly forward, he halted again when he came close to Ben, who with his riding-beast was almost blocking the west end of the span. Then Val looked around. "Are you alone?"

"I wanted to talk to you about that," Ben said mildly, and reined his mount back slightly from the narrow path, giving Val plenty of room to pass. Val urged his own steed forward. A moment later, just as Val was passing, Ben seized him round the waist, and dragged him from the saddle, gripping him fiercely to keep him from drawing any weapon.

Delia came cantering briskly across the narrow bridge with Sightblinder raised to defend her husband.

At the sound of hoofbeats, Ben looked up; and what he saw momentarily paralyzed him.

Before he could recover, Val had knocked him out.

When Ben came to himself—with the feeling of just having made a magically quick and complete recovery—he found himself sitting beside the little path. Valdemar, a Sword in his huge right hand, was standing looking down at him.

Obviously the couple were packed up and in the act of moving on; the sound of a woman's voice came from somewhere just out of Ben's sight around the next bend of the path, as if she were gently fussing with a couple of riding-beasts.

Ben's own mount was waiting patiently, just beside him.

"Where is she?" Ben leaped to his feet, looking around.

"Who?"

"Ariane. I saw her here . . . " His voice trailed off, as some version of the truth dawned on him.

Valdemar shook his huge head. He threw his weapon to the ground, where metal clashed on metal. "One of the two Swords that we are leaving you is Sightblinder."

"That you are leaving me?" Ben inquired stupidly. Following Val's gesture, he looked down uncomprehendingly. Two magnificent black-hilted blades lay crossed on the ground in front of him, waiting to be picked up.

"Yes," said Valdemar. "We are leaving them with you. Chiefly because of a promise we have made. And one of these Swords, I repeat, is Sightblinder."

"I ought to have expected that."

"Yes . . . do you understand now? Whatever woman you thought you saw before I knocked you out was never actually here."

"Ah."

"Yes. The woman with me is my wife. And we're leaving both Swords with you . . . does the Lady Yambu still live?"

"She does," said Ben slowly. "And the Prince too."

"Good. I hoped Mark was going to survive. Heal them, and heal Mark's Princess."

"I will," said Ben, and let himself sit down again, heavily, in the grass. His legs, so recently touched by the Sword of Healing, were as strong and healthy as they were ever going to be, and yet his sitting down was a collapse. He was going to be all right. He was all right. But some losses even Woundhealer could not restore.

Ariane was still gone. Gone forever.

At a little distance he could hear Valdemar mounting, and then the two animals moving away, accompanied by the voices of their riders. But for some considerable time Ben of Purkinje only sat where the givers of gifts had left him, staring at his magnificent paired Swords.